BLACKWOOD HOLLOW

By Courtney Adkisson

Published by Courtney Adkisson

No part of this publication may be reproduced, distributed or transmitted in any form or by any means, including photocopying, recording or other electronic or mechanical methods without prior written permission from the publisher, except as permitted by the U.S. copyright law. For permission requests, contact courtadkisson@gmail.com.

This is a work of fiction. Names, characters, places, and incidences of author's imagination or used fictitiously. Any resemblance of actual persons, living or dead, events or locales is entirely coincidental.

Copyright © 2026 by Courtney Adkisson

All rights reserved.

ISBN Numbers:

Ebook: 979-8-9898860-4-3

Hardcover: 979-8-9898860-5-0

Paperback: 979-8-9898860-6-7

Text in this book: is 11pt. Playfair Display family fonts.

Book Cover Design by: Karri Klawiter [Art by Karri] © 2025

Printed in the United States of America

First printed edition in © 2026

Dedication:
To my good friend, Will (FullThrottleGear), who changed my life:
"We all have demons we fight or dance with."

To all of us who struggle, who suffer in silence, and battle our demons:
You are seen, you are loved, and you are incredible.

Prologue

August 1901

My bare feet sank clumsily into the muddy ground and my lungs filled with the damp summer air.

I struggled to push through the darkness as I watched the lingering mist seem to block the view between the trees.

"*Mother!*" I cried out.

I ran through the scene in my mind. My mother had been dragged into the pitch black, the white of her nightgown flashing in my vision before vanishing out of sight. And now she was gone.

"*CONNOR!*" my mother screamed, pleading in the dark. Her voice was strangled and echoed around me.

I had no way of knowing where she was, but I kept pushing forward.

I sprinted across the fields towards the looming silhouettes of the tree line. Could this have just been a nightmare? I kept playing it over and over but I *knew* this was real.

My mother wasn't in bed, she was *dragged*. Why would my mind play tricks on me? I couldn't fail father, not after what he had done to protect us. I slung my father's hunting rifle around my shoulder ready to act. I would be brave.

I charged ahead until I felt my feet skid to a halt at the edge of the tree line. The night was a black void as my eyes desperately searched for *any* movement.

Finally, my eyes adjusted to the moonlight. I heard it. Footsteps. A branch snapped under the weight of something I couldn't see.

"Mother?" I called out, my voice cracking from the strain, burning as if it turned hoarse.

Nothing.

Then I whipped my head around to the sound of footsteps rushing past me. I looked down, finally seeing *something* in the darkness. My mother's footprints...or at least what *could* be.

I knelt down to examine the marks in the cold mud. Definitely dragged. A trail of large boots imprinted into the mud, pulling the weight of my mother behind them.

I looked up, catching flash of white cotton fabric disappearing deeper into the trees. That cursed place. I felt my skin immediately prickle at the danger that awaited me. What was I to do now?

Be brave. I swallowed, readying the rifle as I finally working up the nerve. I took a quick step into the woods, ignoring my body and soul screaming not to move forward.

The summer haze began to grow as the air remained disturbingly still. No animal dared to scurry through this place; and, now I was diving right into the heart of this ominous plane.

I stopped for only a moment. The church's cross peaked above the silhouetted town. I should have called for help. But...I couldn't afford to lose more time. Not again. I would *not* let another person succumb to this place.

I forced my legs to carry me forward. I listened to every inch of this forest as I searched anxiously for any sign of my mother.

"*Mother!*"

I heard a crack in the branches and a whimper. I followed the sound feverishly, hoping and praying to close the gap, but as the noise ceased, I realized I was approaching a clearing. I stopped.

The adrenaline had my heart pounding. I looked up to where a large, ancient oak tree stood. Its branches were twisted, stretching further and further towards the sky. The muck surrounding my bare feet gave me goosebumps, but my shivering wasn't because I was cold. It was a *hot* late night. No. Something that screamed deep inside me.

Then...I realized the ground below my feet had changed. It was no longer softened by the damp summer air. Now it was this dry, ash and dust as if it wasn't affected by the rest of the elements. Even the sight of it was gray and dare I say *dead*. As my eyes examined the tree, it had an aura about it that dominated the clearing. Something was off.

I looked back down at the ground. My mother's tracks were gone as if she had turned into a ghost in mere moments. I failed. I cursed under my breath and kicked the ground in frustration. My throat stung as tears formed in my eyes and I found myself cursing. I was all alone. I began to feel lightheaded and stumbled, catching myself along the large protruding roots of the twisting tree. All I could hear was the sound of my own breathing.

There was nothing. No more footsteps, not even a *trace* of someone even crossing the clearing. My mother had just vanished, and it was far too quiet. I began to panic as I cautiously searched around. Did something trick me into thinking my mother would just wander out here alone? It wouldn't be too far-fetched considering the curse of this place.

Something dropped onto the ground, making me jump out of my skin. I turned and the hair on the back of my neck stood up instantly.

My mother's cross. I hastily picked it up. It was covered in blood. The lace around the neck was now torn and stained. My stomach turned and my body froze. That's when I felt it. Something was watching me. And it was predatory.

I steadied my grip on the rifle, cocked it and held it at the ready.

I heard a crack and I spun, ready to fight.

Nothing. There was *nothing* in the clearing. I was so thrown off that I felt myself scoffed in disbelief. This place must have a way of tricking people. And I didn't like it one bit.

My eyes fell back to my hands, silver cross dangling on that bright blue ribbon. *Mother.*

I gripped it tightly in my palm. What was I to do now?

I felt the breeze kick up as I looked above me. There was a fluttering of fabric caught on the branches of the trees. My mouth dropped and the necklace fell out of my grip.

Feet dangled then the bright blonde hair, pale skin. I couldn't believe my eyes.

"*MOTHER!*" I screamed, feeling as if my voice could've awoken the whole town for miles.

I turned to run for help, but a cloaked figure with a hidden face forcefully grabbed my neck. The rifle dropped from my hands and landed at my feet.

"*Stupid boy,*" a voice hissed. "*You made this too easy.*"

Swirling, black smoke blasted from their fingertips.

Then everything went black.

One

January 1922

I jolted awake.

My skin was covered in goosebumps, and it took more than a moment to gather my wits. I took in my surroundings feeling my heart pounding out of my chest.

I was more than a little relieved to find myself in my messy but quiet study. It would've been pitch black, had it not been for the dimming fire in the hearth or the oil lamp that glowed in the corner. I managed to return my panicked breathing back to a steady rhythm.

I turned my head and I jumped.

I rolled my eyes, rubbing my face in embarrassment as I groaned at my own reflection in the mirror. Then again my appearance...wasn't the *best*.

I stared myself down for a moment. My auburn hair had grown out to my shoulders after months of growth. My beard had become scruffy and appeared *barely* presentable. My green eyes were tired and my clothes from the night before were more than a little disheveled. I couldn't remember the last time I looked like myself.

The older I became, the more I looked like my father.

And I hated that reminder.

But I was me, and I was no longer that fifteen-year-old boy running in the woods scared and alone. This particular nightmare was an almost daily expectation. It had repeated since the night I found my mother. It haunted me as if I was missing some pieces of a puzzle that I could never solve. And I never found them.

My father had died in the line of duty, but I've always blamed myself for my mother's death, even though she was just as much a victim as he was. This cursed place had a way of reminding you of the ghosts that roamed here. Their lives always ended in vain.

I looked down at the piles of photographs that were scattered about my desk. Some needed more sorting while others remained tacked onto a local map my father had acquired from my cousin who worked as a cartographer for the state. He was thrilled to find it for us since he missed being in his hometown.

The legend read off "*The Town of Blackwood Hollow*" in beautiful print which seemed like a farce if anything with the chaos that happens here. The map was covered in photographs pinned throughout the town. All linked to friends, families that moved, missing people. It was a long-standing project my father had refused to surrender...that I later pursued. Because all of this was his...and I didn't have the heart to get rid of any of it.

In stark contrast, my hastily written barely legible chicken scratch penned names, dates, and other various details to each family. Cases. They were all cases that I refused to ignore, now added to the history mapped out of Blackwood Hollow. Too many *accidents* that were left to rot and die with the victims. It was always a hard pill to swallow, but I refused to put down that torch.

I looked around my desk, then bent over, rummaging around until I felt the neck of the whiskey bottle. I picked it up, noticing the weight. As I looked at it, I cursed realizing the thing was empty...*again*. My father kept his collection in the cellar and I only just recently started raiding the stash that hasn't been touched much since I turned of age. With the prohibition...it's not like we had much in the way of options right now, at least not publicly.

I hated that in the more recent months I had taken to drinking. It was never something I prided myself on. But after the last case, I started wondering if anyone else in this line of work had the same feelings. It got harder to cope the longer I went about things.

A little girl went missing this time...the father I knew, and a dear friend of mine was absolutely devastated by it. Now things were getting too personal. His face when we found her...I couldn't handle it. They packed up their things and claimed they would start a new life somewhere else. Because that's all this town is good for. Death and escape. Where he ended up, I wasn't sure. There was no means of contact after he left. He could've been dead for all I knew.

I placed the whiskey bottle back under my desk as I continued to clear off a few stray papers.

As I moved a few things aside, I stopped, feeling something underneath. I lifted the chaos piled on my desk and spotted a worn necklace with a damaged cross laying untouched. It was still stained.

My mother's ribboned cross. One that I didn't have the heart to bury with her.

I cursed under my breath, pulling out a drawer and tossing it out of sight. I slammed the drawer harder than I had intended.

A shimmer of photograph caught my eye. Despite the lack of color, my memory filled the blanks. In the picture a woman, smiling at me with curled what I knew was honey blonde hair, fair skin and bright green eyes and a man with dark auburn hair and hazel eyes standing next to her. They were dressed for the summer, just the two of them, before I was even conceived. My face twisted with guilt as I stared at their forever smiling faces.

"Don't look at me like that..." I spat.

For a long moment, my parents stared back at me in the eerie silence. I grabbed the photograph, pulled out the same drawer I had thrown the necklace into and slammed it shut. Tears that were forced back released, falling down my face.

My fist slammed onto the desk and I felt my voice yell without restraint.

This was not the life I wanted. But there was no other option.

My mind was swirling then I jumped at the sudden ring of my telephone.

✳✳✳

The small town of Blackwood Hollow was a strange, isolated place.

If it was ever sought out, I never really knew. There was a moment in my life I wanted to run from this place, but that was nearly a decade ago.

I never once explored outside the boundaries of town. Visitors were a rarity, and people wanting to settle here puzzled me. But I suppose that if someone came from the bustling streets of the main cities, perhaps from the outside, it looked like a quaint little town. Most families who came here moved for the sake of privacy, avoiding prohibition, or something they were running from. Others have been here since the very beginning, far before me, generations of accumulated status including my own parents.

Despite the town's grueling reputation, I knew nothing but here. As I got out of my teens I accepted this was home, no matter how chaotic it was under the surface.

Blackwood Hollow was all rolling fields, bordered by grayish pines on all sides. It was as if they were imprisoning us from the rest of the world. My mother used to joke of it being a peaceful little snow globe. Compared to the cities that were rapidly growing, this place seemed like a quiet paradise.

The only history that seemed consistent throughout the generations was a sign greeting everyone:

Welcome to Blackwood Hollow, NJ, Est. 1675.

Now that the winter season had hit us, the town was already blessed with patches of snow and ice. Even though there was always the inevitable chill, it caused many locals to instinctively bundle up in their winter attire.

I found myself mimicking them, tightening my dark, charcoal wool coat that wrapped all the way down to my ankles. It was from my great-grandfather who came from Ireland. It always felt as though my family was perhaps one of the few that basked in this weather. Then again, I always dressed for the cold, including my boots. I kept my newsboy style cap close as well as my dark scarf to keep the wind off my neck.

When I stopped, my eyes rested on the cross at the top of the church. I felt my hand immediately reach into my pocket. I pulled out that photograph of my blissful summery parents staring back at me. My eyes went back to the cross.

It was supposed to be a sign of hope. But to me it had become something that haunted my mind. Something empty. Maybe I wasn't praying enough. And yet that's who called me this morning: a man of the church and an old friend.

"I was worried maybe Michael scooped you up," a voice greeted, startling me.

I whipped around to find the older reverend leaning against the door of his clergy house.

Reverend Bill Donovan was a man in his fifties, showing a bit of age in his eyes and bright red hair that was thinning at the back. Despite bags under his eyes, he still had those cheery laughing lines. Even in a serious time, Bill was known to keep everyone's spirits up and his faith close.

I had known the man since I was a boy and being, for lack of a better phrase "dragged" to the local church. The *only* church. My family went, dare I say, "*religiously*" after the first noticeable incidents. They insisted that praying would keep the demons of Blackwood Hollow at bay, the same ones that took them from me. Of course...that didn't change anything around this cursed town. I'm not sure, but God seemed rather silent in the last few years.

The idea of going to church churned up too many memories that I even couldn't fathom anymore. I had a hard time going after I was old enough to leave my aunt and uncle, and inherited the estate. Plus, in this town, I knew the truth. I expected Bill was smart enough to know the same. He was the eyes and ears of this town before I was even born. And now, here he was...asking me for help again.

Bill was bundled like everyone else, clutching his

jacket with dear life as he withstood the cold even for a few minutes. He leaned further out of the door, squinting as if to be sure as he approached.

"Reverend," I greeted him with a small smile. "Surprised that you called."

"You're allowed to call me Bill or Mr. Donovan, Connor," Bill corrected. "You're a grown man now."

I nodded, glancing at the church. Habit. He was always mindful of everyone. Though I became exceedingly uncomfortable as the pastor made an unsettled face. I felt the need to fill the awkward silence.

"I'm sorry it's been a minute since I-"

Bill put up a hand to stop me.

"I'm sure God will forgive your absences. Everyone has their reasons," Bill reassured, as he stepped down from the clergy house, coming closer to me. He offered a hand, pale and ungloved despite the chill. I reached out and shook it firmly. There was some warmth in the gesture, but...it wasn't what it should've been. Something troubled him, and I could tell by the phone call. I had to remind myself why I was here to begin with.

"I meant to see you for a while now," I mentioned. "How's Mary?"

"Still kicking and making the best Irish stew out of all of us," Bill smirked.

"Remind me to drop by next time," I said. "Is this a good time? You called rather late."

"God knows I have all the time in the world," Bill grinned, leaning in and patting me on the shoulder. I felt his hand push me gently towards the clergy house. "Although I'm not a fan of this chill mind you. Unlike you."

Bill winked at me, opening the door and waving us

inside. I couldn't help but smile at him despite the worries plaguing my mind. He was right, though. I was a fan of snow, and the possibilities of snowball fights and forts. That opportunity hadn't presented itself in a long time though.

Bill closed the door behind us quickly as the screeching of a tea kettle caught his attention, and he rushed over into the kitchen.

"Please," Bill offered, gesturing to the simplistic dining room set up.

The room was as bare bones you could get: a square wooden table and two chairs. There was a third chair, but it remained empty considering the dust it collected. It sat idly by an adjacent window just in case of the rare occasion of more company. There wasn't much room for a party unless you wanted to sit on the wooden floors, though I couldn't imagine anyone stopping by for more than a few minutes. Staying at the clergy house longer than that would mean something was *troubling* such as a post funeral arrangement or a marital squabble.

It was surreal being back in this place. Very rarely did I have a chance to be here. When I was a child, the rowdy children would play in the living room with various toys and games while our parents went to service. I, unfortunately, was *one* of those children. Mrs. Donovan would babysit and keep us entertained while her husband led services for the day. Thankfully, I grew out of at least *attempting* to be a nuisance during such events. The children my age were rather boring anyway or wouldn't play fair.

The kitchen had the basics anyone would need. A wood burning stove that was being used at its absolute best with the current season. Blackwood Hollow had electricity for a while now, but despite all that, Bill tried to keep things humble unless necessary. That's something I've always admired about him.

Bill grabbed a spare teacup included in a plain tea set, clearly passed down or donated judging by its wear and tear. I sat down in the opposite chair of the small dining table looking around the room. Bill grinned as he placed a teacup in front of me filled with what looked and smelled like a strong, black breakfast tea.

"Thank you," I said as I immediately reached for the sugar and stirred it. I couldn't stand bland tea. It makes it hard to focus on anything but the taste.

"Mary just got this, said the Fields family got a new batch for their tea shop," Bill mentioned.

I flinched at the name. I've been rather distant with the family for a while now. Felt like such a ghost after some...*disagreements*. I had to restrain myself from feeling anything other than sympathy as I cleared my throat and I forced myself to smile. "My mother loved their tea. This by far was a favorite in the morning."

I noticed Bill's eyes were on me. My parents were close to Bill in my younger years. I wondered if he had missed them as much as I had or if the town even noticed they were even gone.

Bill always had such a way about him that made me feel as though he could look into my very soul. Then again, I wondered if most religious men could. That's why they were called to this "business" I guess. I wasn't sure if I was ever holy enough to even be in the presence of such a profession. It was probably for the best considering my predicament.

Bill sighed, moving the kettle back in its place to cool.

"So...dare I ask how you are *feeling*," Bill asked, choosing his words carefully.

I put the teacup down, and my leg instinctively started to bounce slightly under the table. It was an unconscious habit as my mind searched for any possible answers.

Bill sat down as I felt the looming silence filled the room, engulfing us slowly. Part of me wanted to be honest, but the other part just wanted to get to the bottom of the call.

"I'm alive to say the least," I replied simply, as my fingers started tapping along the top of teacup.

My mind was racing as Bill watched me, his arms crossed. I had a suspicious feeling he wanted to pry, which I thought was mildly amusing being in a job that requires so much patience.

"Well, I suppose that's acceptable for now," Bill sighed. "However, the *way* you choose to live is still...concerning."

"That being?"

"You know how small this town is. Word gets around," Bill reminded me. Here we go.

"Does it ever," I agreed.

This town had a habit of knowing everyone's business. It was a blessing and a curse depending on who you talked to. I wasn't exactly sure where my position sat yet. A lot has happened in a decade.

"I do pray for you," Bill mentioned. "Hoping you'll one day find your answer somewhere other than the bottle."

I flinched. Of course he would know about that...and lecture me on it. I knew he meant well. Well...there was no way of avoiding even a smidgen of this conversation.

"Did the boy tell you?"

"More like his *mother* but you know how she is," Bill corrected.

Of course it was her. It's always her business. The idea of anything getting past her seemed impossible for me. Even though she had her own life now, and I wasn't in it.

"Have you seen her lately?"

"She comes every Sunday with or without Mr. Atwood," Bill grumbled as he shook his head, almost hissing at the name. "I know you don't want to hear about him. But there's a reason I say to watch the bottle."

In an instant I watched his eyes shift to an almost stern parental warning. I acknowledged the warning and nodded. I knew I had to quit or at least moderate. Even my father warned me while he was alive. He was unfortunate enough to see the worst from family and friends growing up. Now I'm victim to it, some days were harder than others, especially lately.

"She's *happy*," I gritted. "No one asked for my opinion on it anyway."

"I was there...I'm very *aware* of your opinion," Bill scoffed. "And believe me I agreed. And I'm not sure *happy* is the correct word. But no one asked me either. I'm just...sorry I didn't make it in time."

There we go...the flashing of what used to be filling my mind. I rolled my eyes at the memory as I mulled it over as I sipped more of my tea.

Then I grinned. Despite the semi-seriousness of the conversation, I found it amusing of Bill's behavior to be so protective. "Are you about to lecture me on my bad habits and past infatuations," I asked. "Or are we going to talk about why you called so late?"

I knew he meant well despite the teasing, there was a long silence before Bill found the courage to speak again. He shifted before lightening his tone. Yes...I suppose I should be worried about him.

"Oh yes right," Bill sighed. "You know Mrs. Baker?"

I almost spit out my tea.

"Ted Baker is married?!" I demanded. Bill raised his brows, smiling slightly. The tension broke and he nodded. Now this time *I* had to compose myself. "Didn't think that stoic boulder would ever find someone with his *cheery* nature."

"Well, he did. Elizabeth Sutton," Bill chuckled. "I was there. I officiate all the weddings around here you know. Sort of part of the job."

Somehow that was even crazier.

"Elizabeth Sutton?! The bubbly theater girl who sings at the church," I clarified. My tone didn't conceal my utter shock at the news. This was unreal.

"The very same," Bill chuckled. I felt relieved and chuckled with him in disbelief.

"Didn't think she would be his *type*. Chatty and all that," I quipped, sipping more tea. "What about her?"

"Well-" Bill started, his playful smile immediately fading as he began shifting uncomfortably in his seat which was odd behavior even for him. "It's actually about *Evelyn*."

Evelyn.

I felt my body freeze.

Bill noticed and started stammering and started backtracking. "I-it's okay if you say no-"

I felt my teacup land a little hard on the saucer. Bill nearly jumped and I gave him an apologetic look before putting out a hand to proceed.

"I'm all ears," I interrupted smiling politely.

Anything for her. Although...it seemed rather strange that she had any issues at all. If she did, she would've told me. Or at the very least Bryan would've noticed, wouldn't he? Perhaps it was something with her father again. The embarrassment of his gambling addiction was nothing new. Or it could be about the boy. Maybe that's why he wouldn't mention it.

Bill nodded, taking a breath. I leaned forward instinctively, ready to hear every word.

"The Bakers had Evelyn over with Bryan the other night," Bill explained, the words slow and processing. "She showed up with a shiner."

What?!

My jaw clenched at the thought. Someone *hit* Evelyn. But who?

I remember Avery Atwood. He was known to be a rather well-known pretty boy of sorts. He was an uncannily popular boy at school to the girls with his looks. That led to him always flirting with the next girl that would come his way. Though he wasn't thrilled that his parents had insisted Evelyn and him get married since their reasoning was...questionable: a debt payment and her father was the main culprit.

Evelyn was reasonably distraught after finding out she had no choice but to marry Avery. I'm not sure the man was thrilled either with the type of attention he had from other women. I doubt he really stopped. I had a sneaking suspicion that he might've still been seeing others on the side, knowing Evelyn's feelings for him. It was a shame she was trapped in such a conundrum.

But...to *swing* at her?

I felt the urge to break something. I was more than a little relieved to see that Bill was just as upset as I was. He was, after all, her more *pleasant* father figure.

"What happened?" I grumbled, my voice surprisingly steady.

Bill leaned forward and then whispered as if we were out in the open.

"I normally do not condone unreal *gossip*, but the boy came to me directly," Bill whispered.

I furrowed my brows. It was odd for the boy to just up and ask for help.

"Bryan," I clarified. "When?"

"Last night," Bill stated simply. "Before that I had some...suspicions."

I knew Bill had his reservations as well. Knowing the history between Evelyn and I, maybe being away from everyone made me just as blind to what *was* happening.

I stayed quiet as he took a moment to gather his thoughts.

"When they got married, he stayed away from the church. Even the ceremony was on their property," Bill explained. "His family sort of stayed out of things, claimed to have prayed differently or something of that nature. Never felt comfortable in such a small place after moving from their own country. But even so, Evelyn came by herself, alone, then stopped almost entirely for a while. It wasn't until I approached her that she convinced him she would come back."

Bill paused for a moment. She never told me she stopped attending services. The idea of Evelyn not showing up was such an oddity, especially after her mother passed away. She didn't have any comfort with her father being as deep in the dark as he was. Everyone knew her at service growing up. I didn't realize Avery was *that* disconnected from the rest of us.

"I was rather grateful she came back," Bill added. "When she started coming back, however, something changed...*he* changed."

"Was there a tragedy?"

I was already feeling rather betrayed that I was so disjointed from her life.

"I'm not sure. There have been no funerals under his family name, but nonetheless Evelyn came to me a few weeks ago stating he's been snapping at the oddest moments. He's even gotten accusatory and unusually possessive. What's worse is she suspects he's been leaving in the middle of the night unannounced. Then again given his record we shouldn't be surprised, should we?"

I mulled over every detail. Avery was far from stupid, but his family status and his choices were not always made by him.

Perhaps their marital arrangement was only something to hide behind with Evelyn's family being indebted to them. It's not like he was committing murder, just committing a shoddy marriage.

"When Bryan showed up, he was silent and pacing. He said he was worried for his mother's safety," Bill added.

Despite the priest being in front of me I couldn't help but curse, as I leaned back in my chair. Bill seemed to forgive me, nodding in agreement.

"Have you talked to Avery?" I asked.

"No...I rather not stir the pot any more than it is," Bill replied. "As you know, I've already tried *once* to interfere with that family's decisions. Unfortunately, I can't force them to listen. I'd rather keep my flock together, not scatter them and turn them against each other."

I nodded. I could understand Bill's urge to want to protect her. But he wasn't always in the position to do so.

"Mistress?"

Bill shrugged. "It's very possible if he's out and about," he admitted. "But...Bryan seemed more concerned about *her* and wouldn't tell me why other than the incident last night."

I'd have to talk to the boy. It was the only way to get a clear picture of what's been going on. I knew very well that Evelyn would never stand for this kind of behavior from anyone in her family not after what we'd been through.

"I know this isn't the most *comfortable* circumstance for you," Bill added. "But I didn't know who else to go to."

"You think Michael could—"

"There's nothing *against* Avery yet. It's all hearsay and speculation," Bill said. He sighed, looking at me, sympathy in his eyes but there was a shift to pleading. "Is it too late to ask for that favor? You're still working, yes?"

The possibilities caused my mind to simmer. How could she not tell me what was happening? Perhaps she was afraid of getting in trouble. She told me she needed to limit contact with me...perhaps that was Avery's doing. I knew my reasons why I limited things with her. I would never tell her.

I tried to keep my cool as Bill sighed, looking out the nearby window. It took a moment as he watched the passerby before he spoke again. "Elizabeth is helping me run the services tonight," Bill explained. "I encouraged Evelyn to come assist for some peace of mind. If things get out of hand, I want you to *protect* her."

I felt my body stiffen. "You act like he's going to suddenly turn feral on her."

"Something *already* happened, and that man has been showing his true colors in these short months. If he shows up, I need someone to get in between them."

I turned, following his line of sight. Outside, happy, unbothered people passed the clergy house as they ran their errands. I felt as if I were in a snow globe with our own troubles separated from their reality.

"I don't know about you...but there's almost a sudden shift in the air," Bill whispered, uncomfortably. "I can feel it gnawing on my bones. I just don't know *what* has changed."

I knew what he meant. There was something that happens here that gives all of Blackwood Hollow fair warning. Some seem blind to it, while others like myself and my closer colleagues feel it in our souls. But we were never sure of *what* or *who* was going to be in the crosshairs. Ever since my father, I was always prepared for the worst. So why did Avery's interruption feel so wrong. "You always had a way of knowing when something is about to happen."

"So do you," Bill scoffed back. "Will you ask the boy his side of the story? I know you'll listen to him."

I nodded. I just hope the boy was willing to talk.

"He's very fond of you...he's at that age where he won't tell you," Bill chuckled. "Teenagers."

I felt a forced chuckle in my throat. I stood from my chair, and Bill sighed as he did the same.

"Thank you. For everything," I said and nodded as I turned to head to the door.

"Connor," he called out, forcing me to stop.

Bill gripped onto my shoulder; he gestured towards my hand. I furrowed my brows in confusion as I reached out my hand, opening it.

Bill placed a wooden cross into it.

"Token of my gratitude," Bill explained.

I swallowed at the gesture. It was as if it was going to start burning just being in my presence. I felt my hand move towards him to give it back, Bill stopped me firmly, gently closing my hand around it.

"I was going to give this to your mother when she served with us. After your father died. But then...everything happened."

I looked back down, staring at the cross as my throat went dry.

It was dark wood, similar to the one that was around her neck.

"I know you haven't made it to services in a while," Bill stated softly. "Just a little bit of God to protect you, hm?"

Bill meant well. I knew he did, but that didn't mean I wasn't still reluctant to take it. I pocketed the cross into my jacket anyway.

"Thank you," I grunted. "Just hope He can save me from doing something I'll regret."

"Let's start with the drinking, hm," Bill replied with a wink, patting my shoulder as I wrapped my coat back around my body.

Bill opened the door, and we nearly came out of our skin as two women shrieked from behind the door. One of the women lost her grip on some loose sheet music she was carrying. She immediately flushed and dove for it. Then my eyes rested on her and I almost grinned, forgetting the seriousness of the past hour for a mere moment.

"Elizabeth Sutton," I greeted her.

I could tell she was too distracted blushing even harder than before.

"That's Mrs. *Baker* to you now-" Elizabeth began but froze as she finally looked up at me.

She was still breathing heavily from the flustered encounter. She paused, recomposing herself and stood tall as if to show some form of confidence. Elizabeth Baker was a late twenties girl, who recently had been wedded to the "love of her life," Ted. She was a pretty girl. Sandy hair, bright blue eyes and dressed in a red coat that seemed to perfectly match her rosy chilled cheeks and painted lips. I could see how Ted would be infatuated with her. It's not hard with someone like Elizabeth.

I tried not to laugh as Elizabeth's mouth was gaping before grinning to my surprise.

"Mr. Sullivan!" Elizabeth shrieked in glee. "It's been *too* long!"

I scoffed in amusement, nodding towards the papers.

"Do you need a hand?" I asked, as I instinctively knelt down to help her with what she dropped.

She seemed to snap out of her daze and immediately followed suit. I did my best to gather what I could before it collected moisture from the snow. That's when the other woman's voice greeted us.

"Connor?" she greeted from behind Elizabeth.

I froze at the voice. I looked up, my body slowly straightening from the ground.

Evelyn Fields...well Evelyn *Atwood* now. The name gave me a bad taste in my mouth...always had when she had to change it.

The winter did not phase her beautiful nature. Evelyn was almost the total opposite of Elizabeth. Her eyes were gray, her hair was almost auburn, but it had shown darker like her mother in the winter season. She was bundled in a black ankle length wool coat and had a splash of lavender color on a scarf she wore.

We've known each other since we were children. When we were a bit older, I would've told her everything in small doses. I don't know if she'd believe that even now, she still managed to take my breath away.

And then...I saw it. The bruising formed around her right eye.

I tried my best not to show my rage. How could Avery possibly lay a *hand* on her? But my hands were having difficulty not forming into fists. Evelyn stood smiling but I could tell that she was more than a little embarrassed. It wasn't like her to be so aversive. She was a good honest girl and now she wouldn't tell me she was in trouble. Maybe it was such a fluke of an incident that even she didn't know how to go about explaining it. One would hope.

I must've looked awful already with my unkempt appearance and the horrendous nightmares I faced. But, in that moment I didn't care, and I felt myself staring at her. It wasn't until Bill reached out to his arm and gripped my shoulder that I felt myself finally take a breath.

"Mrs. Atwood, Mrs. Baker, I wasn't expecting either of you for another hour at least," Bill interrupted, trying his best polite smile.

Elizabeth nudged Evelyn who was cringing. Though her eyes never left mine. I felt myself staring. Whether she noticed or not, she pretended not to make a bigger deal.

"I'm so sorry Reverend, we just needed the air,"

Elizabeth said hurriedly. "Is this a bad time?"

"No! No of course not," Bill replied with a grin, "Connor was just-"

"Leaving actually," I finished mimicking his polite smile.

I found myself stepping around the women carefully as I made my way down the small stairs. Elizabeth smiled sweetly at me and as I glanced at Evelyn once more she refused to look me in the eyes. That hurt. Hard. More than I was willing to come to terms with. Especially in her circumstances.

I didn't want her to be brave. I wanted her to tell me so I could punch the man if he deserved it.

"Oh! Don't forget we're having a special service tonight," Elizabeth announced. "Maybe you should join us?"

That's when I noticed Elizabeth's eyes flicked motioning towards Evelyn as she stood by the door. I raised my brows slightly.

"Yes, I was just inviting Mr. Sullivan out tonight," Bill agreed.

I felt my eyes look down at the ground and then back at Evelyn.

"Connor's not a fan of being at services he-" Evelyn began.

"I'd be happy to," I intervened. That's when she finally looked at me, sort of stunned at my answer. I'm not surprised. "What time?"

"Seven," Bill and Elizabeth answered almost in unison.

"Great," I chimed. I looked at Evelyn painting a smile on my face. "Will you be there Miss Fields?"

"It's Mrs. Atwood," Evelyn corrected. My stomach

clenched. Even sixteen years later, it was still *hard* to admit she was no longer Miss Fields. "And *yes*, I will be there."

Evelyn seemed to notice the silent pain on my face. That man didn't deserve an ounce of her. And I was going to get to the bottom of whatever the hell this was.

I swallowed as she turned escaping into the clergy house behind Elizabeth and Bill.

I turned to head back. Then I heard Elizabeth rush down the steps frantically and I heard her voice call out, "Connor?"

I turned.

Elizabeth stopped in front of me, smiling sweetly. She leaned in, close enough to speak out of ear shot. "Thank you. Please try to talk some sense into her," she whispered. "That man needs to be reminded who she is to us."

"I'll try," I whispered back.

Elizabeth smiled sweetly and kissed me on the cheek. I couldn't help but blush a little as she grinned. "If only you'd come to church more often," she quipped. "I might actually consider you an angel."

I scoffed in amusement as Elizabeth rushed her way back to the clergy house. Bill gave me a nod before shutting the door behind him.

I had to walk home in the cold, trying not to destroy everything in my path. How could he? What was wrong with Avery and why would he go after *her*? I was going to get my answers. I didn't care how I got them.

If God wanted to stop me, he needed to do it soon. Because I couldn't promise the man wouldn't be dead.

Two

When I arrived at the estate, I felt rather grateful for the bitter cold.

The thought of smashing something became more...*appealing* the more I thought of Evelyn's predicament. And who knows how long it was going on for. As soon as I felt the rage bubble up again, I felt a blustery gust of wind hit my face. *Get it together...you're no use pissed and raging.*

Before I knew it, I found myself standing in front of my two-story brick estate. The curtains were drawn as I approached the rather familiar dark wooden door. This place was home regardless of how empty it seemed from the outside and the tragedy bestowed upon it.

It's hard to believe that I almost ran from this whole town entirely. Everything felt like I was starting from scratch in the most brutal way. But I felt pulled back. I had a feeling my parents' deaths weren't *accidents* which made it harder to leave. It felt as if I was abandoning them if I stepped out and tried a new life.

This whole town seemed cursed even as far back as my grandparents. My mother would tell stories of things they witnessed as children. My father tended to agree with her regarding the many oddities that would happen. They were good people, smart people. Why would they lie over something like that? Either they were caught up in the lore of everything, or they genuinely *believed* it.

Now the only thing that remained of them was this house, a shell of what *used* to be. Ghosts of people who became mere victims of it and unfortunately becoming their own urban legends. But to them and the rest of this town, everything about Blackwood Hollow was all real at the end of the day.

I took off my jacket, finally feeling the bitter cold spread all the way to my fingers as I stepped into the foyer. I glanced at the unchanged décor of the entryway. I tried to respect the estate, keeping it as my parents left it. The elaborate floral green wallpaper that my mother adored saying it would *"brighten up the mood"* always stuck with me. I tended to agree with her. The dark wood that my father insisted that would make the place sharper and more distinguished to the guests who would show.

Their portraits remained along the walls, though I kicked myself for all of them being covered in dust, and...turned around. I didn't have the heart to look at them. Lord forgive me, I couldn't look at their faces anymore.

My mother's crosses were taken down as well. The holy symbol that used to mark her faith was now hidden, missing from the house. Disagreeable or not, God was too busy with the rest of the world to help the small town that was being picked off one by one. At least that's what I told myself. Why else would this be happening over several generations? A bitterness crept up into my throat. My thoughts stopped immediately as I looked down at the floor.

Watery, snow-melted tracks led along the dark floors to my study. Judging by the size and shape of the footprint, they belonged to a certain teenager. I rolled my eyes.

I turned to follow the tracks on the floor, noticing the study was, indeed, open. I peeked in, and of course,

Bryan Fields was sitting at my desk, his feet resting so comfortably on my *father's* desk.

I had to bite my tongue, but I felt my jaw tighten in disapproval anyway. Perhaps my father was rolling in his grave with the amount of scolding I had to restrain.

Bryan Fields was a curious boy, he always had been. Sometimes that curiosity got him in trouble. Bryan was indeed his mother's son. He kept the name Fields as almost a rebellion against Avery. Not to mention his grandfather refused to give up the legacy with the only grandson he had. Bryan never liked the name Atwood. Avery might've taken that as an insult, but he wasn't exactly fond of his son. And as much as Evelyn despised her father, she would not disagree with keeping the name to fill certain legacies.

Bryan being as...brilliant as he was had a rebellious streak that made his mother worried in the recent years. It included going into abandoned places or wandering around the woods as if it meant nothing to the rest of us. Then again, I was like that too, especially after my parents were gone. I understood his situation. His father never bonded with him and Evelyn did her best to pick up the reins.

The more he was absent the more she worried, and I couldn't blame her. To ease her discomfort, she had asked me a favor: putting the boy within arm's reach, keeping an eye on him and my chivalrous nature couldn't fathom saying "no" to *her*. Even the sheriff in town agreed, nudging Bryan to occupy himself in my company.

His curiosity might get him killed one day, the officers would complain and I agreed with that statement. Didn't need him to end up being another news story.

Bryan was sixteen and it's hard to believe he

survived this long, especially when his interest piqued on the odd of the cases I'd been a part of. He refused to keep his nose out, so I kept him in my sight. Outside of Michael and Oscar, I seemed to be the only person who seemed to take Bryan's curiosity seriously. No matter how much his habits got to me.

What he had was not a vice, but a talent. Something to be admired. That's when cases were solved and how people were found. Plus, Bryan seemed to only listen to *my* advice. Which made the responsibility of having him in my dwelling even more grueling.

And now here we are, the boy now taking over my study, his wet boots on *my father's desk*.

As I finally entered the study, I looked over his shoulder as he seemed to be busy reading the local newspaper.

After a moment, I cleared my throat in a greeting which caused Bryan to jump from his seat.

The surprise made him gasp while the newspaper was sent scattering around the desk...the desk which was now *wet*.

"Connor I-" Bryan greeted but I immediately raised my hand to silence him. Bryan nodded, slowly sitting down and lifting his feet back onto the desk.

"*Off!*" I scolded quietly but sternly.

His feet hit the ground instantly with a loud *thud*.

I pointed at some spare cloth for him to fetch. I would not have his mindless action ruin my father's desk. His eyes darted to the water stains on the desk. He flinched and gave me a sheepish look then immediately proceeded to clean up the evidence. I could tell on his face he wouldn't do that again.

"Sorry Connor, I-"

Then I furrowed my brows. *Connor*? When did he start addressing me so informally by my name?

I put up my hand to silence Bryan for a moment. He swallowed, waiting rather impatiently as he put the rag away and sat back down in the chair. "When did you start calling me that?" I asked.

Bryan's eyes widened and his face turned pink as he did when he was younger.

"I uh-" Bryan stammered.

I sighed shaking my head. I wasn't going to scold him again within a matter of minutes. "Never mind."

The looming reminder of needing Bryan to talk lingered in my mind. But him being so disrespectful in my study after seeing his mother just set me over the edge. He must've noticed because his eyes studied me worriedly.

"Did I do something?"

"No."

"I only ask-"

I tsked again, rubbing the bridge of my nose as I leaned against the opposite end of the desk. Bryan sat there in the chair staring at me as I tried to regain my composure. I had to give him the run down. He deserved that much if I were to question him later.

"I talked to Reverend Donovan this morning," I began.

I didn't think the boy's eyes could get any wider. "You found out, didn't you?"

"Depends on what *you* mean about finding out," I replied.

Bryan shook his head, looking away. I could instantly by the look on his face he was angry. Not the normal childlike response he used to have, but genuinely upset.

"He started it!" Bryan growled through gritted teeth, his eyes averted. "That *bastard*-"

"Bryan!" I growled warningly.

Bryan stopped for a mere moment as I saw the rage and almost betrayal in his eyes. I regained some steadiness in my voice.

"Don't talk about your father like that," I stated quietly, holding back my own reluctance. Though...I was definitely on his side right now as much as I hated to admit it.

"But he is!" Bryan objected, a growl in his throat.

When did the boy's voice get deeper? I sighed, needing to keep my cool as well. If I felt as horrible, rage inducing as I did seeing his mother, I couldn't imagine how *he* felt. And who knows how long they've been acting like this. Hidden from the rest of the town. I took a breath and collected my wits.

"Listen...I can't get a clear picture if you don't tell me *what* happened," I explained.

Bryan hesitated, crossing his arms.

"I don't know," Bryan pushed.

I know he didn't want to talk, but I needed answers and I had to do it carefully. "Bryan, listen to me," I pressed gently, his eyes now away from me. "I *need* you to be brave for me all right? Sometimes we must have difficult conversations, right?"

Bryan flinched, eyes tearing but he wiped them away before they could fall.

I waited another moment.

"All I want is to know what happened. For you to be

honest with me," I reassured him as best I could. "Remember how honesty affects what we do?"

Bryan stayed silent and shook his head.

I could see the battle he was having. I kind of took the hint that he was not going to go into it. Boys shouldn't go through this. No one at his age should be dealing with *any* of this. I nodded in acceptance; he'll tell me when he's ready. "Where's your father now?"

Bryan shook his head. "He's home, though I'm not sure if we're going back tonight."

"Where would you be staying?"

"Mrs. Baker's," Bryan replied, grabbing a pen off my desk and fiddling with it. He looked at me and gave an exasperated sigh. "Although not sure if that's any *better*."

"Now be nice. Mrs. Baker seemed like a nice lady," I quipped. "And Ted is no one to sneeze at. They're good people."

Byran rolled his eyes again.

"Why can't *you* just beat him up," Bryan groaned. "We'd be better off without him."

"Oi!" I spat as I grabbed the pen from his fingers. He looked at me grudgingly. "Knock that off. Just because your father had an *episode* doesn't mean there isn't *reasoning*. And *I'm* going to get to the bottom of it."

I felt my voice bite on my words.

Bryan rolled his eyes. "It's not just the one."

I swallowed while regaining my sense of composure.

"Patience is a very *hard* and painful thing. It takes a long time to master it," I reminded the boy as I did in a lot of my lessons. "However, there is *something* you can do for me."

"That being?"

I sighed, sitting on the desk in front of him and forcing a smile on my face. "Keep your mother safe," I replied simply. "Something is terribly wrong and we are going to find out understand?"

Bryan swallowed and looked away, nodding slowly. "Can we talk about something else?" he insisted, grabbing the newspaper rather quickly as if to shut down the conversation entirely. "I got the rundown."

I sighed, nodding slowly as I stood from the desk and backed away slightly so that I could pace around the room. He was a smart boy, and he learned things rather quickly. I could tell he needed the distraction. It's not like my mind wasn't begging for it either, because if I didn't, Evelyn's bruised face would flash back into my mind.

"Give me the run down, Fields," I encouraged.

Bryan hastily grabbed the pages trying to reorder them best he could. He then cleared his throat as he rummaged through each loose paper. He stopped on one and his face brightened.

"Oh! Reports of missing livestock again in the last month-"

Again. More farm animals missing. But unfortunately, that isn't the same as missing people...unfortunately.

"Does it say who's making the claims?"

"It's the pig lady-"

I turned, looking at Bryan. I raised my brows at him, daring him to continue the sentence and sighed.

"She does have a *name* Bryan," I reminded the boy. "Manners."

Bryan's cheeks reddened as he rolled his eyes

despite nodding in understanding clearing his throat. "Right... *Miss Shaw*," he corrected himself. He looked at me as if to confirm any form of satisfaction which I nodded in response, motioning for him to proceed. "She's been missing a few animals throughout the whole year. Says it might be the woods you know."

Miss Jane Shaw was an odd duck around town. She'd been here as long as I could remember. Her family was relatively well known even in my parents' generation. It was odd to have her be such a local legend. She mainly worked on a farm by herself for as long as I had known her. Although she had a bit of a reputation. She somehow always managed to have a massive piece of land, yet her pigs especially would go missing. The butcher never received the livestock, and there was no sign of them *anywhere* in the entire town. It made me wonder if they fled from her poor upkeep.

"Or her incompetence," I commented. "That woman never had a handle on her own livestock since her family set foot here."

Bryan shook his head.

"Any others missing recently?"

"Not since the last one," Bryan replied. "That was months ago."

Thankfully. I stared at Bryan as he flipped to the familiar section of the obituaries. I prayed he was right. But word goes around quickly, and Michael would've told me if something else had been conjured up as suspicious. Unless he had no reason to tell me...

"Are you going to the services tonight?" Bryan asked. "Maybe we can ask around. Mingle."

"Mingling isn't exactly *appropriate* in church," I

joked. "You make it sound like a party."

"Well, it's a memorial regardless. Everyone will be there," Bryan explained.

Bryan flipped through the pages quietly as my eyes rested on the map. All the articles, photographs, and drawings just stared back at me. There had to be a link. Anything. But there was nothing. One by one people seemed to be picked off. Maybe even before that.

Blackwood Hollow was a force to be reckoned with. Unfortunately for me, I was the only one who ever truly looked for an *answer*.

That's when it hit me. The twinge in my gut that forced my hand. I didn't want to be haunted by that church. Old memories were going to be sprung onto me but something screamed down to my bones that I'd be a fool not to go. At the very least I needed to alleviate Elizabeth's worries about Evelyn.

My eyes then rested on an illustrated picture of the home I currently stood in. Without any of my family that stood in a quiet, happy picture. Yet the map labeled the home: ***The Sullivans*** with my father's beautiful calligraphy.

I wasn't sure how long I was staring before Bryan broke the silence. "Are you all right?"

I had to go tonight. For Bill, for Elizabeth, for Bryan...for Evelyn. They were the only real family I seemed to have left. I turned around, leaned forward, grabbed Bryan by the shoulder, and pulled him up from the desk chair.

"Go home and put on your Sunday best Fields," I announced grinning.

"Sir?"

"We don't want to offend God."

Three

The church was always a silent but powerful place.

Its presence lingered from generations of family gatherings from potlucks, weddings, and funerals. It had been a place of hope despite the chaos. To me, unfortunately, what remained seemed to be a ghost of what used to be. Resentment, longing, and loss of faith. With my family long gone, it was hard enough. Facing Evelyn's predicament in this place felt like the final nail on a coffin.

Years...Avery Atwood could have been doing this with her for *years*. I couldn't wrap my head around it. Had Evelyn been hiding this for all this time? No. I would have seen some sort of signs of this. Word would've spread at the very least. This town is too small. Nevertheless I had to get to the bottom of this. Bill knew my feelings about the man. But that wouldn't stop me from protecting her. No matter the excuse for his behavior, I wouldn't allow another incident to happen again. Bryan had unsurprisingly remained quiet all afternoon about the whole thing. I didn't press, but God I wanted to.

So, what happens if he does come by, I thought trying to level my anger. *Whatever happens,* protect *her.*

I didn't want to cause more trouble for anyone, but I couldn't avoid it if it came my way.

I took a deep breath as we finally approached the church. Despite us arriving early, there happened to already be a good handful of busy churchgoers roaming about. Bryan stayed close behind as we entered. It was a perfect time for gossip, catching up and the traditional chatter among those who were preparing for service. Maybe we could find answers with a few or at the very least not make a scene.

The old wooden doors gave an astounding creak as we opened them. I peeked through, noticing only a handful busying themselves with candles, décor, and other things. A good few stopped, glancing in our direction after hearing that old door screech open.

As we slowly walked in, a few nudged each other, and I held my breath. Prying eyes immediately minded their own business as soon as I turned to them, smiling politely as best I could. I guess my reputation is still well-known here.

My stomach clenched uncomfortably. I could handle crime scenes as if it was a walk in the park, but the stares from this town? The attention was always something I had a hard time managing. I remained focused as the whispering continued, now possibly about us instead of the original town gossip. Then again...I didn't exactly give myself *that* much time to clean up my face or my hair despite dressing better than earlier in the day.

I leaned over and nudged Bryan.

"You see her?" I asked.

Bryan looked around. He stopped for a moment, pointing as I noticed Evelyn up front with Elizabeth.

"Keep your eye on the door." I ordered as I patted Bryan's shoulder, and I moved forward towards the front of the church.

I couldn't afford for Avery to crash the party early; or cause even *more* havoc with just about anyone.

Bryan nodded, leaning against the wall of the church while crossing his arms. I taught the boy well as

Bryan began to blend into the background doing his best to not be noticed. Observe, listen, and only interfere when necessary. As soon as he was settled, I made my way to the front of the church.

I felt my heart race but kept focused on Evelyn and Elizabeth conversing alone. I ignored the constant stare of bystanders as I approached. I *had* to ignore it.

I was so focused that I felt a bit of relief and surprise when Elizabeth looked up, smiling sweetly at me. It made the burden of the whole ordeal flee for just a moment. A sudden warmth hit my chest, making my attendance feel more...purposeful.

Maybe I was doing the right thing.

Evelyn turned at Elizabeth's gaze, following her line of sight. I jumped when her eyes reached me, and she gasped in surprise.

Although seeing her face to face, it still took me a moment to process. The bruising under Evelyn's eye was even darker than that morning. I could tell she was trying to conceal it with some form of make-up. But I knew better. It was there, I felt my heart race and my fury build again and there was no mistaking it. It was difficult not to immediately clench my hands into fists. I had a job to do, and I needed to be a friend. I smiled at her with as much kindness I could muster.

"Eve," I greeted gently.

Evelyn was about to turn as if to shy away but I could tell Elizabeth was on a mission. She grinned, turning her and grabbing Evelyn gently back around to face me. "Mr. Sullivan! It's so nice to see you again. Isn't it Evelyn?" Elizabeth greeted me as her smile broadened.

I smiled as best I could. This was going to be rougher

than I had anticipated.

When Evelyn looked away, she looked ashamed. The girl I once knew was now afraid to show me a part of her life that was hurting. It used to be second nature for her to tell me every detail of her troubles with her family. But now, she was avoiding it, and my heart sank. "Yes...well, it's certainly been a while since I've seen you here at church," Evelyn mentioned quietly, keeping her eyes down. "How have you been Mr. Sullivan?"

Formalities. I knew why she was like this, but I hated every second of it. "Come now Eve. Do you have to be so formal with me?" I teased gently, grinning. For a brief moment, I swore she smiled back.

I was relieved as the tension released from her shoulders while she stood in front of me. "Did the Reverend twist your arm?" Evelyn teased back as she relaxed.

"Hardly," I retorted.

"Though he can be quite the charmer when he wants to be," Elizabeth added, nudging Evelyn. "That's why he's the best in this line of work."

"Dare I ask where's your other half," I pried lightly.

Evelyn hesitated. Her eyes immediately darted to her fingers. She glanced into my eyes for a moment. "Do you have to ask?" she replied, her voice small, almost a whisper.

I immediately noticed tears forming around her eyes that she hid well from the others.

"Blackjack at the local bar," Elizabeth grated with disgust. "Possibly dabbling in the latest tail looking for a good time."

"*Elizabeth!*" Evelyn whispered quietly in embarrassment. She flinched as Elizabeth gave an apologetic glance.

I was rather surprised how blunt Elizabeth could be. I wouldn't want to be on her bad side. I shouldn't be surprised word got around. His status doesn't help.

Evelyn's mouth opened as if she was about to say something further until Bill caught up with Elizabeth.

"Mrs. Baker," Bill's voice rang out from the front of the church.

"I have to go," Elizabeth announced as she looked up and put a hand on Evelyn's shoulder. She gave me a cheery smile keeping her composure rather elegantly. "You mind keeping an eye on her for me Mr. Sullivan?"

"I'll go with you," Evelyn protested but Elizabeth gave her a reassuring smile.

"Oh, come now," Elizabeth objected. "I'm more than capable of handling whatever the Reverend needs me for."

"But," Evelyn started closer towards Elizabeth.

"Eve," I whispered urgently. I could feel her hesitation, as her eyes remained on Elizabeth who nodded at her encouragingly. She smiled at me in return. I tried to use that to gain my courage to not fail this mission.

"Oh, go on," Elizabeth whispered. "He's the *last* person I'd be worried about."

Elizabeth winked at me and gave Evelyn a friendly brush on her shoulder as she headed over to Bill for preparations.

We watched Elizabeth leave, Evelyn then turned, looking at me, the tears back again in her eyes. She relaxed for a moment and I was just relieved to not be pushed away in one way or another.

I noticed that her eyes searched around the church and stopped on Bryan. I followed her line of sight, and noticed Bryan, his face away from us as if not paying attention.

"It's good to see you," I whispered, trying to regain Evelyn's attention.

Evelyn almost jumped then nodded, smiling sweetly back at me.

I was relieved to see her so relaxed. I started seeing a hint of the old Evelyn I knew.

"I have to admit the same," Evelyn whispered back. "I'm sorry I haven't dropped off Bryan to you personally. Things have been...rather odd lately at home."

"Eve," I sighed. I needed to get her somewhere privately. I noticed the door furthest from the altar that led to the clergy house from the church. "Shall we?"

Evelyn glanced in the direction of the door and nodded quickly. "*Please*," she whispered.

I led Evelyn forward as I gave Bill and Elizabeth a reassuring look as we headed towards the door. I leaned towards Bill as Evelyn very carefully walked ahead as if to avoid prying eyes.

"Do you mind if we," I asked, pointing to the long hallway that connected to the clergy house.

Bill glanced at Evelyn, and I could tell pity was written all over his face. But he smiled at me, nodding in acceptance. "Not at all," Bill whispered. "I'll be here."

I was relieved to have people at our backs. I patted his shoulder and followed Evelyn into the joining hallway. My hand grabbed the knob, forcing the door closed behind us. It was dark and silence enveloped us. There was no noise from the bustling volunteers. Just us, alone. We proceeded a bit further to gain some distance. I almost jumped from hearing her voice after the seconds of absolute silence.

"You haven't been here in months," Evelyn remarked.

"It's hard to," I admitted.

Evelyn folded her hands in front of her. "I know why you're here," Evelyn sighed. "Please I don't...I don't want you involved."

Of course she didn't, but I had no choice. "Eve, I just want to know what happened."

Evelyn froze, her hand instinctively reached up around the bruising. She grabbed my arm, forcing me to stop. I turned, looking directly at her. Even in the candlelight, she was a beautiful woman. Why in the world was she in this hell?

"Did Bryan tell you?"

I stared at her examining every bit of her face. I needed to help her. I didn't want more harm to come from something like this. "No," I answered flatly. "But, frankly I wish he had if his own father swung at you. Don't play me a fool, Eve. Please."

Evelyn swallowed hard as she nodded and took a breath. "He..." she began as her shoulders suddenly tensed. "He went after Bryan."

I felt my body straighten in an instant. Bryan. He went after Bryan. No wonder the boy didn't tell me. "What do you mean?"

"I got to him before he could get too close," Evelyn swallowed. "It was meant for *him*."

"That's not exactly a *reasonable* way to react," I growled. Hitting a woman helping her own child. Madness. "What the hell is going on?"

"I don't know...Avery's been so strange lately. One

minute he's his *usual* self. You know him. Next, he's...lashing out and aggressive...and *predatory*."

I shook my head, rubbing a hand down my face. "Poor boy is probably blaming himself."

Evelyn shook her head.

"How did it start?" I asked.

"He...he mentioned *you*," Evelyn breathed, looking up at me and biting her lip. "I don't know why but that just set him off. Said something about how he doesn't want me around you anymore."

I wasn't a fan of Evelyn's family marrying her off to Avery for some stupid debt. Regardless, I at least remained *civil* despite the threats against me, though civil and avoiding him were sometimes the same thing. Was the man finally showing unable to hide his jealousy? He knew what we were...

"I think...I think he might be seeing someone else. He's been distant since the pregnancy," Evelyn breathed. "It's gotten worse since Bryan started hanging around you more. Bryan doesn't listen to him but he listens to you, so...there's been more fighting."

"Have you seen anyone with him?"

"You know how he used to be when we were younger. Maybe he's finally sick of me and doesn't give a damn about the legalities," Evelyn flushed in embarrassment. "Not like I blame him."

I shook my head at the idea. It didn't seem impossible considering he didn't *agree* with his family's choice of getting married to her. Regardless of her father's stupid debts.

"I don't want you to get hurt," she whispered.

"I wouldn't worry about *me*, Eve."

Evelyn nodded, looking down at the floor and I sighed.

"Please tell me you have a place to stay."

Evelyn rolled her eyes. It was almost identical to Bryan's way of showing his dismay. "Elizabeth *insists* we stay with her and Ted for the time being," Evelyn groaned softly. "I appreciate the gesture but-"

"Ted's a good bit of muscle," I agreed. "I'd trust him with my life."

Evelyn scoffed in amusement when she smiled at me. I was relieved she still had friends who she could rely on, good ones willing to protect her. It was more than I'd done in the last few months. "I would say it's good to see you, but you look like a mess," Evelyn scoffed. She reached out, fixing a fold in my jacket and tucking the tie that fell just outside of my vest. "When are you *ever* going to clean up?"

"After everything that's going on with you, you're worried about *my* appearances?"

"What can I say, old habits die hard. Or never in my case," Evelyn smiled sadly. "Especially with you."

I swallowed, shaking my head. "Eve-"

Then slamming and almost a bellowing sound roared inside the church.

We ran, and I almost burst the door open in panic and rushing adrenaline. The door swung and as we rushed forward, my eyes went wide in horror at the scene.

Avery. He had shoved Bill aside as he strode for Elizabeth, grabbing her arm, beginning to yank her towards him. He grabbed her by the wrist, grinning at her. It was...vicious and predatory like Evelyn mentioned.

That's when the stoic and large Ted Baker came

charging from the back of the church with no restraint. He was focused and ready for violence. He grabbed Avery and tossed him to the ground in a matter of seconds, forcing a curse out of Avery.

Then Avery started laughing as Elizabeth was pulled away with the help of Bill and Mary Donovan.

I was careful to keep my pace slow and steady with Evelyn behind me. I wasn't going to allow her to get caught in the crossfire.

Ted wrestled Avery to the floor. He was a big six-foot three hulking man, lean but powerful with dark hair and hazel eyes that stared seething daggers at Avery.

Avery Atwood a name that was honey to strangers and poison to those who actually knew him. He was a short but built man, lean, and his eyes were dark as night. His dark hair that was usually slicked back, but, it was now in shambles while his dark three-piece suit was wrinkled from the sudden scuffle. There was some mild satisfaction seeing the man in such disarray from none other than Ted Baker.

"You touch her again I'll *kill* you," Ted threatened in a low voice, his tone dark and quiet enough that it was more chilling than if he'd screamed it.

I glanced over at Elizabeth realizing she was being fussed over by Mary Donovan, Bill's wife. Mary was a broad woman who would come at you like a bear. Her glasses covered her green eyes neat on her face, her sandy brown hair pinned in a tight fit bun. She dressed simply, but everyone knew she was the most motherly of all of Blackwood Hollow. She was also fearless.

"I *told* you after the last incident, Avery Atwood, that you would *not* cause a scene in the Lord's house," Bill warned firmly, his eyes piercing.

"You think *God* will stop me from buying this place out?" Avery asked with a chilling smile. It was an odd facial expression even for him. "Then we'll see how the rules will change."

"We'll see. Until then, the *sheriff* will take care of your *current* status in *my* church."

Avery's eyes roamed. They landed on Evelyn and he stared. My body stiffened, suddenly alert as his head tilted and his smile widened somehow. Then his eyes were on me. His glare was expected, but something was different about his eyes. They were already dark brown, but they seemed almost black in the light.

"*Evee*," he sang. "Is there a reason you're with this *low life*? Should I take care of him?"

I felt Evelyn's hand reaching out and grabbing mine, gripping it from behind. Low life? I swallowed as he chuckled under his breath.

I let go of her hand gently, glancing at her.

I approached Avery slowly. His pupils were oddly big for someone who was in a relatively well-lit room.

"Did you see her?" Avery asked. "She's *mine*. You can't have her."

Evelyn swallowed and my protective instincts kicked in.

I nodded to Ted who gave me a quick nod in return as he kept Avery pinned to the ground, his face turned towards me. I knelt to his level. "You're lucky this '*low life*' doesn't make you see stars," I whispered, my voice daring to come out more threatening. "I heard you had a scuffle with your son."

"That's *my* business," Avery growled. "You going to

take them from me?! If you do I know *exactly* where to find you."

Avery was almost as voracious as a predator on a fresh kill. It was unnerving. Something screamed at me to run or fight back. Unfortunately for me...it was to fight back.

I stood, nodding to Ted. He hesitated before letting Avery go, backing away but we both knew better. If Avery wanted a fight, he would get one. We kept our guard up protecting both Elizabeth and Evelyn alike.

Elizabeth moved quickly out of Mrs. Donovan's grasp and grabbed Evelyn to stand behind Ted as a protective shield.

Avery laughed as he slowly rose to face me. I was lucky to be taller than him. But that didn't stop the man from focusing solid fury towards me. He chuckled lowly, a smile growing on his face. I felt my hands clench into fists, standing my ground.

"What are you going to do about it, Sullivan," Avery taunted.

"You touch her and the boy again like that you'll be answering to more than just me," I stated quietly. "And you'll wish I wasn't the first one to get to you."

I wasn't here to cause more trouble, but I had the urge. I was fuming, forcing myself not to try to tear up his soul despite my voice sounding deceivingly calm and collected. *Just scare him, protect Evelyn.*

Avery scoffed, raising his brows.

"Do we understand each other?" I asked.

"They aren't yours, *mongrel*," Avery scoffed, sniffing the air. "Why don't you die in the grave you drink in, while I *take* what I *own*."

Avery stared at Evelyn. His eyes were fierce. No man in Blackwood Hollow had his demeanor. I felt my skin crawl and my mind screaming in alert. Something was terribly wrong.

That's when it hit me. All the adrenaline, the fuming towards this man couldn't be contained. My fist swung hard, punching him straight into his jaw before I could even stop myself. There was a second of relief to finally do what I wanted for a long time.

There were gasps throughout the church. The patron's eyes were all on us and I could care less with this beast of a man. He deserved so much more than I was about to be ready for.

Avery then charged and attempted to tackle me. I dodged just in time.

My mind was ready to show this man what I was made of.

I kicked Avery to the floor. Avery growled and yelled from the blow. If it weren't for the sudden whistling in the back of the church, I would've gladly had a full-blown battle against him.

That's when the patrol came storming in like a flood. One of the patrol officers bent down, lifting Avery off the floor.

"Well, well Mr. Atwood," the sheriff's voice echoed into the building.

God, I felt myself breathe in relief for that voice. I know I would hear of his *"you can thank me later"* banter of bringing in the calvary. And I was willing to take it for tonight.

Michael Hughes strutted in, the man showing some flecks of white in his dark blonde hair, but kept his hair neat at the sides, long on top. His eyes were a rare amber, and still just as piercing as his younger years. He was only a few years older and he held it well. He still wore his officer's uniform, nodding to the patrolman to keep Avery still. "Causing havoc again?" Michael questioned.

"Unfortunately," Bill grumbled, staring daggers in Avery's way.

"Some poor woman screamed to my men that there was a disturbance at the church," Michael announced. "Do I have to drag you out of here again Avery?"

"Hello *Michael*," Avery greeted smugly, rubbing his jaw I had recently adjusted.

"Sheriff Hughes while I'm on duty, Avery," Michael corrected with an equal, not care about your opinions smirk.

"Well Sheriff," Avery mocked as he strode over to Michael to be face to face with him.

"Careful," Michael warned. "You don't want assaulting an officer added to the charges, do you?"

"May I remind you that the guilty party will just be out as soon as a phone call is made?"

"Sure," Michael grinned. "*But*, since it's *Friday*...you won't be able to make your case until *Monday* morning. And I can't even guarantee that with the allegations against you. Outside of tonight that is."

"What?!"

"I'll explain everything while you have a nice private room, like a getaway. But with bars, and company," Michael mentioned.

Michael nodded to his patrol officers. Avery glared at the two of us and I felt the urge slowly get in between them despite him struggling to be restrained by the other officers. The church going people watched and stayed out of the way as his eyes went back on Evelyn.

"*Evee*," Avery sang at her. "If I see you with this low life again-"

Evelyn swallowed and her chin rose.

"You won't," Evelyn stated sternly.

I felt my body stiffen in disbelief. Did everything I just attempted to do shatter?

Avery grinned at me seeming pleased, his expression victorious and it made me sick.

"I'm leaving."

Avery's face suddenly dropped, and he scowled.

I could breathe. I'd never thought I'd hear those words come out of her mouth. I stared as I watched Avery's eyes turn ferocious. I wouldn't have been surprised if he would've attempted to kill me on the spot if Michael's men didn't already have him in handcuffs.

"You *need* me," Avery growled. "Your family owes me! We have an *agreement*!"

"I'm sure they'll forgive me," Evelyn retorted. I felt so proud at that moment. Felt like the girl I knew growing up was in full force. "But, to be frank, I could care less if they have to disown me. It's better than spending another waking moment with what you turned into Avery Atwood."

"You have *no* idea what you're doing, you wretch!" Avery spat.

Then, his rage suddenly got him out of the patrolman's grip and lunged towards her. He swung, but I immediately stepped in out of instinct. I felt the full blow to the face, gritting my teeth, and tasted blood within seconds. I grabbed my face, my head instantly feeling the rush of pain. I was relieved when I barely made out Michael's men tackling Avery and solidifying their grip on him.

"Get him out of here," Michael ordered calmly as Avery writhed.

Avery's glare shifted to Evelyn, and I even saw him glance at Bryan who immediately ducked further back from view.

Bryan avoided the scene like the plague as Avery was dragged out of the church grunting and screaming like a madman.

Evelyn immediately turned, grabbing onto me and my face. I felt my world shift as I felt her hands around my jaw. "Good Lord Connor you're bleeding," she whispered anxiously. "Mary."

Mary Donovan nodded rushing out of the church towards the clergy house.

I wiped my face noticing the blood coming from my nose. My head was still swimming. "I'm all right," I whispered to her, and she was in tears.

I was too busy with the whole ordeal to notice Michael finally approaching us.

"Well...even in your older years trouble seems to find you, eh, Connor," Michael teased lightly.

"And yet here he is, the big man I can count on to save the day," I retorted, flinching as Mary came back with a pristine white towel.

Evelyn pressed it on my face under my nose and I took over.

"Of course...where would I be without you," Michael patted my shoulder, genuinely looking at me with concern. "He got you good."

"I'll manage," I replied pinching my nose and wiping the blood from my face.

"You got my call earlier I take it," Bill guessed, moving in as Evelyn stayed put alongside me.

"Or else I wouldn't be here," Michael replied. "Had a few already out and about looking for him. With our luck he was already here, of course."

Bill nodded.

"You called him?" Evelyn asked Bill.

Bill looked over protectively. "Someone has to keep an eye on you," he nodded to her.

Evelyn instinctively touched her eye. "But-"

"Eve..." I whispered giving her a small smile of assurance. "Please."

"You didn't think we'd just let this go, did you?" Elizabeth asked as Evelyn looked over at Elizabeth who strutted over to her and hugged her in full force.

"Some serious accusations were placed Mrs. Atwood," Michael gritted at her last name. "I have reason to believe that they were true."

Evelyn sighed before nodding in agreement.

Michael looked over at her, showing the same protective nature as Bill or even Elizabeth had earlier in the day. His face was grim and serious. "Then...I highly suggest you gather what's yours and stay with someone else tonight."

"She's staying with us," Elizabeth piped up with Ted nodding in agreement. Bryan came out of his hiding place in the back rushing up to his mother and giving her a hug. She seemed caught off guard at first, but I could tell she was grateful.

"I'm proud of you," Bryan whispered, and she hugged him tighter. Bryan looked at me nodding and I nodded back.

"We'll get your things after church," Elizabeth stated gently and Evelyn nodded.

"Eve," Michael whispered looking at her rather sympathetically. "We'll work on paperwork tomorrow to get you out of this."

"What if he gets out like he says?"

"I promise with the evidence, and your testimony...he can be put away for a long time," Michael reassured, "You can always call if you're concerned."

He motioned to me.

I swallowed and Evelyn looked at me for a long moment. She's safe. That's all that mattered at this moment. For a second I could see her eyes staring at me as I clumsily worked with the towel Mrs. Donovan gave me.

Bill sighed and clapped his hands. "Well...shall we get on with the service then?" he suggested. "Lord knows we need some cleansing after that whole fiasco..."

"I think I can agree to that," Evelyn whispered quietly.

I felt relieved as she smiled. She was finally free.

Four

I felt as if I came out of some lucid dream after the whole ordeal with Avery.

I didn't stay for services, since Michael and Evelyn both *insisted* that I take care of my nose. I tried to pass it off as nothing I haven't experienced before. Rather a bloody nose and a bruised face than the others being in trouble.

Knowing Evelyn was okay though, I finally felt like I had the blessing and willpower to leave. Bryan would stay behind and keep an eye out for any more trouble. He was a good kid that way. Michael, Ted, and Bill all agreed to keep the peace. And knowing Avery was behind bars tonight, as odd as that seemed to be, that did give me *some* comfort.

Avery's eyes kept replaying in my mind...how crazed and dark they turned.

They felt *inhuman*.

I wasn't sure if this new behavior was temporary or always had been behind that fake charismatic mask. I had to be sure that Evelyn and Bryan were safe regardless of the answer.

The walk home felt longer than normal as the events of the night kept circling in my mind. I was rather grateful for Bill inviting me. It wouldn't have been just Evelyn in trouble tonight. The Bakers could very much be in danger now.

Avery seemed *predatory*, even the air around him made me sick to my stomach. I recounted every incident before tonight, and I should've trusted my gut about the man. Something was always strange about him since we were kids.

I opened the door to the house. The place felt empty and dark despite the semi-happy outcome of something so...*dismal*. I felt the urge as soon as I walked in. I grabbed a small glass of whiskey. I would be good tonight and not drown myself in it. I took the glass with me as I headed into the nearby washroom.

The only thing telling me its reality was the blood on my face and clothes. Well...that and the pain in my nose. I was just grateful my nose had stopped bleeding...

I found a clean shirt while throwing off my current one. The stains would be a nightmare. I ran the sink and threw the shirt in cold water to let it soak. I hoped that I'd remember to thoroughly wash it later while I washed the rest of the blood off my face.

Knock, knock, knock.

I nearly jumped out of my skin as I faced the direction of the front door. I checked the clock and noted the time. It was 10pm...a little late for a visit.

I washed my hands, then buttoned up my shirt as I made my way to the door.

I opened the front door, and Elizabeth gave me the biggest cheery smile. It had been a while since I had someone smile at me like that. And...with cookies?

"Mrs. Baker," I greeted her, feeling myself almost laugh in surprise. She only beamed brighter and the delicious fragrance of those cookies were making it hard to concentrate. "A little late, isn't it?"

"These, sir, are for your valiant efforts," Elizabeth announced, handing me a small tea towel wrapping a rather big batch of warm cookies. My mouth started to water as soon as I smelled them in full force. It made it easier to ignore the iron taste in my mouth.

I wouldn't ignore something this good this late. Not after our victory of keeping everyone safe. As much as it made me a little uneasy. "If you say so," I smirked, taking the cookies gently from her. "How is she?"

"Ted and I grabbed her things. Bryan was a huge help," Elizabeth replied. "Although she insisted not to bring much. She'll sort more out once that...scoundrel is more *legally* settled."

I nodded as I instinctively reached into my unexpected gift of morsels, grabbed a cookie, and took a bite. I felt victorious and I owed all of them for letting me interfere, as selfish as that seemed in the moment. "Good," I muttered as I motioned inside the house. "Do you want to come in?"

Elizabeth shook her head. "No, I really just wanted to drop off your gift," she replied.

I nodded. She watched me eat part of the cookie and I raised my brows at her.

"I..I don't know how to thank you," Elizabeth remarked. "She talks about you often. As much as I don't know you personally...it's almost as if I do..."

"Well, I color me surprised," I quipped, smirking. "Gave you all the dirty details I take it?"

"Only what mattered," she retorted back with a smirk of her own.

I laughed, taking another cookie.

"Well...I can see why you won Ted's heart," I teased.

Elizabeth giggled and looked behind her. "She um," she began, biting her lip as if thinking how to proceed. "She's very grateful that we helped her. But..."

"But?" I repeated as my stomach dropped at

Elizabeth's hesitation.

"She was wondering," Elizabeth continued, "if she could see you tomorrow?"

I immediately froze. Evelyn wanted to be here tomorrow with Bryan. I must've given a deer in headlights look because Elizabeth immediately stammered embarrassed.

"If you're not busy that is," Elizabeth started. "I'm sure you could-"

"Of course," I agreed instantly before I could even mull it over.

Elizabeth took a breath and smiled broadly.

"Tell her to pick up anything she wants for dinner."

"I'll let her know Mr. Sullivan," Elizabeth answered with a grin and turned to leave. "Enjoy those cookies."

"Connor," I corrected. "You're Evelyn's best friend, might as well drop the formalities."

Elizabeth nodded, not at all refraining from the wicked grin on her face.

"And tell Ted thanks for you know...being him," I winked at her.

Elizabeth giggled as she waved and headed out. "Good night Connor," she said, walking down the steps and onto the street.

I smiled and waved, shaking my head in amusement.

I took another good bite of the cookie as I shut and locked the door behind me.

Despite the bloody nose and a definite bruise in the morning, I was definitely feeling like a hero.

***

February 1905

The chill in the air was biting at my face, but that didn't stop me from the magnificent night ahead of me.

I found myself rushing down the road, my pace quickening at every step. Tonight was the night when everything was about to change, and I couldn't help but grin like a mad man despite the nerves in my stomach.

I almost tripped up the steps of the clergy house and finally got myself to the door. I knocked, but I didn't have to wait long before Reverend Donovan swung the door open, sharing almost the same stupid grin in return.

"My boy you're early," the reverend teased, the smile never leaving his face. "I guess I shouldn't be *too* surprised."

I found myself rushing in, but it was damn near impossible to hide the smile plastered on my face. "Is Evelyn here yet?"

"She's with Mary," Bill replied gently. "I would love to personally congratulate you again."

I nodded quickly. Grabbing the box in my pocket, I started fiddling with it out of a mix of nerves and excitement.

Bill smirked. "I heard you officially inherited to the estate," he mentioned. "That's certainly a good way to start the honeymoon."

"Just this week," I confirmed. "I've been having a hell of a time cleaning it."

Bill crossed his arms. "Well, I have to say God really has a way of showing his blessings," he chuckled.

I fiddled with the box in my hand. My mind was swirling that night. We waited for so long to get this done in private. But...there was a part of me that had no idea if this was going to work.

"No matter what comes of this," Bill said, snapping me out of thought. He walked over, putting a hand on my shoulder and squeezing. "I know your parents would be proud of you. Of her. You *both* deserve this."

Bill stared at me for a long moment and I couldn't help but smile. I was grateful for him. He had been nothing but a father figure to both of us through our family ordeals.

"Thank you Reverend," I replied, finding myself at a loss for words.

The house was now mine to own and to hold and to now find my next chapter in. I felt my hand squeeze around the box in my hands as the back door connecting to the church opened. The reverend's wife came through first with a big smile on her face.

That was the moment, I felt my breath catch. Evelyn Fields stood in the doorway behind her. She was blushing, but her smile was beautiful. She was wearing such a beautiful dress. Something her mother probably gave her a long time ago.

I felt my heart racing and grinned as I dared to move forward to her. She grinned seeing me which made my heart skip even more. I grabbed her and hugged her tightly. She sighed into my chest and I could have lived in that moment forever.

Then there was a tap on my shoulder.

"Are we ready?" Mary's voice asked, mirroring a smile that was almost as joyous as ours.

I felt myself break away as Evelyn looked away

embarrassed. She nodded and I did the same. Though my smile never broke.

Mary grinned, clapping her hands and motioning to Reverend Donovan. He nodded and escorted us through the back way towards the church.

We followed them, our hands intertwined. I felt Evelyn's grip tighten around mine. She glanced, and I could see some fear in her eyes despite her happiness.

Bill and Mary finally reached the door to the church. I was about to follow but felt a tug pulling me back.

Evelyn stared at me, her eyes filled with worry.

Bill turned, looking at us.

"Can you give us a moment?" I requested lightly.

Bill smiled and nodded, motioning his wife to follow him into the church. Mary closed the door behind them to give us a hint of privacy.

I looked at Evelyn in the little darkness that was in the hall. Her face illuminated by the twilight that peeked through the windows. She smiled, a tear falling from her face. "I'm sorry," she whispered.

I dared to move closer to her, gripping onto her hand. "It's all right," I whispered back.

"What if...what if father finds out?" Evelyn asked. "What if he doesn't approve?"

"Evelyn..."

"God what if he hurts you?"

"He can't."

"But-"

"*Evee*...I'm not here for *him*," I assured her, grabbing her hands. "I told him everything. I will not let your father stand in the way of us."

Evelyn hesitated, looking out the window. "What if

this is a mistake?" she whispered.

I scoffed, grinning at her. "You are *never* a mistake," I answered. I found myself hovering over her, lifting her chin to look up at me. "I will do *everything* in my power to protect you. Because I know you've done the same for me my entire life."

Evelyn scoffed, she smiled and she reached out, as she wrapped her arms around my neck.

"I've always been yours Evee," I whispered into her hair. "Now I want even God to know."

Evelyn chuckled into my chest and squeezed me into her. "I love you," she whispered.

I squeezed her tighter before pulling away and offering my hand. "We will break the news tomorrow. But tonight is ours alone. Before God and ourselves," I offered. "If you'll still have me."

Evelyn nodded, smiling widely as she wiped the tears off her face. "You think I'd complain about marrying you?"

Evelyn grabbed my hand, and I pulled her to the door.

"You've complained about a lot of things Evee. Marrying me, I hope, is not one of them."

We made our way to Bill and Mary. They smiled when they saw both of us smiling.

"Are we ready?" Bill asked.

I looked at Evelyn again and she grinned. But this time she answered and I felt myself falling in love with her all over again.

"Yes..." Evelyn whispered.

***

January 1922

  After dreaming of that night with Evelyn years ago...I did something drastic the next morning. I went to the barber.

  Evelyn was right...I needed to clean up. It was something I hadn't thought about doing for a long time. I didn't realize how bad I let it go until I looked at the seemingly careless version of myself in the mirror. I knew it wasn't my best but I must've let it get in the way.

  I got my hair cut along the sides, keeping it long along the top and my beard trimmed. I didn't want to totally shave it off, not with the winter being here. God forbid the change was *that* drastic.

  I almost hesitated as my barber revealed my cleaned-up hair and face in the mirror. It was almost as if I was looking at the ghost of my father's younger self. I never believed I looked that much like him until more recent years.

  I tipped the barber more than I usually did in the past. I needed to be at my best. *She* was coming today.

  I tried to find *anything* that was suitable to wear...nothing crazy, just something I didn't feel like a total slob in. Then again, she'd seen me at my absolute worst in rather recent years. I couldn't help but feel a small swell of excitement as I cleaned and arranged the house by myself.

  I finally found a thick button-down shirt, suspenders and casual pants that were cleaned from my father's closet. Hard to believe they fit me now. I grabbed my boots and made sure they weren't particularly dirty. They were worn but not catastrophic.

I was in the middle of getting the study organized when I heard a knock at the door. I made sure to close the door of the study as I strolled to the entrance.

As I opened the door, Evelyn, Elizabeth, Bryan and Ted greeted me in their own charming ways. I nearly jumped when Elizabeth gave off a gasp.

At first I was puzzled by the sudden stares I was getting.

Then I realized this is the first time any of them had seen me this cleaned up. Even Bryan did a double take, his eyes wide, his grin big.

I tried to keep my cool. I wasn't a fan of such attention, but I felt more or less *human* today.

"Connor! Gracious I almost didn't recognize you!" Elizabeth gloated. "You look like a totally different person!"

My eyes reached Evelyn who was gaping. She turned away blushing. Well…I guess I can still do that to her which was hard to believe. I tried not to let it get to my head.

She wrapped around her dark wool coat and lavender scarf around her tightly.

"Have to say Mr. Hackett should be famous by now. He's probably the best barber I've ever had," I complimented with a smirk. "Care to come in? I doubt you want to be out in this frozen paradise."

Evelyn looked over at Elizabeth kind of sheepishly.

"Actually, *she* will," Elizabeth replied with a grin. "Ted and I are taking Bryan."

That's when it hit me. She did say Evelyn was coming, but I didn't realize it was just *her*.

"But," Evelyn protested.

"It's all right mom," Bryan reassured her. "I'll be fine."

Bryan looked at me as she turned, smiling slightly. He winked motioning towards the house.

"I trust you be good to her," Bryan teased playfully.

Was the boy trying to push his mother on me? I rolled my eyes at the thought.

"You know me," I replied, but Bryan just grinned as he turned to leave with Ted.

Evelyn grabbed Bryan before he could get away. I almost laughed at the sudden dragging of the teenage boy.

"Ah, ah!" she interjected and motioned towards her cheek.

Bryan rolled his eyes. Even at this age she still had *some* authority over him.

"Mother...I'm not a little boy anymore," Bryan groaned.

Evelyn raised her brows at him.

"Bryan," I said lightly. "A *man*, knows when to be good to his mother."

Bryan's mood changed for a mere second. His eyes shifted from their playfulness to glaring. That however, only lasted a moment before he rolled his eyes again and sighed. He kissed her quickly on the cheek as if not to be seen by anyone within miles of the estate.

Evelyn turned towards me mouthing "thank you" and blushed a little harder.

I nodded in assurance, and felt the sense of ease with her despite my nerves getting the best of me. I haven't seen her this happy in so long. It was something I didn't think I'd see again. At least not in front of me. Now if I could not ruin it in a single moment that would be ideal. But not guaranteed...

Bryan pointed at me as he fell into step with Ted who gave a polite smile and wave.

"Be good," Bryan joked and left.

I wasn't sure if I should've been proud or confused over the boys antics regarding his mother. But at least at the moment he seemed cheery. Better than brooding. Especially after last night and perhaps the last few days.

Elizabeth gave Evelyn a kiss on the cheek and whispered something in her ear as she hurried behind the boys. "Have fun you two!"

I found myself unable to hold in a scoff of amusement as they left, leaving Evelyn alone in front of me. She was shivering in the cold. The sun didn't do much on frigid days like this other than give some comfort in a dreary time of year.

I stepped down brick stairs.

"Well...he seems rather cheery this afternoon," I mentioned.

"Mmmhmm," Evelyn hummed in agreement. "He's a piece of work is what he is." Evelyn smirked.

"Gee, I wonder where he gets that from," I teased. Evelyn glared at me and I laughed, offering my arm as I winked at her. "Come on. Your friend brought me cookies last night. I can't be the only one eating them."

Evelyn hesitated for a moment, looked up at me, smiled, and brushed past me. Well, she didn't take my offer, but at least she got out of the cold. She stepped into the house as I followed her, closing the door.

The air seemed to shift almost immediately. It started with the sound of Evelyn's heeled boots hitting the wooden floors. The sound alone seemed to echo as I closed the door behind us. I would've never noticed it, but the eerie silence felt like a lifetime.

I watched as her eyes scanned over every picture like a gallery. They were in such poor condition, dusted and untouched barely hanging along the walls. Their backs remained facing towards us as if refusing to be totally erased from our memories.

Evelyn had been here most of her life, but...she hadn't seen what had happened to this place since our childhood years. It was partially my fault. Well...*mostly* my fault. It was hard to rebuild this place after I inherited it and things didn't go as planned. It was just hints of father and mother all around me. It was tempting to tear it all down and remove them completely. I knew that even then it would've just made things worse.

Still as I looked at her in that...*moment*, I felt as though I was stuck in time with the ghost of her former self. Older...but still Evelyn Fields.

My heart fluttered at the familiarity and comfort of her presence, something I buried since Avery took the reins. His jealousy really took a toll on us. Or, maybe, it was just me.

When we were young, she was the girl that followed me into the woods, bringing her books from school and running off to avoid problems at home. Her father wasn't exactly the best man. Drinking and gambling were his specialty, even in this small world we live in. Everyone knew, making everyone avoid or pity her...except my family.

My mother absolutely adored her, doting on her every second she had. My mother always wanted a daughter. She always told me, "*don't let that one go*". I wouldn't be surprised if she's still match making in her afterlife. Seeing Evelyn now was killing me. Loss of time, loss of comfort...loss of a chance that we wanted.

This is where she was always allowed to escape. And now she was here, and I could not make heads or tails of it.

"Connor?" Evelyn whispered.

I shook. Her voice felt as if it cracked into my soul and dragged me back into the present.

Evelyn was staring at me concerned. "You look like you're seeing a ghost."

I hesitated, cleared my throat as I crossed my arms. "Well...would it be too crazy to say I sort of am?" I asked simply with a forced smile. "Can I take your coat?"

Evelyn blushed and looked away. The color that rose in her cheeks made me smile. At least that's something that wasn't lost between us. I missed her smile. It felt so fleeting the more she stayed away. Maybe I'll see more of it after Avery's affairs are dealt with.

She took off her coat revealing a dark maroon sweater and a brown wool skirt that passed her knees. The dark stockings complimented her shoes. She always had a way to look well in simplicity.

It took me a moment to realize I was staring and proceeded to hang her coat. She wrapped her arms around her chest. "I'm sorry I haven't been here since," she paused, looking at me as if to read my mind.

I swallowed, nodding. She missed being here.

"I know," I answered, reassuring her.

I knew it killed her not being where she felt at home, but she was married. Well maybe *was* is more accurate now than it was even a few days ago. Her husband, or what *used* to be her husband, was never fond of me.

Avery was one of my former bullies when Oskar, Michael, and I were children. And, given the circumstance, he wasn't afraid to keep his new wife from being around me. He knew what she meant to me, and...he knew everything about our history. I had a sneaking suspicion he might've loathed me for it.

"I went to the town square this morning," Evelyn mentioned. "The reverend helped with being a witness with Avery."

"For?"

"No longer being Mrs. Atwood," Evelyn replied simply. Her eyes seemed to be searching my face. I tried to remain as neutral as I could. "We made it official thanks to him and Michael."

"Are you...all right with being Miss Fields again? I'm sure it feels quite sudden," I asked, choosing my words carefully.

"You knew how I felt about him," Evelyn sighed. "We both knew he never loved me. He didn't even want to try after his family intervened."

I knew tension was high with the marriage when it started. I hated that I watched it from a distance for so long.

"I still can't believe he went straight for Bryan. It was like he finally cracked," Evelyn said as she looked at me and swallowed.

I watched as Evelyn rubbed her hands along her arms as if brushing off the outer chill. I motioned to a chair in the study. She nodded, moving to the leather couch, sitting up straight, her hands folded over. I went over to make sure the fireplace was still lit and warming up the room. I felt her eyes bore into my back as I did so.

"It's been a long time since you've looked like that,"

Evelyn stated.

I turned, seeing her eye me up and down. I raised my brows. "Looked like what?" I asked as I stood and made my way to the chair behind my desk.

Evelyn hesitated, looking down at her fingers and smiling. "You look so grown up," she complimented and smiled. "Almost the spitting image of your father when I met him."

Seeing Evelyn smile made my heart stop as she blushed again. I missed her being in this place. She was like a home I lost. I stared at her for a long moment. I felt my mind nagging at a question in the air, but I wasn't brave enough to ask it yet. She must've noticed because her smile faded. I could tell she was trying to avoid the conversation, but I nodded in reassurance.

"I'm not upset for leaving," Evelyn admitted. "I regret that I didn't do it sooner."

I furrowed my brows.

Evelyn shook her head. "You know it's so silly," she continued. "But even as a boy, that man was always a fool for women's charms. As good looking as he always was, his confidence relied on it. I guess it only got worse recently and why he's been so...distant. Besides marrying me wasn't exactly *his* choice. I don't think anyone believed it was. I still have no idea how they got away with it."

"Some of us *hoped* he'd turn around...for *your* sake," I mentioned.

Evelyn scoffed in bitter amusement. "That man was *always* straying," she remarked. "There was hardly a day he didn't. I barely saw him in the house even when I was with child."

Alone...in a mansion. No family or friends. Was she

really that isolated for so long?

"Why didn't you go to Bill? How do you know if he doesn't have a child with some poor girl?"

"Believe me, he *doesn't*," Evelyn insisted. "Even if he did, it... it doesn't *matter*. He was *obligated* to marry me by *his* family and my *useless* father. All I'm good for is repaying a debt that isn't even mine. That ungrateful man."

I looked at Evelyn as her cheeks flushed, as her anger fuming just slightly underneath the surface. I swallowed and nodded. I never liked the man either.

"After what Avery would've done to Bryan and did to me instead...I'm done. I don't care what reputation comes. Bryan doesn't deserve to have such a life," Evelyn snapped and shook her head. "A distant father and a mother afraid of him."

I nodded, as I slowly walked over to her. I squatted down to her eye level. "Well...you seemed to have made a good friend with Elizabeth," I pointed out, with a smirk. "Although Ted is a very smooth talker, isn't he?"

"You mean *if* he talks," Evelyn teased and risen her brows at first holding it in, but then laughed.

I found myself grinning. She stared at me for a moment and smiled sweetly.

"Well...Elizabeth was *very* convinced you didn't mind the visit today," I stated, as I stood and headed out of the study.

I grabbed the cookies from the dining room table and turned to leave. Evelyn was almost immediately behind me as I picked up a cookie and smirked at her.

"I'll make you an offer Miss Fields," I stated.

Evelyn smiled as she grabbed the cookie from my hand. "And what would that be Mr. Sullivan," she chimed in as she did when we were younger.

"You remember my father's library?" I asked.

Evelyn's eyes widened.

I grinned. "You bring some of your family's tea, and I'll be more than happy to oblige sharing a room and some of the collection," I bargained.

Evelyn beamed. "Your mother's rules?"

"Well maybe out of respect," I teased. "But we can break *some* of those rules."

Evelyn tapped the cookie in her hand against my own. "You, Mr. Sullivan, can be very persuasive," she grinned in agreement, taking a bite of her cookie. "I see that hasn't changed."

"Is that a complaint Miss Fields?"

"Not if I'm allowed to take that offer right...*now*!"

Evelyn reached out and stole the bag of cookies from my hand then rushed up the stairs to my father's library. I stood there in shock before racing up the stairs behind her. For the first time in years...I felt like I had my friend back. Evelyn Fields.

✳✳✳

I nearly jumped out of my skin at the frantic pounding at my door.

I knew it was late. There was no reason for someone to be at my door. Unless...did something happen? The sudden rush of adrenaline hit me as I bolted out of bed and rushed down the stairs.

I heard shouting from outside as I finally opened the

door and found Evelyn in tears with Bryan and Michael Hughes next to her. If Michael was here...something must've been bad.

"Thank God," Michael breathed.

I looked at him rather confused, my body in full alert. Michael's expression was on the edge of losing his calm demeanor. "What's going on?" I asked.

"Something's happened," Michael growled. "I need you out here."

"What do you mean?"

"Elizabeth," Evelyn cried in distress. "She's missing!"

My heart rate rose furiously without warning. "What," I demanded. "What happened?!"

"Still figuring that out," Michael spat. "But I need your eyes. I have a feeling something dangerous is roaming about."

"Mr. Baker is missing too," Bryan chimed in his eyes wide with worry.

Michael sighed as if he wasn't going to add that detail. "He went looking for her after she didn't come home," he supplied

My stomach dropped. I remembered the look Avery gave Elizabeth at the church. He was charging for the woman. And if he was roaming around...this could end badly.

"I'm taking them to Bill's," Michael insisted. "I need you with me."

"Me?"

Evelyn stepped forward, tears in her eyes and down her cheeks. She had been crying for some time. "Connor please," she begged. "What if something happened to her and Ted too?"

If Avery was behind bars, then what in the world would be coming after the Bakers? There was no protecting Evelyn and Bryan while we were out patrolling for something dangerous. Ted was gone, which meant he would either find Elizabeth or was a soon-to-be victim.

We couldn't allow the town to panic. My mind was whirling with all sorts of possibilities that I didn't want to think about.

"Connor," Michael insisted, his eyes stern. "Clock is ticking."

Michael was right. We had to get moving before another victim got hurt. Maybe not by some lore monster this time, but from a dangerous man who wanted no one in his way.

I looked over at Evelyn and saw her pleading eyes. I couldn't have the man roaming this town freely after being such a threat for so long. And, now, Elizabeth. She was in danger too. I frantically grabbed my coat and wrapped it around me tightly from the ghastly chill.

"Show me," I said as I stepped out of the house.

Five

It was one of the coldest nights of my life as I searched high and low with the search party.

The only thing that gave me comfort was knowing Evelyn left to stay with Bill and Mary Donovan. I felt guilty leaving her behind, but it was better than leaving her alone or, God forbid, we found something we didn't want her to see.

Bryan insisted on helping as back up in case something went wrong. I wouldn't have it at first. He needed to protect his mother with the Donovans. Then...Evelyn agreed that he should be part of the search party.

"You know where to go," Evelyn reminded Bryan.

My eyes darted to her.

Bryan gave her a reassuring nod. I had a sneaking suspicion he knew where his mother used to hide when we were children.

"Be careful."

As the night lingered on, I was determined to find Elizabeth before it was too late.

Though Avery was trapped behind bars...something made me wonder. Was he somehow a part of this? It couldn't be possible that he was out attacking others, was he?

I'll have to find Ted once this is over. If *anything* suspicious happened while they were out, he would have been the first to see it. He was built different, and I trusted his instincts as much as I trusted Michael's.

A dreaded feeling loomed over me. What if Avery *did* find a way out? No...there was no way with Michael's officers. They were too loyal to let that man out. No one in town liked him *or* his family at least not in my generation. They always rubbed us the wrong way. Our flashlights were the only things that guided our steps, helping us avoid sliding in the ice. I walked carefully alongside both Michael and Bryan as Michael ordered a separate search party to patrol the rest of the town. He was making sure there wasn't some animal or if Avery *did* escape his cell. And if he managed to break free, I wouldn't have it...not after what he's done to Evelyn.

I was grateful to have Michael with me.

Every second searching for Elizabeth felt like an eternity. The entire night, we searched everywhere in town: store fronts, a few friends' houses, nothing. It didn't help that no one had seen or heard from Elizabeth since earlier that day.

The idea of having another scene on our hands made my skin crawl. I couldn't afford another disappearance. Or a death.

That's when my eyes darted in the direction of the dark, looming woods. It was pitch black and as ominous as it always had been. Just like all those years ago when my mother was being dragged into it's depths. This time it was cold and frigid, but I was more determined than ever. I was armed with friends and colleagues willing to fight. We still prayed we avoided another horrid "accident".

We stopped for a moment as I stared through the trees, looking for any signs of movement. I felt Michael and Bryan immediately stop alongside me. There was a tense silence as they both followed my line of sight.

"Something doesn't feel right," Bryan noted.

I kept my eyes on the woods; if something were to be a danger outside of Avery, it would emerge from that wretched place. The boy had a knack for sensing things as much as I did. I trusted his instincts more than most.

"Tell me," I prompted.

Bryan hesitated but Michael nodded as well. We were all ears.

"You know those stupid feelings that scream that you're not alone?" he asked. "The ones that sit in the pit of your stomach?"

So, he was getting that too. I shouldn't be fictionalizing Avery's escape as if it were real. There's always been something else here. Maybe that was the threat. "I wouldn't call them *stupid*," I reassured. "I'd call it *talent*."

"What? Why?" Bryan asked as he looked at me puzzled.

"Because your gut is trying to save you," I explained.

"Save me?" Bryan asked. "How would it save me?"

"Think of it this way kid," Michael pitched in, grabbing a cigarette and lighting it in his mouth. "Gut is like your guardian angel. If you feed it, if you trust it, it'll be good to you. And when something is lurking…it'll alert you of all the trouble that you don't see."

I felt the hairs on my arm stand up. Bryan swallowed and nodded, rocking uncomfortably in his place.

My eyes narrowed as I tried to focus more in the darkness of the woods.

I suddenly felt an instant tap on my shoulder. I nearly jumped out of my skin as I spun around and a small shriek came from the woman standing in front of me.

Evelyn.

"Eve," I breathed.

Evelyn rolled her eyes for a moment. "You're a hard man to find," she whispered. "I had to ask the other patrol where you went."

I was relieved for a moment, but then I felt my stomach instantly drop. She was out here with us. Bryan must've heard my thoughts since my fears went right out of his mouth.

"Mother," Bryan hissed. "You promised you'd stay with Mrs. Donovan!"

Evelyn looked between us and gave that worried look. "I'm sorry...I couldn't stay in that house for another minute," she objected. "Did you find her?"

Of course she was worried. If she wasn't then I'd be concerned she was being replaced by something supernatural.

"Not yet," Michael interjected. "We've looked almost everywhere. There's been no signs of her."

I grabbed Evelyn's arm and pulled her gently aside, away from the others. "What are you doing out here?" I whispered.

"Look I know you're trying to protect me," Evelyn protested. "But I *need* to make sure Elizabeth's okay-"

"What if something, *someone* is out hurting people?" I warned, feeling my voice growl in my throat.

"The only thing I'm afraid of is locked up in his cell right now," Evelyn protested. "What's the matter with you?"

"You know there's more than just *him*."

"You think I'd fall for a few ghost stories?" Evelyn whispered.

"They *aren't* just ghost stories and you know it," I

spat. She stayed silent, processing and giving me a few moments of silence. That's when I had to remind her. "And what of Avery? Hm? There's a very good chance he is out here."

Evelyn's body stiffened at his name. "He would've been searching for me if he was," Evelyn commented, hugging her arms. She looked at me with scared eyes.

I swallowed at the thought of her being scared of this man. My mind flashed from the memory at the church. The look Avery gave Elizabeth was an unmistakable hungry, menacing look of someone clearly out of his mind. An almost predatory stare of someone or *something* you wouldn't dare cross.

And…Evelyn was alone and terrified.

"Please," Evelyn whispered. "Connor…I…I don't want to be alone."

"Evee," I whispered, going up to her and hugging her tightly. I felt her grip tighten around me, a sniffle from the cold, and the tears fell from her face. "Listen I-"

"Sir!" one of Michael's men called out.

Evelyn and I broke free as they approached us. Michael alerted to the patrol party.

"You've got to see this!"

✽✽✽

The town disappeared behind us as we ventured further into the dark.

All we had were a few flashlights gripped in the police officers' hands. Anything from the old traditional oil lamps to the newer flashlights that were handheld and gave us more range.

The streetlights were far from view as we ventured further from the outskirts and into open fields. I felt engulfed in the darkness as I held Evelyn's hand tightly. She was gripping mine and refusing to let go. Bryan stayed behind us, protecting his mother as we moved forward.

When we reached the top of the hills, the hair on the back of my neck stood up immediately.

We approached a large tree that stood alone in the dark winter night. Lovers Lane, at least that's what the town called it. The massive tree's solace was no longer a pleasant scene as it has been in our youth.

As we approached, I heard Evelyn gasp.

I wasn't sure what spooked her at first until a light flashed along the ground. My blood ran cold.

It was Elizabeth Baker. Her face was bruised, her body limp and covered in the snow below. Now motionless...and cold, her face already pale from however long she had been out here.

I was staring at the poor girl's face when Evelyn's gasp turn into a full scream of horror and despair. She let go of my hand, as she almost lunged towards Elizabeth's body, but I grabbed her before she could get to the scene.

"No!" Evelyn screamed. "No, no, no, no!"

"Evee," I hissed as I pulled her back towards me. I covered her face from the scene as she sobbed uncontrollably.

I looked at Elizabeth's body, mindlessly keeping Evelyn away from everything. We were too late.

Michael marched forward shaking his head at the scene. "*Jesus*," he cursed as the patrol officers stared at the pale body.

I glanced at Bryan who stood in shock. I looked over at Michael who glanced at me. I motioned to Bryan. Michael nodded, putting his hand on Bryan's shoulder, gripping it firmly. He mildly shook him to snap him out of his trance. I recognized that look Michael gave him. Like a father protecting his own son.

"Take your mother home," Michael ordered quietly.

Bryan remained quiet as he turned to me. He looked at his mother and swallowed. I moved my way toward him with Evelyn still in my grip. I was hushing her as she was in her own reality.

When we were far enough away, I pushed her slightly to face her.

"Evee," I whispered.

Evelyn looked at me with blurred eyes. "I should've gone with her," she whispered.

"Eve," I interrupted again through her cries. "You need to go home."

"I can't leave her here," Evelyn whispered desperately.

"We will take care of her," I assured as she took a moment to breathe. "I need you to go with Bryan."

Bryan glanced at the body before grabbing his mother. His face grew pale as he pulled her away from the scene. "Come on," Bryan whispered as she followed her son and didn't look at the others.

I grabbed Bryan by the shoulder gently from behind and whispered so his mother wouldn't hear. "And keep eyes out for Ted," I reminded him.

Bryan glanced over his shoulder.

"And, whatever you do, lock your doors and *do not*

leave the house for the rest of the night," I warned.

Bryan nodded, hesitating before leading his mother away from the scene.

I turned as they left the scene, focusing my attention back on the body. Michael barked some orders and some men scattered to secure the scene.

This poor girl was just smiling at me hours ago. Now she's here pale, dead, and cold in the snow. I dared to step a bit closer, trying my best not to disturb too much of the scene.

The snow was littered with dark red around her. Her eyes were wide, her mouth opened and a bit of blood had dried at the corner of her lip. There was no sign of a weapon anywhere. The snow had already been so disturbed from her struggling that it was hard to find any tracks at a glance.

But, I noticed something vile as I approached.

Elizabeth's neck. Her scarf was absolutely soaked. I glanced at Michael then reached out and pulled the scarf aside. I felt acid reach my throat.

Elizabeth's neck was *torn*. Not just cut, but *ripped* and a chunk was taken out. This was no puncture or cut with a knife, although if it was...it was brutally hacked. It was as if the attacker had no care but to aim for the neck multiple times.

I sat back, examining the body from head to toe. I looked down, noticing more blood, this time coming from her wrist. That one was different but equally confusing. It was punctured, but not by a weapon and draining from her veins. She was gripping onto something on her injured hands. I looked around and saw something peeking out.

It was a cross just like my mothers. Why in the world would it be in her hand?

I felt myself standing as I took a slight step back from the scene.

"Michael," I called out to get his attention.

Michael was still running some orders around the patrol. I wasn't sure he heard me until I heard the crunching of the snow behind me.

As he stopped, he did his familiar habit of grabbing his cigarette case. I made an effort to stand next to him as he found a cigarette and his lighter.

"What are we looking at?" I asked as he put one in his mouth and lit it in the darkness.

The warm glow was so isolating in comparison to the scene that stood before us. I glanced at Elizabeth.

"Well, it couldn't have been Mr. Atwood," Michael announced.

I furrowed my brows at him.

Michael took a long drag of his cigarette and blew out the smoke. "My boys are still watching him pace the jail cell," he stated. "Although he's been...behaving rather *oddly*."

My blood ran cold. If Avery didn't somehow escape, then there really was something more dangerous. "You know he's got friends," I suggested. "Maybe it was one of them?"

"If it was...well we're in trouble," Michael admitted. "That doesn't account for Mr. Baker."

"You think he's seen her?"

Michael blew out more smoke and looked at me as he stepped a tad forward to examine Elizabeth from afar. "We better hope not," Michael groaned. "Or Mr. Atwood will need more than my guard to save him from a *very* angry husband."

"If it were someone, they were pretty barbaric," I growled. "Her neck is torn, even her wrist is ripped open."

"Couldn't be an ax?"

"Not with the markings," I replied. "There wouldn't be much left of her."

Michael nodded, shaking his head. "I'll have to question Ted when we see him," he mentioned.

"Avery's the only one fits the bill," I insisted. "Before you arrived, he was charging at her. It was...unlike him."

Michael raised his brow and shook his head. "And, yet, he's behind bars," Michael swallowed. "The man can't be two places at once."

I looked at Elizabeth and swallowed.

"I wasn't expecting something like this so close to town," Michael whispered.

The hair on my neck stood up and I looked at him, his eyes lingered around the woods and his mentality shifted. The air gave a sudden chill that struck to my very bones. "Michael?"

"If you see Ted, send him to the station."

"Do you think it's linked?"

"You know as well as I do that none of this is ever *that* simple here," Michael warned. "For all we know we're looking at the mind of a lunatic or it's a horrible accident."

"If people ask questions?"

"An *unfortunate* accident," Michael replied as he sighed. Michael stayed silent for a moment, taking another long drag of his cigarette before stomping it out. A few patrol officers approached with a coroner's vehicle. It drove up slowly through the snow, the lights illuminating the scene. "I'll send for you when Mr. Lowe gets her to the morgue. I'm sure he'll be thrilled..."

Six

Ted never made it home.

I checked the Baker house and saw no sign of anyone on the premises. Strange. Even if Ted didn't spot Elizabeth anywhere, you'd think he would've headed home to regroup. Perhaps both of them were in trouble.

I was there to check in, to tell him my condolences; but, it was my poor luck that he wasn't there. I decided the best course of action was to make my way back to the Donovan house. It was late, but I had to make sure Evelyn and Bryan were safe after the whole ordeal.

Finding Elizabeth sent a chill down my spine. I made sure to stay put until she was well on her way to Lowe's office at the morgue. As I watched her get lifted into the vehicle, I felt my stomach drop. She had greeted me warmly this week. Now, she was as cold as the ice I stood on.

It was a dreadful way to go.

Michael's investigation team stayed behind as they examined every bit of the crime scene like they had in my younger years. I knew the routines at that point by heart.

Michael didn't need me to stay for the photos and clean up. If he saw something odd, he would've told me. We've had that trust for a long time even after I left. Besides, Mr. Lowe wasn't one to hide his opinions from us. Maybe to the public, but not me or Michael.

Ever since the odd deaths began, Mr. Lowe had seen what was really happening with the bodies, and he would keep everything archived. However, he would *never* scare the public any more than they already did by themselves with their folktales.

Michael assigned me and the other officers to have a few patrols roaming in case Ted somehow turned up. And, from what Michael told me, the *prime suspect* of at least Elizabeth's death, never left his cell.

The only person who might've known about the whole ordeal was the one who was missing or dead.

I stopped at the Donovan's small, simple house. It was late, yet there was at least one light illuminating the porch as well as a small light inside. Someone was up.

I knocked very quietly so I wouldn't disturb the whole household. To my surprise, there was a bit of rustling behind the door. After a moment, it swung open. I thought maybe it would've been Bryan, but instead, Bill was standing in front of me. "Connor," he whispered, as he glanced behind himself. "Thank goodness."

Bill reached inside, pulling out a thick wool jacket that he quickly threw on over his robe as he stepped out onto the porch. He stood in front of me, rocking a bit, his grip tightening. I looked down noticing his hands gripping onto a small cross necklace. Of course he was still up. I couldn't imagine the type of fear that was running through the house. His eyes were weary as they were on most solemn occasions, but he stared at me with determination.

"I'm sorry it's so late," I greeted Bill gently.

"Emergencies take priority," Bill reminded me quickly.

I motioned behind him. "How are they?" I asked.

Bill flinched and sighed. "Scared, confused," he answered, looking at me. "What happened?"

Bill's eyes watered as they did in most of his funeral services. I couldn't imagine how he felt now, knowing Elizabeth being a light within the church. I stared at him as he was trying to read anything about my expression which was hard to keep neutral. Knowing her now...I wish I hadn't known her. Maybe then the blow would've been different.

"We found Elizabeth."

"I *know* that," Bill groaned, rolled his eyes but then sighed in frustration before he bowed his head. He was struggling to keep his composure. "What *happened*? An accident?"

The flashes of Elizabeth's dead body haunted my mind. I swallowed and tried to approach it in a logical, almost scientific manner. It wasn't easy telling people their loved ones were missing or brutally injured from God knows what. But I had to remain steady for him. "I highly doubt it," I disagreed. "From what Michael and I saw...it had to be *intentional*. But from *what* I don't know?"

Bill's eyes glazed over in anger before he could stop himself. "Is it Avery?" he demanded quietly.

"Unless the man can walk through walls let alone bars, I'd count him out."

"And Ted?"

"Hopefully somewhere safe," I replied honestly.

I did hope for that. I didn't want to tell Ted the bad news, but to be frank, I didn't expect him to just disappear either.

"I don't like this...not one bit," Bill shifted and shivered in the cold. "I pray he didn't get out."

At least I wasn't the only one who assumed the worst after Avery's outburst.

Multiple people, multiple theories all led to Avery's

erratic behavior. But the man was *in a cell*. There was no way he would possibly get out with the type of security Michael had. It was tight, and they never strayed.

Bill gave me a sympathetic look. "The boy is a little shook up," he added. "He found her you know."

I furrowed my brows. Bryan found Elizabeth? But...

Bill noticed my expression and mimicked me, tilting his head. "He didn't tell you?" he asked.

There was a moment of silence. He came with Michael and Evelyn. It was possible that he saw her. But then why hide her location? I needed answers.

"No, he didn't," I replied.

If that *was* the case, he didn't even tell Michael where to look when they came to find me. Why would he lie? Bill shook his head.

"Poor boy was probably shocked," Bill replied as if reading my mind.

I swallowed and nodded. "Do me a favor and tell him to come by in the morning?" I requested.

Bill nodded. "In the meantime, Miss Fields will stay here with us until Avery's conundrum is straightened out," he said. "Michael is confident he'll be dealt with within the week."

I nodded. "Get some rest," I encouraged lightly, turning to leave.

Bill nodded, rubbing his arms from the cold as I stepped off the porch. "Connor," he called out gently.

I stopped and turned to him.

Bill gave a grave, gritted response. "Do me a favor and find the bastard who took that poor girl. God forgive me if I don't find them myself."

"For someone of faith, you seem to be

rather...*violent*," I mentioned.

Bill twisted his jaw. "I tend to my flock, and I must defeat the wolves. You forget Mr. Sullivan. I am a shepherd of the Lord."

I stared at Bill for a long moment. His gaze serious as he walked down the steps slowly to face me fully. His voice was barely a harsh whisper. "Believe me, if a wolf comes to my home and takes another lamb, you bet your soul I'm not going to stand for it anymore. I'm sure God will forgive me."

I swallowed as he nodded slowly, turning and heading back inside.

I watched him in awe as the door closed behind him.

Bill was always protecting his people. This was just...another side I never expected to see.

※※※

 I barely slept that night.

Elizabeth's crime scene kept screaming in my mind. Repetition took over in my dreams: the wounds, the cross in her hand, the blood. I tried to imagine what it could've been. A man hacking her with a knife of some kind? An animal biting causing punctures and ripping in her neck? But what roams here in Blackwood Hollow?

Whatever lore the town believed even resonated with the animals both wild and domestic. Nothing ever came out of those woods. The pines were always quiet, looming, and dangerously ominous. I was stupid as a boy and thought nothing of it until I was faced with the death of my own family.

That morning, I found myself staring at the Bakers' picture trying to wrap my mind around the last twenty-four hours.

A dead body of a young woman who, as far as I knew, had no enemies and a protective husband who wouldn't have let her wander out that late without some form of well...*security*. Especially with their new housemates.

So where was *he*?

I only hoped that Ted was home after I met up with Bill. I wondered if he had heard of his wife's demise and how much I loathed the idea of how he would find out.

I shook my head as Bryan knocked and waltzed into the study. "Did you sleep?" I asked.

Bryan shook his head and I didn't blame him. Anyone who saw what happened last night I doubt had a wink of sleep or comfort.

First his father having an episode in the church, and now just saw a resident...killed off. Whether it was a total accident, which I doubted, or someone who did that horrific deed, it was not something you can unsee.

"We stayed at the reverend's house," Bryan mentioned. "I never saw Mr. Baker..."

I shook my head. I prayed Ted wasn't in immediate danger. Or else another search party was called for. Then again, anyone who decided it was a good idea to mess with an over six-foot man was daft. I had to hope that luck and sheer common sense were on his side.

That's when it hit me. I looked at Bryan who sat down at my desk. He seemed exhausted. I tried to be as casual as I could be despite the circumstances of the conversation. "Who grabbed Michael last night?" I asked.

Bryan looked up and hesitated as he looked through the previous newspaper he left the day before.

I raised an eyebrow.

"I did, after Ted left. He said he was going to go find her," Bryan answered simply. "When he didn't return, mother insisted we'd get help."

"Did you go straight to Michael?"

Again...*silence.*

I walked over, looming over the desk. "Bryan," I urged calmly.

Bryan flinched and shook his head. "You're just going to lecture me," he protested.

I felt the sudden urge to roll my eyes but I pressed again keeping my tone level.

"Bryan...*please.* Someone's life was already in danger last night," I insisted. He swallowed. "Did you go straight to the sheriff's station?"

Bryan shook his head slowly. "I was...going to help Ted-Mr. Baker," he corrected himself. "So, I went out for a little while."

I motioned for Bryan to continue.

Bryan's face paled. "I heard screaming," he whispered. "I ran up to where the yelling was, I saw someone attacking someone else. But it...it sounded off."

My eyes widened. "What do you mean *off?*" I asked.

"*Inhuman.* Like a creature, growling and snarling and *hissing,*" Bryan stated quickly. I swallowed. "When I got too close, I saw something almost like a horse nearby as well."

I put up a hand to stop him, then pointed at him. "Did you tell Sheriff Hughes *any* of this?" I demanded.

Bryan shook his head.

"Why not?"

Bryan flinched, looking down. When he finally found the courage to look at me, he looked terrified. "Whatever that thing was...I think it *saw me*," he whispered.

My jaw tightened.

"I ran to find anyone to help. But...I wasn't sure *who* was getting attacked. I was just as surprised as you all were."

So it was something malicious. I couldn't be upset with the boy. He was afraid and he genuinely didn't know it was the person he was searching for to begin with. But that didn't mean we couldn't take action now.

I leaned forward and grabbed him by the arm, lifting him up from the chair.

"Hey!" Bryan protested.

"We're going to see Hughes," I insisted, refusing any objections.

Bryan resisted for a moment and growled at me. "Did you not hear me?! That thing might come after *me!*" Bryan objected.

I stopped, pulled him to me, and looked him straight in the eyes. "Listen carefully," I said. "*Nothing* is getting past me."

Bryan stared at me, his eyes widening at my anger.

I swallowed, calming my tone but remaining firm. "*Nothing*. Not to you, or your mother, or anyone else," I assured, my tone calm but firm. "Understand?"

Bryan stood there, shocked, and for a mere moment I didn't think he'd ever be mildly afraid of me. He's known me for a long time, but I suppose this side was not something he's seen much of. He nodded slowly as I go of his arm. He rolled his shoulders and moved around his neck loosely. He was probably just as stressed as I was.

"Okay," Bryan finally agreed.

"You tell him everything," I instructed.

Seven

The Blackwood Hollow Sheriff's Department was busier more than usual; the blinds were drawn, and the door was closed in Michael's office.

I had forgotten how pristine, orderly, and simplified Michael kept his office. It had been months since I stepped foot in here. His large wooden desk filled the room where his notebooks remained neatly stacked and set aside.

What I also forgot about was the décor. The reminder of *why* he was in this room.

Pictures of his family were neatly framed along the walls as well as a photo of him and his wife and children on his desk facing him. Then there was the gleaming titled name plate on his desk: **Sheriff Michael E. Hughes**. He earned that title. It's what he wanted in his younger years as children.

I was lucky enough to meet the man during our school days. His parents moved from New York City, wanting a quieter life. Although *quiet* might not have been the most accurate term. There were other things that kept this town busy. Including keeping *me* out of trouble with some of our classmates.

Michael was always the kid defending the "weird ones". I asked why once and got the "I don't mind" answer. Because he was so straight-laced, he got bullied originally. Until I was one of the ones who stood up to them. They backed off for a bit. His reward in returned seemed to be an infinite friendship with an odd duck. We were inseparable for a while and even were partners once at this station...in this very department, rookies and willing to save this place.

That was...*before* the missing people started piling up. It only got worse in our older years.

Michael went from run of the mill patrolman to sheriff real quick. The last sheriff that replaced my father after his death had one bad case he couldn't handle anymore, retired, and fled town.

Michael seemed to be the only one who was tough enough to deal with this sort of chaos. He heard stories from his own father, a patrolman in a bigger city, with bigger problems. Missing people and monster stories were next to nothing in comparison.

Today was no different. Just a poor, innocent woman in an unfortunate, rather grueling crime scene we've seen in a minute.

Regardless, Michael was looking rather haggard when we came, his blonde hair was still clean, but his jacket was off, and his shirt was unbuttoned at the top. He was just getting a round of coffee that morning when we arrived.

And...Bryan told Michael everything. Told him of his night searching on his own. How he did it alone after Ted left them behind to search for his wife. The unbearable screaming he was faced with. All leading to Elizabeth being the actual victim.

Michael finished a note as he dropped his pen, allowing his rather quick cursive write down details on his notepad. Michael stopped as he wrote down every detail and looked at Bryan in confusion. "You said there was a horse?" he asked.

Bryan nodded.

Michael's jaw twinged, pausing as he stared at Bryan.

Bryan hesitated then with the man's stare.

"What?" Michael asked, seeing the boy's sudden uncertainty.

"Well, I *think* it was a horse, for all I know it could've been something else," Bryan mentioned.

"Like?"

"Well...anything with *hooves*," Bryan scoffed almost in amusement.

I saw Michael's eyes harden.

"Don't be smart with me," Michael scolded. "You already," he began then stopped.

Bryan's eyes widened as he straightened in his seat, keeping his lips closed and tight. The *last* person anyone wanted to be on the wrong side of was Michael.

Michael sighed, rolled his eyes and shook his head I could tell this case was hitting him different. "You withdrew information from a Elizabeth's potential murder case-" he informed.

"*Michael*," I whispered warningly.

I motioned to Bryan from behind him, hinting to take it easier on the boy.

Michael's shoulders tensed as he shook his head. When he regained his composure, Michael watched Bryan tiredly. The man looked like he was restraining himself from punishing a son.

Bryan seemed to get more and more nervous as he sat in the opposite leather chair. His body went rigid, trying to sit up straight but his leg was bouncing. I noticed his thumbs were twitching. The boy was acting as if he was going to be disciplined at school for being rowdy in class. I put a hand on his shoulder tightening slightly and he seemed to relax.

Michael stared at him for a moment, stretching out a few fingers before tapping on the desk. "Anything else," he asked, keeping his tone even and professional.

Bryan shook his head.

Michael's eyes stayed on him for a moment before looking at me. "Why don't you get me another cup of coffee and one of those donuts from the front lobby?" he suggested.

He didn't have to tell the boy twice. Bryan instantly stood as if not to trouble the lion any more than he did.

Michael smiled plainly as the boy rushed to the door. "Make it black as you can get it," Michael called out as Bryan scrambled out of the room, slamming the door behind him.

I raised my brows at Michael as he sighed, rubbing his forehead. I sighed, shaking my head as I sat down in the now vacant chair across from Michael.

"Thank you for letting him speak," I said gratefully.

Michael looked at me, tapping his fingers on the desk as if still having the gears grinding in his mind.

"He's had a rough few days," I remarked.

"Hate to break it to you Connor we *all* are," Michael groaned. "I had several people this morning already asking for the girl. I assigned someone else to break the news after the first two."

It *was* a rough morning.

"Any sign of Ted?" I asked.

Michael shook his head. "Not sure how we lost someone *that* big," he groaned. "And *because* he's missing it makes things near impossible right now."

"How?"

"People get suspicious," Michael reminded me, as

he got up from his desk.

"You know no one thought oddly of the two of them," I objected. "Outside...you know the usual. Bubbly girl with a muscle man that barely says anything."

Michael scoffed, as he leaned down reaching for a folder in a nearby drawer. "My team worked all night," he said as he rummaged through the drawer and finally dropped an envelope on top of his desk. "Photos are in there."

I grabbed the folder from his desk. The photos were graphic, but nothing I hadn't seen before while being here. It was every step and detail as they gathered Elizabeth's body.

The scene, the girl...the blood.

"Anything on the autopsy?" I asked.

"Nothing *official*," Michael said carefully as he moved to sit on his desk, grabbing a spare small ball from his drawer he fiddled with when he needed to think. "But Lowe saw the body. He's...a little concerned. I was hoping you and I could stop by tonight. Without the boy of course."

I nodded. There was no reason to make Bryan tag along.

I flipped through the pictures. The image of her neck looked horrendous. It was worse than if someone cut her with a knife or even an axe. A whole chunk had been ripped out. I cringed a bit as I continued through the photos.

"You still think it's an animal?" I suggested.

"My team certainly hope so," Michael groaned. "God forbid we have a killer on the loose."

My skin prickled into goosebumps at the thought. Michael noticed and rolled his eyes. "You worried about *him*?" he guessed.

"Should I not be?"

"He's more than a little unhappy but that's expected from a bastard like him," Michael concluded. "Evelyn?"

"I didn't have time to," I started but then stopped. I froze at one of the pictures. It was of the scenery and the setting around it. The snow was just disturbed enough from the chaos but just outside of it there was something else. Prints...*hoof* prints.

"Connor," Michael alerted seeing my shock on my face.

I pointed at the area of the photo and Michael hovered over me. He scoffed in amusement.

"Well...I'll be damned. Maybe you were right about him Sul," Michael shook his head. "The boy's got talent."

The door opened and made us both jump. Bryan came in with two cups of coffee and a few donuts in his arms haphazardly.

"Christ Fields! *Knock* next time," Michael breathed.

Bryan shrugged trying not to drop the donuts. "Sorry," he groaned, handing the coffee to Michael while trying not to spill it.

Michael grabbed the coffee and snatched a donut from the boy. Bryan looked at me, I noticed he had the second cup of coffee. He reached out his arm towards me.

"Sugar and cream right?" he asked.

I raised my brows. "Since when do I ever take it with cream and sugar?" I asked.

"Mother says you used to," Bryan replied.

I swallowed. Evelyn remembered how we used to get coffee well over a decade ago...and she still talked about it? I shook my head trying not to smile as I took it and he handed me a donut, keeping one for himself.

"So...hooves huh?" Michael questioned. "Well, I got just the place to start."

Considering the circumstances of the death, and the location, it was odd that there were hoof prints. So Bryan *was* right. If it was going in the direction we expected, there was only one place to go. Later in the morning, Michael made the comment "check the mule" when we finally decided to leave. I thought it odd until I realized what he was talking about.

The only one who could possibly be that close to Lover's Lane and what was a well-known isolated little farm. That would be our first clue while I waited to visit Lowe that evening with Michael.

As soon as we left the sheriff's office, Bryan walked ahead of me.

"Check the mule?" Bryan repeated the phrase in confusion. "Doesn't he mean check the *ass*?"

I rolled my eyes. The boy was really testing his swearing...then again, he wasn't exactly *wrong* with the terminology. "Technically it's a *mule* not a donkey," I corrected.

Bryan smirked. "Well, the only *mule* is the one with Happy Jack," Bryan said now grinning. "Sweet thing if you can get close enough. Happy Jack cries something fierce when you leave though. Swear it's an alarm bell."

That would make it a little hard then if someone did separate them even for a night. Donkey screaming while it sees you at night. You'd think the whole town would hear you. But then again, I wasn't familiar with all the farms or their animals. "And *where* exactly is Happy Jack?" I asked.

"Uh...the pig lady's farm," Bryan hesitated, keeping

his hands in his pockets to keep them warm from the bitter chill. He the look of disappointment on my face and immediately corrected himself. "Oh, I'm sorry *Miss Shaw*."

Of course it was...the one lady who dominated this town since at least my parents' generation. Known for her livestock just disappearing due to her negligence. I always thought it was because they were trying to run from her. She wasn't exactly the most pleasant person. If she did finally come out of hiding, she was one of the glary-eyed, silent people. Then again, I wasn't sure if that was because of how the younger kids reacted to her. She was somewhat of an urban legend.

Kids who were at the edge of being adults would dare each other to run over to her property and dash before she could get to them. There was a part of me that had some sympathy for the woman, being made into a game of chicken for the kids when all you want is to be left alone.

Bryan began humming some chant about the pig lady coming to get you with the ax and I rolled my eyes. I nudged him to stop, giving him a warning glare and he blushed.

"Bryan?" a voice greeted us as we walked further into the town.

I looked up and my heart leapt.

Evelyn. I was surprised to see her out and about but she was there alone. I felt a pang of guilt as I saw her swollen eyes.

"What are you doing here?" Evelyn asked. "I thought you were spending the day with Mr. Sullivan at his house."

"We took a bit of a detour," I replied, glancing in Bryan's direction.

"I just had to talk to the Sheriff mother, nothing big,"

Bryan tried to brush it off.

"Why would *you* be talking to the Sheriff?!"

"I–"

"Bryan," I interjected. Bryan looked at me but stayed quiet. "Why don't you grab the notebooks and meet me at the house?"

Bryan looked back at me, nodding.

I nodded back as he mouthed "thank you" and moved quickly past his mother. Evelyn looked at me as if to object, and I shushed politely putting up a finger as Bryan left the scene. She watched as Bryan headed off and then proceeded to look at me.

"What was *that* about?" Evelyn objected.

"Teaching him a lesson," I answered.

"A lesson on *what* exactly?!" Evelyn spat, ready to argue more but I looked at her gravely.

"Evee," I interrupted firmly.

"Don't *Evee* me, what was he doing with Michael?"

"He withheld information."

Evelyn stopped, her slowly filling with worry. "What do you mean?" she asked.

"He was the first one to see Elizabeth getting attacked," I whispered to keep away from earshot of other people.

Evelyn's face instantly paled.

"I made sure Michael was aware of the details."

"Lord help us," Evelyn whispered as she put a hand over her mouth. "I should've known."

"You know that's a load of hogwash," I objected, keeping my tone even. "Now the question is what are *you* doing here?"

"Well I...I came to see what's come of Avery," Evelyn

swallowed. "Maybe he knows what happened to her. God forbid he's the reason Elizabeth's dead."

"Eve...You shouldn't-"

"She's dead?" a voice said from behind her.

I looked up as Evelyn turned.

It was Ted Baker.

❈❈❈

"*WHERE* IS HE?!"

We nearly rushed into the sheriff's office with a raging husband. Ted Baker was a beast that was ready to maul someone.

The small team of officers that were in the building were all rushing to determine the source of chaos. It didn't help. Ted was no joke when it came to getting people out of his way.

He pushed them aside or they avoided him in his state with his monstrous stare.

Evelyn and I ran behind him as he stormed into the section of the building with the holding cells. Michael heard the commotion and was following behind with other officers.

Ted finally reached a very ragged-looking Avery who was stuck in his cage.

Even in the short time that he was in that cell, he looked *broken*. This was not the same man I grew to know in over a decade. To see his hair totally unkempt, his clothes disheveled, and his eyes dark in the cell was something I never thought I'd witness. He was sitting in the cell, and grinned seeing Ted as he approached the bars.

"Hello Teddy," Avery greeted in an almost sing-song voice. "To what do I owe the pleasure?"

"What did you do to her?" Ted growled.

"*Her?*" Avery questioned, his voice not leaving that odd rhythm. "I'm sorry I don't know who you're referring to."

Michael stormed into the jail cell and grabbed Ted's arm, but Ted pulled it away.

"Ted! For God's sake back up," Michael ordered quietly. "Let's talk about this in private."

Michael tried to grab Ted's shoulder, but Ted shoved him off again. The man was angry with good reason. His wife's passing was...devastating.

Michael glanced at me. He kept Evelyn behind him protectively.

Ted refused to move, looming at the cell doors. Even at his height, there was something worse coming from *Avery*. Something about his demeanor had my gut flaring. Avery stood up very slowly. Despite his ragged appearance, he strolled towards Ted confidently. Ted stood his ground, keeping close to the bars.

"Oh...that's right," Avery whispered. "The girl."

Avery grinned and I saw Ted's back stiffen at the gesture. Something was shifting and it wasn't right.

Avery almost licked his lips and I furrowed my brows. His eyes were *dark*...darker than I'd ever seen them. His skin was a lot paler than I remembered too. His eyes then rested on me and then saw Evelyn. His eyes narrowed. "She was a sweet smelling one," he whispered.

I felt my hand immediately grab Evelyn's. Avery's gaze became predatory. I felt Evelyn flinch and try to stay next to me. "Avery," she whispered. "What's wrong with you?"

"I'd hate to break it to you, but as *sweet* as that girl is. I'm afraid she's gone," Avery concluded nonchalantly. "Such a pretty thing. But you can make up with *her*."

Avery motioned to Evelyn and she flinched.

SLAM! Ted slid his hand through the bars and gripped onto Avery's shirt, and slammed him on the empty spot next the door of the cell.

I launched for Ted as Michael pushed Evelyn to an officer and helped get in between Ted and Avery. Avery just laughed as Ted wrapped his big hands around his throat.

I grabbed Ted's arm trying to pull the over six-foot man away from Avery.

"Ted stop!"

That's when Avery grinned, he pulled Ted's fingers that made him wince in pain as they were wrenched back. He grunted in pain as Avery then did something that I didn't expect him to do.

Avery *bit* Ted. Full on teeth and blood.

Ted yelled in agony as Avery's teeth sank into his wrist.

"AVERY! LET GO!" Michael growled as Ted tried to pull back with no luck.

Michael pulled back, grabbing the keys and fumbling with the lock.

I looked over and saw a nightstick in an officer's hand. I grabbed it from him.

Michael threw open the door as Ted pulled with all his might into the cell bars but Avery just held on. I charged in, nightstick pulled back and immediately swung at his back.

The man *finally* let go.

We rushed out of the cell as Avery fell to the ground winded by the blow. Michael immediately locked the cell again.

Ted stood there shaking from adrenaline. He was bleeding, a lot. The man actually drew blood.

Avery's laugh resonated into the cell as his mouth was full of blood that wasn't his own.

"When the full moon rises, you'll all know, that this town is *ours*," Avery sang.

I furrowed my brows in confusion.

"What you are is a lunatic," Michael growled. "Ted...head to the infirmary. Get that bleeding patched up."

Ted stared at Avery in anger and uncertainty as an officer escorted him out.

"Am I not to have more visitation?" Avery grinned, staring at Evelyn.

Evelyn backed away from him, grabbing my hand behind me. I could feel her terror in her grip.

"Not a chance," I growled back.

Instinctively I led Evelyn out of the holding cells as the other officers filed out and prepped to lock the doors.

Michael shook his head. "I'm submitting that man to the sanitarium on the verdict of *insanity*," he growled tiredly.

There was something wrong with Avery Atwood and I hated that there was *no* evidence against him for Elizabeth's death.

However...Ted was an immediate victim. Only a matter of time before he cracked too.

Eight

"Are you coming?"

Bryan stood there in the field next to the makeshift wooden gate lining the property. He was staring at the sign that swung next in the chilly air reading: *Shaw's Family Farm*.

I was relatively familiar with the property. It's been here since I was a boy, and was always just as quiet. The Shaw farm seemed like a breath of fresh air compared to Avery's visit with Ted. Evelyn stayed behind to make sure Ted was taken care of after the incident. Apparently, she'd come with him as emotional support to see, and confirm, Elizabeth's body. He needed to see it for himself. *"I searched all night,"* he said to me. Even for someone who didn't talk much, I could see the light leave his eyes. *"She's everything."*

I knew giving up the love of your life, but not like this. I couldn't imagine how he felt in the moment of seeing her. Part of me hoped it was an accident for his sake. But my gut screamed danger, and I needed to start with our first clue: the mule as he stood by the separated barn. It didn't seem to notice us yet.

I looked up, feeling the rush of burning daylight. The sun was already setting by the time we got to the farm.

Bryan seemed to finally take notice of me as he fumbled with his notebook and a spare pen. He nodded quickly, continuing to follow me.

"So...does she really chase you with an ax?" I asked, smirking at him.

Bryan laughed a bit. "Well, not *me*, but I know one of

my classmates before we got old enough got chased with his girl," Bryan explained and swallowed at the memory. "She's always so *scary*."

"Let's hope for our sakes that he's lying," I commented as we approached the quiet house.

It was an old farmhouse, having survived at least three generations in Blackwood Hollow. No one really went this far away from town. It was too close to the woods, and no one wanted to be near the forest anymore. But today, I noticed an older boy playing ball with his dog when we reached the edge of the town and headed towards this lonely structure. It was a rarity, but not impossible.

There was no smoke coming out of the chimney, which seemed unusual especially with sunset approaching. The temperature would only drop further than the already frigid cold.

We climbed up the old porch steps and the wood creaked under the heels of our boots. I was just grateful to not be trudging through the snow, while the wind picked up the chill that was coming at us fast. Bryan seemed to keep his distance behind me, holding his notebook close to his chest.

I raised my brows as I knocked on the door.

"You ready?" I asked.

Bryan swallowed, nodding. "Keep notes ready," he repeated my instructions.

"And?"

"Be polite," Bryan groaned, rolling his eyes as if *that* was going to be the hard part.

I pointed at him, as if giving him a warning as I knocked again.

Then there was stomping from inside. And it was

loud. I found myself backing away from the door as I heard the footsteps charge towards the door I was standing in front of.

Before I could react, the door swung open.

Bryan moved back and immediately fell on his butt. I'm surprised I didn't do the same as I backed away out of instinct.

There was an instant click of a shotgun that made my hands immediately shoot up.

Bryan mimicked me from the ground, his notebook and pen on the porch floor.

"I TOLD YOU BASTARDS TO GET OFF," a female voice with a thick Scottish accent yelled. She froze seeing us, shotgun pointed directly in my face.

The mule hollered from the barn at the sudden ruckus causing more tension.

I quickly stepped out of the way to avoid more conflict.

Jane Shaw, was a woman twice my age. She would be closer to my mother's if she were still alive today. She had short, dark bobbed hair, her nightgown was covered in a thick wool coat and she wore a pair of matching slippers.

"Well good afternoon Miss Shaw," I greeted her, trying to keep my tone pleasant as the barrel of the gun was now aimed away from me.

Jane was about to aim the gun at Bryan but I deflected it. Her eyes seemed to adjust and widen at me. "Detective Sullivan?" she questioned her tone confused and shocked.

Apparently even she knew *my* reputation. "Yes well," I replied, clearing my throat. "I'm sorry to intrude-"

"Oh no dear, my apologies!" Miss Shaw exclaimed,

lowering the shotgun and resting it back behind the door. "Damn boys have been *terrorizing* my property for *weeks* at all hours of the night."

I turned to grab Bryan and lift him from the porch as he brushed himself off and grabbed his things. As he straightened, I noticed that Jane's eyes glared at Bryan as if studying him. "Is *he* one of them?!" she demanded.

Bryan nearly jumped as he kept himself behind me.

I put my hands up and put on my most professional smile. "Bryan? No, no," I assured her and motioned to Bryan. "You remember Evelyn Fields' son?"

Bryan stepped forward hesitantly as I put my hands on his shoulders. I was trying to reassure him, but he still flinched from her stare. He stayed silent until I gripped onto his shoulders.

"Bryan...*manners*," I whispered.

Bryan swallowed as he cleared his throat. "Hello," his teenage voice that was usually lower now, went up an octave.

Miss Shaw sort of laughed followed by a sweet smile and her glare disappeared. "Forgive me boy," she apologized cheerfully. "You can't blame me for being on my toes with the likes of your *friends* showing up on the property."

"They *aren't* my friends," Bryan reassured nervously.

Jane nodded. "I'll get the kettle on," she announced. She leaned out towards the mule. "IT'S ALL RIGHT JACK. THEY'RE JUST VISITING."

She smiled as the mule calmed down and stepped back inside.

That's when Bryan's body turned and shifted to run.

I immediately grabbed the boy and turned him around in an instant. "No, no, no," I objected quietly as he groaned in protest. "Smile, be *polite*, and *write* your notes."

I pushed Bryan into the house. Miss Shaw might be the woman we needed to get to the bottom of this mystery. Even if it's an odd fragment of information. My gut told me to keep my eyes open here.

The place was almost as austere as the clergy house. A simple kitchen, a wood stove, jars that were sealed for the season and a few odds and ends that littered the shelves. I wasn't sure of *what*, exactly, were in those jars. Herbs? Fruit? Some didn't look great against the dusted walls. The furniture was bare as the wooden floors and smelled musty. Trinkets were scattered here and there which I assumed to have been passed down from family, but there was nothing too extravagant.

Miss Shaw kept to herself and I don't blame her for considering the legend of being the "*witch*" of the town.

The kettle was heating as we carefully walked into the living room.

"Please excuse the mess, I wasn't expecting company," Jane sputtered. "Especially from the Sheriff's boys! How is Mr. Hughes?"

"He's well. Although we've been rather bombarded recently," I answered.

"He's married and with children now, yes?" Jane asked as if casual conversation.

Considering this woman was never seen around town, she seemed rather observant. "Growing like weeds," I answered simply.

"Good! And you've been a good man keeping the criminals at bay!" she praised.

"I'm sorry I don't work with them directly anymore," I mentioned as the kettle boiled over the stove. "Just me."

"Now why is that Mr. Sullivan?" Jane asked, her eyes studying me. "Don't tell me there's corruption in that little building."

"Priorities have changed," I stated.

That was not *entirely* true but she didn't have to know that.

There was something off about this whole exchange. She seemed distracted with setting up a simple tea set as she waited for the kettle. I watched as she fetched herbs from a drying rack.

My gut screamed to not touch it.

The whole place felt wrong, but I couldn't put my finger on it.

I scanned the room for anything that would hint at why my mind was on high alert. I started noticing small things that were missing from any average home.

No family portraits anywhere. The trinkets that I thought were heirlooms were encased in strange hutches or cages, almost as if they were older than she was. Ancient relics maybe? Crows. There were several, and they were all in cages with jeweled eyes, while holding something in their mouths. My eyes found one, its eyes wide and red. I looked in its beak. A blackened coin? Bryan and I were leaning in to look at the thing.

We jumped at the sound of the kettle whistling violently.

"Is this about my farm?" Jane asked, breaking the silence.

I motioned to Bryan who immediately opened his

small notebook and scrambled for a pen.

"What about it?" I asked.

"The teenagers! The ones who dared to waltz in and start vandalizing my farm," Jane growled. Then her eyes went sad. "Poor old Jack, the poor dear will have a heart attack. *And* my pigs keep escaping due to their escapades!"

"Well...as much as I'd love to help," I replied, trying to sound at least somewhat sympathetic. I couldn't let her assumptions steer us off course. "There's been an unfortunate incident the other night."

"Oh?" Jane asked, pausing and glancing over at me.

"You might...want to sit down Miss Shaw," I suggested.

Jane looked at me oddly before settling herself into a worn rocking chair that creaked under her weight. She stared at us with what looked like curiosity. I took a breath.

"There's been a potential attack. Someone died rather...tragically," I explained carefully.

"Oh dear," Jane replied quietly. "Attacked by what exactly? An animal?"

"We aren't sure. For all we know it could be a dangerous person roaming about."

"Then why come to me?"

"We found hoof prints leaving the scene," I answered. "They were heading in *this* direction."

Jane stared at me for a long moment before her face scrunched in disgust. "Are you...accusing *me* Mr. Sullivan?" she demanded.

"Not at all," I objected simply. "However, if you'd seen anything out of the ordinary-"

"Nothing," Jane stated quickly.

I furrowed my brows. Quick...that was quick. "Yet

you have teenage boys roaming your property," I replied. "Are you sure there's been nothing else? Did they perhaps steal at all?"

Jane hesitated.

I narrowed my eyes.

"There was...*one*," she mentioned carefully. "He came by late that night."

"What did he look like?"

"It was dark...he was a rather quiet man. Had an odd feeling about him. Not someone I want to get into trouble with. I chased him off the property," Jane explained almost stuttering.

Could it have been Avery? It was dark, whether it was him or someone else it would be hard to prove. But maybe someone was to blame for Elizabeth's death after all rather than *something*.

"Did he say anything?"

"He was talking nonsense. Something about finding a girl."

"And?"

"And I chased him off the property," Jane repeated, her voice releasing a mild growl. "What more could I do?"

"And, your horse stayed here?"

"Listen here Mr. *Sullivan*," Jane snapped, suddenly standing up.

Something shifted in the room. I felt my gut tell me to back up. I felt my legs backing away before I even processed it. She stood, but I kept my distance from her getting too close.

"I told you what I know," Jane pushed. "The man *barely* made it onto the porch before I threatened more than what I did with you and the boy here."

I put up my hands in a placating gesture and searched for anything to defuse the situation. "All right, all right," I accepted quietly.

Jane looked at me with frustration in her eyes, her cheeks turning red.

"I just need to...cover everyone's story."

"Cover their *story*?!" Jane repeated with acid in her tone. "Are you implying that I'm hiding something?"

"No, but you have to understand that if what we saw was true, it could be a murder case-"

Before I could even level the situation, she pushed forward. Bryan stood up and started towards the door. Miss Shaw grabbed my arm with a grip like a vice and I was dragged towards the door.

"Miss Shaw!" I protested.

Jane shoved me out the door with Bryan scrambling to get behind me. He tried to create as much distance as he could to get anything between him and the very mad Scottish woman.

Jane loomed over the door frame as we stood there speechless on the porch.

"I said my peace, now you have overstayed your welcome," she growled. "I have *enough* attention as it is without a supposed *murder* being added to my list of hogwash."

"Now Miss Shaw-"

That's when she stepped back inside, and I saw her hands reach for her shotgun again. I backed up protecting Bryan as we made our way further off the porch.

Jane sneered as she gave her ridged farm door a push. It creaked and slammed shut.

We quickly made our way off the porch. Bryan was

gripping his notebook so hard his knuckles were white. We were down the stairs when he finally spoke. "And you said *I* had to be the polite one," Bryan commented with some fear in his voice.

I rolled my eyes. "Come on...before she changes her mind," I started as I looked back towards the house.

As I turned, Bryan was already running away from the property and into the safety of the barren hills.

As I caught up with him, we were far enough to be safe from earshot. Bryan finally calmed down when we got to the hill on Lover's Lane. The same place where we found Elizabeth. I couldn't help but scan on the ground.

"Does that always happen when you investigate someone?" Bryan asked as he kicked a few spare rocks around the snow.

I paced under a barren crab apple tree, trying to replay the scene in my head with Elizabeth being there. "Not always. But panic does odd things to people," I replied.

Bryan found some pinecones under the snow and started tossing them in random directions. "Why was my mother at the station?" he asked.

I hesitated.

Bryan noticed and swallowed. "Did she go and see father?" he asked.

I nodded slowly.

Bryan shook his head. Even at sixteen, I couldn't imagine.

I knew what it was like to lose a parent under strange and horrible circumstances. Mine didn't just upright change overnight, though. The way Avery looked in the church or even the jail. This was far beyond me.

"He's always been a little off...just been worse in the

last few months," Bryan mentioned.

"Your mother agrees," I added.

Bryan looked at me. "You think he might've done this?" he asked. "Might've hurt Mrs. Baker?"

"Do you?" I found myself asking aloud.

Bryan shook his head. "I'm not exactly close to him," he admitted. "Does that make me a bad person?"

I walked up to him, and put a hand on his shoulder, gripping it slightly. "No...no it does not," I said. "Whatever happens I'll-"

Bryan's eyes then widened as he looked out towards the woods. I furrowed my brows in confusion as I followed at his line of sight.

Before I could ask, Bryan started sprinting towards the woods.

"Bryan?!" I called out, sprinting after him.

As we reached the border of the tree line, he stopped.

"Oh my God," Bryan whispered.

I looked down.

There was blood...a *lot* of blood that was trailing further in.

Bryan moved forward without hesitation as I stayed close behind. Then the blood trail stopped, with a body looking still in the snow. The boy was no bigger or older than Bryan.

I looked over and saw a dog next to him, dead and almost torn apart as if it were mauled. I swallowed as Bryan flipped the boy over, his breath catching.

"Trevor!" Bryan whispered harshly.

I swallowed and grabbed Bryan pulling him away from the boy.

"Get the sheriff," I ordered.

Bryan hesitated.

"Now!"

Bryan sprinted back to town as I sat with the sixteen-year-old boy.

"It's okay I got you," I whispered as the boy's labored breathing filled the silence.

I gently sat next to him. I looked down, his shirt was shredded, and soaked with blood. His face was pale, his bright blue eyes were wide with terror, and his dusty blonde hair mixed with snow and mud.

It was Trevor Hughes...Michael's son.

Nine

I was never fond of the morgue, but I'm not sure the dead are either.

Oskar Lowe was a precise man. His family had worked in funeral homes and this morbid business for generations in Germany before moving to this speck of a small town. Death wasn't anything new to him. When he took the reins of his family business, however, he had witnessed death and cases like he had here in Blackwood Hollow. Because of this, outside of working the usual funerary services, he assisted the sheriff's department.

Oskar's curiosity was a blessing to this station. He had an eagerness of wanting to solve the unusual accidents as much as the next person. Both Michael and I had been grateful to him for taking up the job since no one else would. Despite that, even with someone like him to run the report, I wasn't looking forward to it...especially this one. Seeing that beautiful young woman's face being taken away by death so quickly was...rather depressing. Plus the *way* that it came about...it was unlike anything I'd seen. I wondered if my father experienced this in his time on patrol. If he did...I didn't envy him.

After a few grueling hours, Michael met up with me back at the station. He'd been home tending to his son after the incident. His wife and Trevor's siblings were on the edge of desperation and prayers for hours. When he arrived, his face was pale, and he was sweating as he motioned down the hall to make our appointment.

"How is he?" I dared to ask.

"He's not *good*, but he's *alive*," Michael answered, his voice tired but level. "He's lost a lot of blood, but it's all surface...just needed a few stitches. If it wasn't for the dog...might be in a worse position right now."

Dog was a damn guardian angel, then, remembering how badly torn up it had been. The patrol rushed him to the hospital as quickly as they could without making the wounds worse. Despite the scene with his son, Michael insisted I'd meet him at the station for the coroner's report. I wasn't *exactly* sure why.

"You don't have to be here," I assured him. "He's *your* son."

Michael stopped and gave a long exhale, shaking his head.

"You know I can't just let this lie. I don't care if it's a killer, an accident, or a damn bear," Michael said quietly as we ventured further down the hall.

We reached the entrance to the morgue and Michael gave me a grave look. "We're going to get to the bottom of this," he stated as if making a promise to himself more than anyone else.

I nodded as I motioned him into the room.

Michael opened the door and we stepped in slowly.

Oskar was already preparing Elizabeth's body to be seen as we stepped in. A white sheet covered her from head to toe. He wiped his brow, showing his brass rimmed glasses and slicked back black hair. His eyes were dark but he gave off a kind demeanor.

"Ah, guten abend Herr Hughes," Oskar greeted. He still had a relatively subtle German accent from his family line, but it came out more in his fluency in the German language.

Michael nodded in common courtesy, but even Oskar could see his face. Michael tried hard not to be spent from the whole ordeal.

"Good God Michael...what happened?" Oskar asked.

"Long story..." Michael breathed.

Oskar looked at me and smiled as best he could despite the situation.

"Though I won't doubt a miracle happened tonight," Michael added.

"Well...if you need something go to my office," Oskar mentioned. "I'm still working on my father's liquor."

"You're lucky I don't report you for that," Michael groaned from his exhaustion as he walked out of the autopsy room and into the adjacent office.

"Ja, ja, I've heard that before," Oskar retorted, unfazed. "Just because the rest of the country is in prohibition doesn't mean we're all lining up for the law. You know as well as I do that *no one* cares about this place."

I heard clattering from Oscar's office as Michael rummaged through the desk.

Oskar's eyes turned to me, his expression shifting to something serious. "If they did, we would've had *someone* out here by now considering our *accidents*," he commented as if only speaking to me. His gaze was fully on me as he smiled reaching for his gloves. "Same offer extends to you Connor."

"No thanks," I rejected politely.

Oskar raised his brows at me in surprise. "Off the drink? That's a first in a long time," he commented.

I rolled my eyes. I suppose I deserved that. "I...need to keep my head on straight," I pressed.

Oskar smirked and nodded, seeming pleased.

"Good you came to that," he remarked.

I felt a bit proud of myself. Getting Oskar's approval was almost as hard as Michael's. I nodded and smiled. I did miss Oskar on more than one occasion, despite the circumstances.

I met Oskar through that tiny school with Michael one day in similar circumstances. He was my friend during funeral services since he got stuck ushering people with his father on every occasion. He would talk about how they prepared the bodies, what were common customs, and much more that went into the business. He even had a few chilling ghost stories.

And, yet, somehow his family lived in the house of all the funeral arrangements. Which...made me question their sanity.

Oskar was another weird kid who turned to a strange line of work in Blackwood Hollow. As soon as Oskar and I became close friends, Michael became our protector of sorts. Defending the weirdos from the bullies at school ended up becoming his job I guess. Not sure if I ever properly thanked him for that.

"Did you get a chance to look at her?" Michael asked as he came back with a glass of some strong-smelling liquor.

I could smell it from a few feet away.

Michael took a sip and immediately winced. "Christ Lowe," he whispered and immediately poured it into a nearby plant. "That'll make demons scream out of hell."

"My father's taste was what you say, *bold*? *If* he had any at all after that," Oskar quipped. "I keep it more as a sentimental piece than anything. Unless you find other strong Germans come into the area. I'm sure they'd appreciate that."

I chuckled in amusement at Michael's face as he shook his head and wiped his lips.

"*Burns*," Michael croaked, coughing slightly.

"And, as for your question," Oskar continued. "No not *thoroughly*. But in passing my curiosity has piqued for sure. One of your boys already got her stripped down for me and submitted what she had on her person for evidence...so be prepared."

Oskar finished securing his gloves as he nodded to me. We nodded back in acknowledgement as he went towards the end where her head rested at the end of the table. Then, he carefully pulled the sheet down. I swallowed, the smell already affecting the pit of my stomach.

Elizabeth's skin was pale but almost turning an odd shade of gray. That wasn't normal for most of the bodies we'd recovered in the past. Pale yes, but...there was something even more striking about it. She was frozen from the snow and from death's embrace. But the wounds...they looked grotesque as they had dried on her neck.

Oskar moved, lining up with the top of her head as Michael and I stood on either side of him. He looked down at her. His eyes rested immediately on her neck.

"Christ," Michael whispered.

Now that it was dry, it really did look like a tear. It was as if something was hacked or even *bitten* off. She looked more inhuman than most post-mortem bodies I've seen in my career. Even Oskar seemed to notice.

Oskar with his gloved hand lifted her eyelid and immediately flinched and backed away.

"What's wrong?" I asked, my voice more alert than usual.

Oskar shook his head, blinking for a bit before he dared to come back. Michael's hands were up. He hated dead bodies as much as I did. He was the one that was always more prone to being frightened of the ghost stories Oskar used to tell us. So it wasn't too surprising that bodies made it worse.

Oskar took a breath, leaned down, and lifted her eyelid again. That's when I saw it. Elizabeth's eyes weren't her normal color or even faded from blood loss. They were black. Pitch black. It was...*unreal*.

"Well...that's a first," Oskar swallowed. "Could be an anomaly."

"What anomaly would make someone's eyes like *that*?" I demanded.

"I'd have to dive into records. My father mentioned something about it in Germany. But...not here."

"Could it be the season?" Michael suggested.

Every answer felt *wrong*.

"It's the first for me," Oskar mentioned. "I'll have to retrace my father's journals from before we moved here."

I looked down, finally breaking the spell of staring at the body. My eyes stared at her exposed wrist, where punctures were clearly visible.

"Oskar," I interrupted, pointing.

Oskar furrowed his brows, moving to her wrist where another wound formed. It was punctured as if bitten by an animal or some strange creature. He looked between the neck and the wrist.

"So beside the strange eyes, what's the verdict?" Michael asked, trying to keep his eyes away from the body.

"Blind guess," Oskar began. "Attacked by *something* for sure."

Oskar opened her hand near the punctured wrist and found scarring on the palms of her hands. I swallowed. The scarring formed imprint of the cross in her hand as if it was burned into the skin.

"What-?" Oskar started.

Then, the body suddenly jumped and twitched making the rest of us jump in horror.

Michael nearly yelped, his hand instinctively landing on the gun holstered at his belt. Oskar jumped back from the body and I had my hands up as if afraid to touch her.

Then silence.

We all stared at each other as the body remained still. No movement. All we could hear was our own breathing.

Oskar looked between us and cleared his throat. "Well...that's another first," he tried laughing it off as he straightened up and shook his head.

"That...doesn't happen," Michael stated.

"No...no it doesn't. Not this late," Oskar replied. "She's been dead far too long."

"Great," I sang.

"Whatever this is," Oskar began pointing at Elizabeth. "Either is a grave accident or something...more."

"How?"

"Those my good sir," Oskar started straightening up taking off his gloves. "Just by *looking* at them...are *bites*. Wretched, ripping *bites*."

Michael and I looked at each other. I stared at the wound on her neck. So, it *was* torn.

"Why it hadn't taken the woman fully for a meal...I'm not sure. Something could've scared it off."

Bryan...Bryan saw her getting attacked, but it wasn't a creature.

"What if it was a person?" I asked.

"If *that* was a person, then I'd call them insane, *psychotic* even," Oskar announced, dropping his gloves on the gurney beside her and walking back toward the desk. "And if that's the case," he added, crossing his arms. "Then there's something *far* more sinister happening here."

I looked at Elizabeth's body.

"How long 'til we get the full report?" I asked.

"Hopefully before another body shows up," Oskar stated, sighing and looking at Elizabeth's corpse.

I only hoped he was right. Michael nodded to me and motioned to the door.

"Thanks Oskar," I thanked as I patted his shoulder and Michael and I left Oskar to his work.

It felt odd to leave him alone with Elizabeth considering the circumstances...and how her body reacted. Out of all the bodies I've seen in the past, *nothing* looked like this. We stood in the hall after gathering our wits.

"Of course my luck it's some psychopath," Michael groaned.

"It could *still* be an animal," I reassured.

Michael shook his head. He knew as well as I did that it was something bigger. "You heard the boy," Michael reminded. "Someone was there with her."

I swallowed, nodding.

A killer in Blackwood Hollow.

This town is so small, yet this person seems so hidden. Then it hit me.

"Do you think this is linked to what happened with Trevor?" I asked.

Michael froze and looked at me. He was silent for a good long moment.

"I'm not asking to pry on him now Michael," I clarified.

Michael swallowed nodding. "I'll talk to him," he agreed. "At the very least we can see if something is wandering those cursed woods. Maybe there's a reason for those ghost stories."

"What about Avery?"

"He's growing more irritating and stranger by the day," Michael replied. "I doubt he'll be much help. I already sent in a request to the State Psychiatric Facility to have an examination admitted here for him."

Michael looked at me. "Are Evelyn and Bryan with you?" he asked protectively.

"I have room."

"Keep an eye on them," Michael said. "I'll come get you if anything happens."

I nodded, putting out my hand. Michael looked at it, and took it firmly.

"Get some rest," I insisted.

Michael nodded reluctantly as I turned to leave. "Sullivan," he called out.

I turned and looked at him.

"Don't do anything stupid."

Ten

To my surprise, Ted was standing outside the station when I left.

I felt my body stiffen seeing him leaning against the station's brick wall, freezing from the cold.

"Ted," I greeted him.

Ted didn't immediately look my way. His expression seemed focused but not on anything around him. His hand was bandaged up from the scuffle with Avery the other day. It still had the occasional weeping of the wound, but it was nothing too serious. He seemed rather pale, even though he hadn't lost much blood.

Ted grunted, finally nodding in acknowledgement.

I furrowed my brows at him. He was sweating a bit despite the bitter chill in the air. Maybe he was running?

"You all right?" I asked with concern.

"Would you be in my position?" Ted asked, his tone stern.

Ted's wife was dead and we still have no idea how. Just a bunch of theories and no culprit. It must've been eating away at him.

I nodded in understanding. "Fair enough," I replied simply. I reached out and patted him on the shoulder and for an over six-foot hulking man, he flinched. I hesitated as I pulled my hand away from him. "Get some rest."

I turned to leave but Ted's voice called out. "Hey," he said, his voice forming under a low growl.

I stopped, turning to face him. His eyes. The night must've been playing tricks on me, because *something* wasn't right about his now dark, unrelenting eyes. My body went into high alert.

"You don't really think it was an accident, do you?" Ted asked, his voice hoarse. Before I could answer he glared. "It might be *him*."

"We don't know for sure," I assured Ted, keeping my voice steady.

"You saw the *look* in his eyes. You saw what he almost *did* to her," Ted insisted, now facing me fully.

Ted's posture set off alarm bells in my head. It was almost as if Ted wasn't Ted anymore...but something *predatory*.

"Ted," I began.

"Avery...I *swear* I'm going to-" Ted growled.

"TED!" I barked, raising my voice in an attempt to bring him back to his senses.

Ted froze in his spot, blinking rapidly. He shook his head, and wiped his face.

"I'm sorry about Elizabeth," I continued. "But I *promise* you: we're going to figure this out."

Silence.

Ted remained perfectly still, the tension was rising and the cold was biting onto my face.

For several long moments, Ted didn't show any sign of relaxing. I couldn't blame him. His wife died and he had no remaining family to turn to. He seemed *strained*.

Then Ted sighed, shaking his head and looking down at the ground. He shoved his hands in his pockets, but his fists never unclenched in his wool coat. He managed to finally move from his spot and brushed past me.

"They will be staying with you," Ted said flatly as he walked further away from me.

"Who?" I asked.

"You know who."

***

Evelyn and Bryan were already at the estate when I arrived.

The glow of the fireplace from inside the study was a warm welcome compared to Ted's unusual demeanor.

Questions swarmed through my mind as I entered my home. What was Ted doing at the police station? Was he asked to come back for Elizabeth's body again? My skin prickled with goosebumps remembering the way he stared at me. The seething hate that radiated off of him, and how he spat out Avery's name like venom.

Despite the stress Ted must've been going through, something wasn't right. It wasn't like a lot of other cases, when I've had to deal with widowers. He was *angry* and ready to fight.

I had to remind myself to focus on Oskar's reports and whoever could potentially be behind Elizabeth's murder, if in fact it *wasn't* a fluke.

"Connor?" Evelyn's voice called from the study. Before I knew it she was approaching me. Her eyes widened. "My God you're shaking."

I looked down. She was right. "I'm fine," I replied simply. "Just colder than I was expecting."

I prayed it was partially true.

"How was Mr. Lowe?" Bryan asked casually.

Bryan had that gleam in his eyes. His mother on the

other hand looked between him and I questioningly. "Oskar? You went to see him?" she asked.

I nodded glancing at Bryan. "There's always at least *one* trip in cases like this," I replied, trying to lighten my tone.

Bryan looked at me eagerly, but I motioned further into the house.

"Mr. Baker told me you *and* your mother will be staying with me until someone says otherwise," I informed them.

Bryan's eyes widened. "Can we?"

"Well," Evelyn started, looking at me rather hesitantly.

"It's better than Mr. Donovan's," Bryan groaned. "*Please?*"

"Do you have your things?" I asked.

Bryan nodded, motioning towards the wall of the study. A few suitcases were lined up in the space.

"Good," I praised the boy, nodding.

They were staying with me...in this empty house.

I put my arm around Bryan and led him to the stairs. "In the meantime," I continued. "Why don't you pick your room? You already know which one is mine, yes?"

Bryan called out with a "yes", rushing up the stairs as he went down the hall.

Evelyn watched him and then looked at me. "First Oskar and then Ted," she whispered. "Such a full night."

I locked the front door and motioned to the study and Evelyn followed me.

"What did Oskar want?" she asked.

"Another pair of eyes on Elizabeth's examination," I replied, sitting myself down in my chair by the study.

Evelyn stood in front of my desk, her fingers fidgeting. "And?"

I got up, grabbing a small chair from the side of the room and placing it in front of the desk for her to sit. She looked at me for a moment and nodded in acknowledgement. I sat down back in my place behind the desk.

"It's bad Evee," I sighed.

"How bad?" Evelyn asked.

Evelyn's tone was curious, but I could tell there was a tinge of fear laced through it. "If it was *intentional*," I started carefully. "Then...I'd hate to see the person who had the wherewithal to do it."

Evelyn swallowed.

I explained the oddities of the wounds trying not to go into too much gory detail. She wasn't one to be squeamish growing up, but I wanted it out of respect to her friend's current state.

"And Ted?" Evelyn asked. "You saw him?"

"He was out there when I left," I confirmed, shaking my head. "He's not looking good Eve."

"Of course not! He just lost his wife," Evelyn retorted.

"It's a lot more than that. It's *different*, trust me," I said.

Evelyn saw the look on my face and her jaw tightened. "Is that why we're here?"

"Outside of his orders, I agree with him," I replied. "After seeing how he is and how he's coping, it's best to keep you and Bryan out of his way."

Evelyn nodded.

"Unless you prefer to be at Bill's until Avery's

situation," I started but she straightened, looking at me and shaking her head.

"No...no that's not necessary," Evelyn interrupted. "As much as they feel like family. I'd...prefer to be here."

There was a lingering silence.

Evelyn looked at me and smiled slightly.

"So...you'll stay?" I asked.

"Through the bowels of hell...this is where I'd rather be," she whispered. I stiffened and she cleared her throat. "For Bryan of course."

I scoffed and found myself smiling despite the chaos and uncertainty of the entire day. "Of course," I agreed. "For Bryan."

Eleven

"I talked to Trevor," Michael mentioned as he glanced over at me.

His face was pale. Michael had come early in the morning to check on things and to talk with him.

"And?" I asked gently. "How's the boy doing?"

"He's...struggling. The stitches will get pulled in about two weeks," Michael replied as if giving a report. "We got him in there early enough that the doc wasn't worried about an infection. And of course *because* of how close of a call it was, my wife's been *hovering*."

I would rather the hovering than the alternative, but I wouldn't say that out loud.

Michael grabbed his cigarettes from his jacket pocket and lit one. He looked like he hadn't slept in days, but it was deeper than that.

"You have this look on your face," I noted.

Michael glanced at me giving a "no shit" look and proceeded to take a drag of his cigarette. "You know Trevor's Bryan's age."

I nodded.

"He's been having nightmares flare up again," Michael mentioned, his tone grave. "Claiming nonsense is real."

I felt my stomach drop.

"He keeps screaming for the dog," Michael stated. Something about his tone sent chills up my spine.

Michael shook his head.

"You got that look again," I remarked.

Michael scoffed in bitter amusement, looking at me uncertainly. "I know you always had a *feeling* that something is bigger here," Michael said as he motioned towards the woods. "I've always been a bit skeptical…"

"But?" I prompted when he hesitated.

Michael sighed. "When your own family is face to face with *whatever* this is…it makes you wonder," he replied. He shook his head and made a face. "Makes me wonder if God really does exist. If He does…why would he watch us be pulled apart bit by bit?"

I thought about it for a long moment, unsure of what to say. His eyes searched mine. "I've been asking the same question for a long time," I replied feeling a bit of pain in my throat. "I've come to the conclusion that maybe we don't deserve saving. Not unless we do it ourselves."

Michael scoffed, dropping his cigarette and stomping it out. "Well…already on it," he agreed. "Although despite my skepticism, hoping for something good is preferable. The worst that happens is what's been happening. Silence…and uncertainty."

I nodded.

Michael reached out a hand.

I furrowed my brows as I reached out grabbing his hand firmly. "Michael…"

"We gotta figure this out Sullivan," Michael insisted. "Lock your doors. God might not be listening right now, but a little more protection by your bed won't hurt."

"Connor..." her voice was...haunting and heavenly. I watched as she came into view.

A woman with a smile that was just as bright and warm as her yellow dress. Her cross swinging around her neck. She reached her hand out.

Mother...I reached out to her comfort and embrace, but things started to change. Her beautiful eyes mutated to solid black as her skin followed suit stretching into a sickly leathery gray form. Her teeth grew into monstrous, elongated spears.

"Come here!" The monster hissed at me. Before I could move away, she lunged and I was screaming.

I bolted upright in my bed, gasping for air. My eyes darted around the room to find a silhouetted Evelyn hovering over me. She stepped back in shock, trying to remain near as I gathered my wits. My heart was pounding and I could feel the cold sweat on my brow. "Connor! It's okay," she whispered earnestly, as she finally stepped forward.

Evelyn placed a hand on my heaving chest. It took a few moments to catch my breath. Nightmares were such a common occurrence that I forgot a time where I wasn't haunted by monsters. Now someone was in my house, living out my nightmares in same the room. And...I was finding it difficult not to stare.

Evelyn's hair was a mess from sleep, a warmer nightgown clung to her as she watched me. Her eyes were filled with concern and something else I haven't seen in a long time. Worry and comfort. Her presence started to calm my mind.

Finally, my mind started waking up with the rest of

me. My heart shot up from adrenaline now suddenly at a stand still. Time was barely moving. She was here...*alone* in my room. A decade since I caught her breath in the same room. I watched as her eyes shifted. Maybe she finally realized the distance as well. It wasn't the first time she was in my room saving me from my nightmares. But it felt *different* this time. It had been so long since the last one.

"Are you okay?" I asked, almost shocked at the quietness of my own voice.

Evelyn scoffed in disbelief. "Am *I* okay?" she objected smiling slightly. "You never change, do you?"

I rolled my eyes as I raised one of my knees, leaning against it. "I guess I don't."

Evelyn smiled, taking my hand and squeezed it gently as she continued to sit on the edge of the bed. "Thank you," she whispered, her eyes darting to me.

"For what?" I asked.

"All this time and you're still here."

I swallowed. I felt my hand tighten around hers. "I made a promise, didn't I?" I reminded her, managing to smile at her in the darkness.

"If you want me to stay-" she began.

I swallowed. "No...no I'm fine," I whispered, when she trailed off, squeezing her hand in reassurance.

Evelyn stared at me for a moment, swallowing. Before I knew it, she leaned in to kiss my cheek. A rush flooded and my face instantly became cold when her lips parted from my skin. Whatever rush of fear and adrenaline was gone. Now...my mind was just wanting her comfort. "Eve," I breathed as I felt my hand reach for her, but her other hand slipped away.

Evelyn stood, turned and headed towards the door.

My chest ached at the familiar presence leaving the room. I was finally seeing the spark of her that I felt so deeply empty over.

※※※

"It doesn't make *sense*," Oskar groaned into his coffee.

Oskar was pacing with a worn down journal in his hand, comparing it into the reports he'd divvied up. Michael had closed the door to his office and drawn the blinds while we went over the records.

Oskar *insisted* on seeing us in the morning. The coffee didn't stop the throbbing in my head from the night before. I found myself with my head in my hand and a barely touched mug of the stuff on the desk as I dared to examine the photos for the hundredth time.

"I'm telling you Lowe," Michael began. "It's just got to be a fluke."

"Mrs. Baker's volume was higher than it should have been. Not to mention it was still a proper mixture, though it came out *dark* almost *black*," Oskar growled. "This is *far* from normal."

"It's winter. Doesn't that affect things? If it was an accident, then it very well could be-"

"Her skin, her eyes, everything," Oskar interrupted almost shouting.

I'd never really seen Oskar so shaken.

"*Oskar*," Michael interrupted before he could go further.

Oskar seemed to realize he was yelling. He cleared his throat as he pulled out a rather elaborately embroidered handkerchief from his pocket. He started wiping his glasses first and then his brow. "Michael...this is *concerning*," he emphasized, putting his glasses back on. "And what's *more* startling is what I *found*."

I watched Oskar held a beaten and battered journal in his hand. I furrowed my brows in confusion. "What's that?" I asked, pointing at it.

"My father's records. Autopsies, funeral logs, everything from the very beginning. As far back as when my family lived in Germany," Oskar explained. "And I found...*something*."

Oskar opened and speedily rushed his fingers through the worn pages. There was a fold in the paper as if he had bookmarked it as he stopped on a page. I looked over his shoulder seeing the rather beautiful calligraphy, but it was all in German.

Oskar's eyes scanned for a moment and then translated.

"*January 20th, 1886: Herr Bernard Hoffmann, age twenty-seven, cause of death: unknown, potentially wild animal. Autopsy: Wounds in t the neck and chest as if mauled. Skin pale but almost gray, dark black blood and twitching during procedure.*"

The sound of the flipping pages filled the silence as Oskar proceeded to another marked page.

"*February 4th, 1886: Fräulein Ava Geiger, age twenty-two, cause of death: Strangulation? Autopsy: bruising on the neck as if gripped, odd punctures on both wrists. Blood changing to black.*"

Oskars hands were trembling as he read off more

and more from the records. It all happened in the same year, some within *weeks* of each other. All younger people. What chaos did this poor area of Germany fall into?

Then Oskar stopped, his eyes rapidly scanning the page.

"Oskar?" I asked.

Oskar swallowed.

"*December 22ⁿᵈ, 1886: Fräulein Emma Lowe...*" he paused.

Lowe...another Lowe? But...she wouldn't be *that* much older than Oskar. I don't remember an Emma in his family. I saw his face turn pale, his body starting to shake.

"Relative?" Michael asked, furrowing his brow in confusion.

"*Age...16,*" Oskar whispered. I cursed under my breath. "*Cause of death: Murder. Autopsy: blood loss, ripping of the neck, wrists and bruising at the ankles. Anemic.*"

Oskar paused, staring at the note as I hovered over him. I could see the writing getting less logical and methodical and more frantic by the way the ink splayed on the page. Oskar seemed to notice and frantically turned the page. There were many blank pages after it until he flipped back at the page.

"*Emma*," Oskar whispered, swallowing. "My father told me about a long-lost sister. I didn't realize..."

So...it was his sister. I felt my stomach drop at the idea of a sibling being murdered. My hand reached out as I gripped his shoulder. His hands stayed firm on the journal.

"That's odd," Oskar remarked gathering some semblance of control and taking a breath. "There's a personal note here. It's...it's from my father."

I felt my chest tighten. A note? I hovered over the page, the writing was different and the pages worn.

Michael watched, nodding slowly to proceed. Oskar calmed himself as he read over the blotchy ink.

"*This will follow me to my grave,*" Oskar translated, his voice getting unsteady. "*This year there had been so many cases in only a matter of months. People are dying in the street, sometimes even in their own homes. It's almost like a curse. One by one they come to our funeral home and are buried. Some have family fall not far behind them.*

"*But, then, my daughter was murdered. I couldn't protect her. As I feel responsibility for her death, her spirit must've sought revenge for her early grave.*

"*My daughter rose from her examination table, grabbed me and tried to attack! She stared at me with black eyes, and an evil grin. There was no heartbeat. There was no* breathing. *But that was not my daughter...this was a creature. With no choice, I had to take her down...saying goodbye by my own hand this time. For the sake of my family, I must leave this place. Or else it would be the death of all of us.*"

Oskar shook his head then looked at me.

"Rising from the dead," Michael scoffed in disbelief. "You can't be serious."

"What about Elizabeth..." I suggested.

Michael flinched at the memory.

Oskar took off his glasses. The closing of the book was like the slam of a door with how it filled the silence.

"My father was a serious man," Oskar reminded us. "He would not make light of this, especially not involving one of our own blood."

"If she died of murder...are we sure it's not a side

effect of grief?" I asked. "Guilt is a rather dangerous thing."

"The only one who knows is gone Connor. I'd ask him myself if I could," Oskar replied. "However...I *know* him. I'd have to trust that the year of reports in Germany were nothing but oddities. Similar deaths, just like Elizabeth? Just like the other ones we found here in Blackwood Hollow since your parents. Maybe even *before* them."

I swallowed. A curse? The one we've all been living with since we were children. Whatever this was, the cycle needed to stop before it got even more out of hand.

"So, what are we looking at?" I asked, my voice unsteady. "A superstition that followed you here?"

"I'm not sure," Oskar whispered. "But whatever it is, I don't think it's an accident."

Michael stared at us. "Well...now what?"

"Perhaps we should ask the person who would know," I stated.

"Who?"

I shook my head. It was the *last* person I wanted to face, but he might be the only one to trail back towards an answer.

"The man who started this whole mess," I grumbled. "Avery Atwood."

Twelve

Avery's eyes were staring directly at me. My gut was screaming that something was wrong.

Michael, Oskar and I were standing in front of Avery's cell. What little light there was, came in sparsely through the barred windows of his new enclosure.

And there was Avery. His body was tucked away on top of his small cot, huddled in the darkness, acting like a rat avoiding detection. His eyes glared at us through the bars, and his breath seemed more labored than usual.

He grinned when I approached, sending a chill down my spine.

"Mr. Sullivan," he growled. His voice...it was *angry*.

The hair on the back of my neck stood on end. "Avery..." I greeted him, keeping my voice level.

Avery grinned, but there seemed to be some strain on his face. He was pale and sweating and his eyes appeared darker. He was so different compared to how he was only days before. "How's *Evee*?" he purred. "Don't tell me you forgot her?"

My eyes hardened. The voice in the back of my mind was screaming in alert and fighting to stay calm. "*This* wasn't a planned visit," I replied coolly.

"Well," Avery scoffed, staring at me menacingly. "She seemed *much* more favorable of you anyway."

I inched a little closer to the cell and felt Michael's hand on my arm, gripping in warning. I glanced at him. His gaze rested on me protective but uncertain. It felt almost as if we were children dealing with Avery back then. But now...he's caged and dangerous. Even Oskar's body went rigid as his eyes remained on Avery. He held that journal in his hand like it was the key to all of this madness, even though I for one, had no idea how to crack it.

"What's that supposed to mean?" I asked.

"Like it or not...she's *mine*," Avery hissed, his eyes refusing to leave mine. That's when I heard Oskar behind me. "And best you know that now so when I find you with her-"

"Mr. Atwood...are you feeling all right?" Oskar asked as his fingers started fidgeting around the journal.

"*Starving* if you care so much," Avery growled, shaking his head.

I looked down.

There was a tray of breakfast donuts, water, and even a porcelain mug of black coffee just sitting on the floor. Nothing was touched.

"And it's *boiling* in here," Avery complained.

I looked at Michael and furrowed my brows. It was frigid. Not as bad as outside but it's not that the stone walls could keep the cold from leaking in. I grabbed Michael and Oskar, and we huddled away from Avery out of ear shot.

"Have you had him looked at?" I whispered, glancing back at Avery as he started pacing the cell.

"Not yet...a medical "professional" was supposed to come this afternoon," Michael whispered back.

"Could be fever," Oskar pitched in. "He looks...*ill*."

Then there was a bone chilling laugh that radiated from Avery's throat. It made us all jump and stare at him.

Avery grinned. "I've never been better," he said, approaching the cell doors and gripping onto the bars. I took an involuntary step back. "So...what brings you to my new abode if you're not here to deliver my wife to me?"

I felt my blood boiling. I would *never* give her back to this lunatic. That much was crystal clear.

Avery eyed me as if he noticed my change in behavior. It felt like an odd predatory challenge. But I tried to keep myself in check. He was leading us off track. Michael must've felt the room because I felt his hand grip onto my shoulder.

"I was hoping we would talk," I replied simply.

Avery leaned his head on the bars keeping his eyes on me. "About?" he asked.

"Someone told me you've been roaming about," I replied. "Meet anyone interesting?"

"Whatever do you mean?"

"Don't be coy Avery," I bit. "Everyone knows you haven't been exactly...*faithful*."

Avery's eyes narrowed then smirked. "That's quite an accusation," he muttered then pushed off the bars and started pacing in his cell. "Your point?"

"Who have you been with?" I asked bluntly.

Avery stared at me. "Why does it matter?" he demanded.

"Because we have reason to believe maybe someone or *something* is...influencing you," I proposed.

Avery smirked. "You're acting like I *didn't* want this," he said. "You have no idea what I'm capable of."

That's when he lunged towards me, reaching out to grab me. A hand reached out and pulled me back from my jacket hard. Avery *hissed* at me before laughing. It wasn't like a person either. He hissed at me...like some feral cat.

I turned to find Michael still gripping my jacket to save me from the predatory jump.

"No, no," Michael growled. "We're not biting again."

Avery shifted his grip to the bars, grinning wildly. And finally, I saw it. Avery's wrist bared, showing faded scars identical to Elizabeth's and the victims that Oskar's father encountered. My mind raced at every possible connection.

Avery grinned. "You act like our little town has a choice," he remarked, laughing. "The moon will shine, and your holy ground will be no more. And then...we will return."

"I think I've had enough of this lunatic," Michael muttered. "I'm going to make some calls."

Avery smirked. "I'll find a way out don't you worry," he chimed.

Michael turned toward Avery, and dared to walk up to the bar doors, keeping his distance.

An officer came in, a woman at his arm.

"Sir," the officer called, and we all turned.

Jane Shaw stayed on the arm of the officer. She had wrapped herself in an old wool coat, and wore a scarf that neatly covered her salt and pepper hair. Her eyes widened as she looked at Avery.

"Miss Shaw," I exclaimed in surprise.

Jane then turned her attention on me. "My goodness. Is that Avery Atwood?" she asked.

"Hello Jane," Avery sang.

Jane froze, eyes terrified.

"You owe my family a visit." Avery mentioned, his posture changed and he started licking his lips, his brow still sweating.

"Perhaps they should come to me," Jane retorted.

Avery smirked. "With that awful tea?" he quipped.

"No, I think you deserve *our* hospitality this time. It's *long* overdue."

I watched Avery quietly. He stared at Miss Shaw, then slowly started grinning. He went back to pacing but his eyes were on her. A wolf spotting an older deer. My hair was standing up. I tapped at the bars, getting his focus back on me. "We're not done here Avery," I snarled.

Avery smirked, still eying Jane.

I backed away as I stared at a rather shaken Miss Shaw.

Michael walked up to Miss Shaw, quickly putting out a hand motioning to the door. "Miss Shaw, why don't we escort you to my office," Michael suggested, glancing back at Avery.

"I wish to talk to Mr. Sullivan too!" Jane pipped.

I raised my eyebrow.

Michael cleared his throat. "Yes of course," he accepted. "He'll join us shortly."

Michael looked at me, nodding and mouthing "*five minutes*". I nodded as he whispered something to the officer before leading her out of the cell block.

Oskar swallowed, grabbing my shoulder. "I need to take care of a few things," Oskar whispered. "Meet me in my office when you're done with Miss Shaw."

I nodded.

As soon as the door closed, I was standing face to face with Avery alone with an accompanying officer.

Avery grinned. "So...why are you really here Sul?" he asked.

Avery's tone made me twinge uncomfortably, but I tried not to show it. "I already told you," I swallowed.

Avery smirked. "No you *didn't*," he objected. "But I

can make a wild guess."

I stood there, crossing my arms.

"You're trying *so* hard to blame me for her death," Avery speculated. "Well I hate to tell you *Sul*, I've been right here the whole time."

"That's what I've been told," I agreed. "But I saw you with that girl the night before she died."

Avery grinned. A glimmer of light showed something off about his teeth. I couldn't place it, but it was horrifying. "Maybe it was fate," he suggested.

My jaw tightened.

"Maybe the bitch should've left her nose out of *our* business," Avery continued. "Perhaps she'd still be alive."

"You're acting like it's *not* an accident."

Avery shrugged, leaning his arms against the bars, his forehead resting to stare at me. "Perhaps she wasn't as *holy* as your church made her out to be," he continued indifferently. "Maybe the devil finally got to her."

I nearly jumped out of my skin when the officer called out. "Mr. Sullivan, Sheriff Hughes is calling you," he announced.

I nodded.

Avery grinned, making a clicking of his tongue. "Looks like our time is up," he whispered playfully.

"We're not done here," I retorted, turning to leave.

"And tell my very stubborn wife that I'll be coming for her," Avery stated, laughing lowly.

I stopped and turned around. Avery was watching me, almost as if he were processing my face. "*Ex* wife," I corrected cooly. "And if you touch her again, I'll make sure that you regret it."

Avery narrowed his eyes, a smile forming on his lips

as if not at all threatened.

"You have no idea what you're up against Connor Sullivan. This is far beyond anything our parents feared and I'm on the winning side."

I left the holding cell without another word, nodding to the officer. I felt my pace quicken to Michael's office and was relieved when I finally made it to the door.

I opened the door and made the others jump for a moment.

Miss Shaw was staring at me from the leather chair that seemed to envelope her small frame.

Michael was sitting on the corner of the desk. "Ah there he is," Michael greeted me, as I closed the door.

"Miss Shaw," I greeted the old woman.

Jane's eyes were staring at me, wide and scared. "Is that boy okay?" she asked.

"I told you before, Jane, we're looking into it," Michael assured. "I have someone coming in to check on him while he...well...lets say he's accused of several offenses that now require a grand jury far bigger than Blackwood Hollow."

"Offenses? Goodness," Miss Shaw whispered.

I cleared my throat. "Miss Shaw," I started, redirecting her back on topic. "Might I ask what you're doing here?"

"I was telling Sheriff Hughs here that I think his son might be a part of the group of boys who have been harassing my livestock-"

"And I told you again Jane, that my son has had an accident and hasn't been out of the house in a few days," Michael reminded the old woman.

"Well *someone* has been on my property," Jane

accused harshly.

I furrowed my brows, crossing my arms about my chest. "How do you know? The weather has been harsher than usual," I mentioned.

Jane looked at me, her frustration plain on her face. "Last night, I was tending to my farm," she recollected. "I've been preparing for the cold. And as I reached the pen, they were...they were gone!"

Janes eyes teared up as she grabbed a handkerchief from her crocheted handbag.

"Who's gone?" Michael asked.

"My precious babies," Jane cried. "My pigs!"

Michael looked at me and raised an eyebrow when Jane turned away from him. Pigs...her livestock was gone. *Again.*

"I searched and searched," Jane cried. "But it was too cold and I'm sorry to admit that age has not been the best to me. I want there to be a search party."

"Miss Shaw..." Michael coaxed. "I'm sorry but I can't spare any of my officers from here. Perhaps you can go to the church."

"The church?!" Jane screeched. "Reverend Donovan wants *nothing* to do with me nor I him."

"The newspapers," I suggested. "Maybe a missing poster?"

"I don't have the money," Jane whimpered. "The farm has been struggling all year."

Maybe if she would just be more...reliable with her own livestock.

"Can you not do anything? Michael please, do an old woman a favor. Just a small one," Jane tried to coax. "I'm sure your wife wouldn't be happy leaving an old woman out to dry."

Michael sighed, giving me an exaggerated "oh boy" look. "Fine," he sighed. "I'll alert my officers to keep an eye out for anything while they're doing their rounds. Tracks, maybe one will be wandering near their routes."

Miss Shaw looked up, her sniffling lessened.

"Really?" she asked.

Michael nodded.

"We'll make sure to alert you if we see anything. One of the boys can send you a message," Michael replied.

Jane grinned, smoothing out her wool skirt as she stood. "Thank you Sherriff," she stated, patting him on the shoulder. "You're a good lad. Always have been."

Michael flinched at the Scottish woman's touch and nodded politely.

Jane wiped tears from her face as she headed towards me. "And I'm sorry to you and the lad for being so harsh in the last visit," she apologized quietly. She made a polite smile. "I saw the girl's obituary in the paper. Such a shame. So young. No wonder you were so wound up."

I nodded, swallowing.

"Just...be careful you never know what lurks in this place," Jane whispered.

I furrowed my brows. "What kind of things?" I asked.

"Bad things. Things I haven't felt since I left my home," Jane answered. "You best be careful." She reached into her pocket. "Here," she whispered, motioning my hand.

I furrowed my brows as I put out my hand. The old woman placed something cold in my palm, immediately closing it. She patted my fist and smiled gently. "Keep this with you. It'll give you protection," she supplied.

Jane then glanced at Michael, waving. "Thank you, Sherriff."

She opened the door, left the office, and closed the door behind her.

I grimaced as I finally opened my hand. The coin...the same one I saw in the crow's mouth while we visited the farm.

"What in God's name is that?" Michael asked.

I swallowed. Something in my gut felt off. The coin was almost blackened, cold to the touch, and carved with otherworldly sigils. I flipped it, the coin was etched with an ancient crow on the back side. "Something I don't wish to lose," I assured.

Thirteen

"I'm not exactly sure what we're going do with him," Michael announced. "My men have been a little put off by his strange behavior."

Later that afternoon, I walked with Michael and Oskar as we made our way away from the station. Avery had been causing more trouble even in his enclosed space.

"He keeps saying he's *hungry*," Michael growled. "The man has every meal in that cell *untouched*. I swear it's because it's not some fancy pants bull he's used to."

"I don't know Michael," Oskar objected. "This doesn't feel right."

"Yeah well...I'm trying to avoid another biting incident," Michael retorted. "You saw the damage he did to Ted."

Oskar swallowed, nodding.

I felt my fingers flipping the coin in my pocket. I was so focused on it that I nearly jumped when I heard Oskar's voice. "Connor?" he asked. "Are you all right?"

I stopped flipping the coin and shook my head. "The man is just trying to scare us," I replied.

"Well, until the doctor gets here to examine him, we won't know anything for sure," Michael said and shook his head. "His behavior is unlike anything I've seen before."

"He had the same puncture scars that Elizabeth had," I mentioned. "Maybe it is *something* that affected them both."

"I'll believe it when I see it," Michael growled. "As it stands he's a lunatic."

"A lunatic who knows too much about Elizabeth's demise," I added.

"What do you mean?" Oskar asked.

We stopped in front of Michael's house.

"He said something...off about Elizabeth," I replied. They waited for an answer. "Claiming she wasn't as *holy* as we made her out to be."

"Bullshit," Michael cursed.

I swallowed. "What...what *if* she was involved with him?" I asked, rolling the thought around in my mind.

The idea of Elizabeth being in any way involved *with* Avery seemed unlikely. That bubbly smiling face.

"Again...I call bullshit," Michael repeated, giving me a rather disgusted look. "That girl couldn't squish a spider without screaming how we killed something *innocent*. There's no way."

I nodded in agreement.

Michael walked up to me, face to face, his eyes stern. "Don't let this bastard get in your head," Michael warned.

Oskar nodded. "*Something* is going on," Oskar agreed. "Elizabeth was just in the crossfire."

I nodded again, surely they were right.

"And with the way my boys are watching him, I wouldn't be surprised if he's not *somehow* involved even indirectly," Michael added.

Michael watched me and I felt myself fiddling with the coin again. He put his hand on my shoulder and squeezed.

"We will figure this out," Michael whispered. "We always do."

I nodded. If I was to figure anything out with the case...I rather it be with these two.

Michael patted my shoulder, motioning to his house. "Shall we?" he suggested, leading us into the house.

✳✳✳

"**Trevor! Hold *still*,**" **Margaret Hughes fussed as the teenage boy rolled his eyes.**

"Mother you pull any tighter, you'll suffocate me!" Trevor objected.

Michael cleared his throat, rapping his knuckles on the doorframe. They both froze, staring at Michael, Oskar, and me in the doorway.

"Maggie," Michael whispered reassuringly as he leaned on the door.

Margaret was tending to a newly wrapped bandage around Trevor's ribcage that was knotted into place. The wounds were still seeping here and there, but they weren't as bad as I would've expected given the attack. He had a few scrapes on his face as if he tackled a rose bush.

"Trevor...you mind?" Michael asked, motioning towards the living room.

Trevor blushed in embarrassment as he quickly pulled his shirt fully down.

"Michael," Margaret protested and Michael gave her a swift smile as Trevor nearly ran past us. "He *needs* rest."

"Maggie," Michael whispered. "We've been over this."

Margaret's eyes rested on us, and she swallowed hard.

"Hello Margaret," I greeted, Oskar waving from

behind me with a polite smile.

Margaret's honey blonde hair was in a state of disarray from all the work she must've done during the day with the other children. Her eyes were a stunning shade of blue as they darted towards us. Michael was always a sucker for her in his younger years. It wasn't a surprise when we found out she was head over heels for Michael too. Their love got stronger as they got older. It was no surprise they had at least three children and one on the way from the looks of it. Michael didn't tell us...no wonder he was so stressed.

"Connor...Oskar," Margaret greeted us lightly. As she stood, she stumbled, immediately resting her hand on her stomach and giving a weary smile. "Oh my goodness I'm a mess," she groaned as she worked her fingers into her hair. She spoke quickly and fussed anxiously, "If you told me we would've had company-"

Michael walked up to her, glancing towards us as he smiled, kissing her temple. "Maggie. I told you to *rest*," he reminded his wife soothingly. "I've got Trevor. Where are the others?"

"Still in school," Margaret whispered.

Michael nodded.

"Go lay down," Michael suggested, kissing her on the forehead.

"Will you be staying?" Margaret asked.

I shook my head as Michael guided her to their room on the lower floor. "Go...to...bed," he whispered, pushing her gently.

Margaret smiled slightly, and kissed Michael on the lips for a split moment before darting into their room, closing the door behind her.

Michael gave a bit of a smile until he turned to us. His face immediately changed to serious as he motioned to their living room.

Trevor sat on the sofa twiddling his thumbs as he watched his father walk into the room. I followed as Oskar sat in a spare chair, my back against the wall and Michael standing in front of him. "Am I in trouble?" Trevor asked, glancing towards us.

Michael tilted his head and scoffed in amusement. "No of course not," he replied as he squatted down, his eyes level with his son's.

"We came to check in on you," I reassured the boy. "And to see if you're willing to tell us what happened the other day?"

Trevor glanced at me and swallowed looking at the floor, his eyes wide.

I furrowed my brows in confusion when his leg started twitching.

Michael seemed to notice as well.

"I don't-I don't know," Trevor stammered.

"It's okay," Michael reassured his son.

Trevor swallowed, and Michael tensed at the fear in his son's eyes.

"You'll...you'll all think I'm insane," Trevor whispered.

"No boy," Oskar objected lightly. "Believe me...we've seen our fair share of demons here."

Trevor scoffed in disbelief as Michael leaned in grabbing the boy's shoulder and squeezing. "Trevor...please," he whispered.

Trevor hesitated for a moments, his mouth opening and closing several times before he finally spoke. "He saw it first," Trevor swallowed, his eyes still on the floor.

"Who?" I asked.

"Brutus," Trevor replied, his eyes turning to tears. "I should've listened to him when I didn't see anything."

I swallowed. The dog. The dog that protected the boy by being mauled in his stead. The boy was shaking but sat up.

"Trevor...what did you see?" I asked gently.

Trevor looked at me and scoffed with a bitter smile. "You'll think I'm crazy," he insisted.

Michael squeezed, but I looked at the boy gravely as I stepped to be next to his father. I hovered over him. "Believe me, Trevor Hughes," I replied firmly. "I've seen far more crazier things in my lifetime."

Trevor stared at me for a long time. He swallowed before finally opening his mouth. "It was a demon. A monster," he stated confidently. "I thought it was a person...but it was far worse. Teeth, claws, gray skin. It lashed at me before I even knew what was happening. It was so fast. Before I knew it Brutus was attacking it and it screeched or something like that...It was a *horrible* sound."

"Is that all?" Oskar asked, although his voice sounded shaken behind me.

"Its eyes were black. Like it was soulless," Trevor finished. "If you and Fields didn't find me...I don't think I'd be here."

Trevor looked at me, tears in his eyes that finally fell.

"Trevor," Michael whispered.

The boy stood suddenly, forcing Michael to stand with him. Trevor looked at me, nodding in thanks as he took a step around me. "Tell him thanks," he said as he left the room, going to his own upstairs.

Michael sighed, shaking his head.

"I uh...it all sounds like the monsters in his nightmares," Michael commented. "I'm starting to wonder if the shock is blurring his sense of reality."

"I don't think so Hughes," Oskar piped cautiously. Michael furrowed his brows looking between us. "Whatever he saw, he fully believes it to be real."

A long silence stretched as Oskar stood next to Michael and I.

"So what does that mean?" Michael asked.

Even for such a stern solid man of stone, his fear was slowly starting to show.

"It means we need to be careful," I replied.

"Patrols?" Michael recommended.

"Bigger," I replied. "We need to be armed and ready."

"Jesus, Sullivan. You act like-"

"Michael...I *know* whatever he's talking about is real," I insisted.

Michael stopped and shook his head. "How?"

"Because my family was the very victim of this..." I reminded Michael quietly.

And I wasn't going to let it happen again.

❋❋❋

Trevor's testimony repeated through my mind on the way home.

As much as I didn't want to believe the boy's nightmarish story, a part of me felt the familiarity of the chaos he experienced.

I sat there in my study mulling over the whole series of events from Avery, to Miss Shaw to Trevor's testimony. They were all separate, but each had harrowing similarities. Something ominous was going on. Question was...how do we stop it?

I looked over, noticing Bryan asleep on the spare couch parallel from me.

Thinking about Avery's behavior seemed to make things worse. I told Evelyn everything. I didn't have the heart to tell Bryan that his father was a raving lunatic yet. But even in the insanity of it, and I knew in his anger...Avery was speaking the truth.

Why would it be so far-fetched to even think what he was saying wasn't true? And, if he was after Evelyn...I wouldn't allow it. After all the deaths, the destruction, everything he would be no where *near* her.

I felt my hands drift to the whiskey under the desk. Damn it. Just one. One to make me forget this horrendous day, then I'll quit.

I wrapped my fingers around the bottle, moving it carefully as I lifted it. I placed it on the top of the desk. As I went to look for a glass, though a hand grabbed the bottle and snatched it away from me.

I nearly jumped, seeing Evelyn holding the bottle of whiskey. She lingered near the doorframe of the study.

I hesitated to look at Bryan to make sure he wasn't disturbed. He wasn't. That boy could sleep through anything.

I raised my brows at Evelyn, and put my hand out to grab the bottle but she pulled it further away from me. "Evee," I sighed in frustration.

Evelyn rolled her eyes, moving out of the study and I instinctively got up to follow her. "You said you'd stop!" she called out as she rushed to the kitchen further from the study while I caught up with her.

"If you saw what I happened today, you wouldn't *blame* me," I whispered harshly. "Just one!"

I grabbed Evelyn's free wrist and pulled her to me. She yelped, keeping the whiskey bottle away from me as her body fully collided into me. "You promised," she insisted and then we both stopped.

My hand was still on her free wrist, her body in front of me and close. She stared up at me and blushed hard as if she realized the same mistake I made. "I'm..." I whispered.

"Sorry!" Evelyn whispered, her eyes staying on me. She backed away slightly putting the bottle on the counter and pointed at it. "All yours."

Evelyn turned to leave but I immediately grabbed her arm. She stopped and I felt my heart racing. I pulled her back gently. "No you're right," I agreed. And I felt her come closer to me. "I promised."

"I'm sorry," Evelyn whispered again.

"Stop apologizing," I grumbled. "You don't need to-"

"I meant for this..."

Evelyn wrapped her hands around my neck and pulled me down to her level. Her lips were on mine. The shock of her touch and sudden warmth of her skin made my head spin.

Then it stopped as fast as it came.

Evelyn leaned back so close to me now. I felt my hands wrap around her waist as if I was afraid she'd just disappear. She stared at me as if to read every thought that sped through my mind.

"You know what I am promising you now?" I said, daring to break the silence.

"What?" Evelyn asked.

I reached out my hand cupping her face gently. She shuddered, closed her eyes, and blushed.

"I am never leaving you again," I whispered.

"Connor-"

"*Ever*. You hear me? You and Bryan. You're staying here with me."

She smiled, her eyes almost tearing, as I leaned my forehead against hers. She took a sigh of relief as she pushed me back slightly. "Connor there's something-"

SLAM!

Bryan yelled and cursed in the other room followed by a massive crash in the study. My heart stopped as we looked at each other and then at the study. "Bryan," we said in unison as we rushed to the study door.

The window was shattered. A brick lay on the floor.

Bryan was standing up and looking out the window in shock trying to avoid the glass.

"Bryan are you all right?" Evelyn shrieked.

"Someone was standing by the window!" Bryan yelled.

A horse whinnied followed by rushing hooves that sped away from the house. I rushed to the window to see a cloaked stranger galloping away from the estate.

I turned, rushing to my desk as I pulled out a revolver hidden in one of the drawers.

"Where are you going?!" Evelyn demanded.

I tossed her another revolver from a separate place in the desk.

"Wait here!" I growled. "Protect yourself and Bryan until I get back."

Evelyn looked at the weapon in shock as I grabbed my jacket and ran out the door.

I heard Evelyn's voice crying out my name from the estate. I ran outside sprinting out into the cold, holstering my revolver as I scoured the darkness.

I saw them.

The cloaked figure riding into the woods, and it hit me. The sudden flashes of my mother being dragged. It was coming back. I had no time and rushed to make sure I could keep up. I felt my feet flying in front of me until I got near the tree-line.

My legs rushed, and I forced myself forward. I could barely see the figure. Then, they disappeared into the darkness, and I was left breathless in front of the clearing.

The company of the cursed, ancient, twisted tree loomed over me. I took out the revolver, feeling as if every crunch of snow or branches was much louder than it should be.

It took me a moment to realize I was alone.

I cursed and caught my breath. Again. They got away *again*.

"Dammit," I growled. "DAMMIT!"

I kicked the ground so hard that I that some snow flew in the air. But as I saw it...it was dark. What? I furrowed my brows as the deep snow turned a blackened color. I had almost missed it in the rush of adrenaline.

I finally noticed the smell...the putrid smell. I looked down. A blackened ooze formed a trail further towards the ancient tree's roots. I hesitated as I followed the trail, revolver in hand.

The blackish trail led towards the back of the twisting tree. The smell grew steadily worse, forcing me to pull my shirt over my mouth. There it stopped, and I froze in utter disgust.

Pigs. A pile of fat pigs rested at the base of the tree. Their black eyes lifeless and their bodies torn apart, missing limbs or mauled as if from a carnivore that stumbled on a feast.

What did I just walk into?

The flashes of the camera kept blinding me as the investigators photographed the scene at every angle.

The morning light seemed to make the gruesome scene even worse than when I found it and the stench was horrid. The flashing of the photographer was all I could hear and the other patrolmen who joined us on the cleanup.

Michael and I were in the midst of it all. We stood in front of the pile, our noses covered with our scarves. We originally used them for the cold, now they masked the stench. The scarf, however, couldn't protect us from the scene. It wasn't the first time animals or livestock got attacked in our lifetime, but this was an absolute massacre.

"Well...looks like we know what happened to the livestock," Michael quipped.

The thought of Miss Shaw at the sheriff's office flashed. "What do we tell Shaw?" I dared to ask as I knelt in front of the maimed bodies.

A poor hog stared back at me with its unblinking

black eyes, a face of terror. A massive hole was ripped into its belly. I sort of hoped that the thing was long dead before the butchering, but something in me screamed otherwise.

"Michael," I called, motioning him over.

Michael, giving me a rather reluctant look, came closer. He hated this sort of thing and I'm sure the smell didn't help. He made a face as he made his way towards the hog. He was covering his mouth even further within his scarf as he cursed.

I stood when Oskar appeared, nodding his head to a patrolman as he slowly approached the scene. "Good God," he whispered as he approached us. "What happened?"

Oskar knelt down in a spot near where I had just been examining the nearest hog. His face a mix of intrigue and disgust.

"We found Shaw's pigs," I replied. "Followed some ghost of a person out here last night."

"Which I *still* can't figure out," Michael growled, turning his back as Oskar pulled on some gloves to examine the nearest hog.

Michael hated this stuff, and he flinched when Oskar reached out, touching the neck and cut up parts of the hog.

"Anything?" I asked.

Oskar furrowed his brows, grabbing a nearby stick. He lifted the pig slightly to show a mangled part of its underbelly.

"Ruthless," Oskar growled, whipping off his leather gloves. "Michael..."

"What? I'm not really up for a biology lesson," Michael groaned. "You two were the experts with your fascinations with-"

Oskar looked up at me in horror. "It's gone," he stuttered as he swallowed.

Michael turned his head as I knelt down next to Oskar.

"What's *gone*?" Michael spat uncomfortably rolling his eyes as he finally faced us.

"Everything," Oskar breathed.

I watched as I saw the large tear in the underbelly of this poor creature. Nothing. There was absolutely *nothing* left. A husk of a terrified animal.

Michael was frozen for a moment, his skin paling even further.

"Perhaps the butcher forgot to tell us of his new dump site," Michael tried to reason but Oskar and I looked at him sympathetically.

"No...something worse," Oskar objected.

Then I looked down.

There were tears everywhere on the pig's body, similar to those on Elizabeth's neck. I looked around. Those marks were on every pig within reach. Some on the throat, others in the stomach. Whatever it was, it had a feast I couldn't fathom. I pointed it out to Oskar and he swallowed.

"Ruthless. Whatever this thing is, is an absolute *devil*," Oskar grumbled.

"I don't care *who* or *what* this is," Michael growled. "This is getting ridiculous."

Everything was a mess. Mauled, torn, and just overall brutally taken down. Then I saw it. There was barely *any* blood considering the *number* of carcasses here. I nudged Oskar and motioned towards the ground.

"Lowe," I whispered, and he stopped. "Something

missing? Something *familiar?*"

It took only a moment before I saw his eyes widen.

"The blood...there should be a *lot* more of it," Oskar whispered.

"What?" Michael asked as he walked over, standing beside us.

There was a small blood trail but it was too small for several pigs. It added to the mystery of nothing left behind.

Michael shook his head cursing as he walked up to a photographer whispering something. The photographer nodded quickly. I reached into my pocket, my fingers feeling the coin that I kept on me. I was twirling it instinctively as I watched. I could see Michael's body tense as he made a quiet order.

"You said there was a person last night?" Oskar whispered to me as we watched Michael do his work.

"Cloaked, ran off on a horse like a damn ghost," I informed him. "Something *familiar*."

"We *need* more protection," Oskar whispered.

"Trying everything we can," I replied evenly.

My fingers kept spinning the coin. Oskar's hand gripped onto my shoulder. I froze for a moment, avoiding his gaze.

"I know you have *history* Connor," Oskar reminded, his voice stern. "*However*, at this moment with this *thing* roaming about...we can't afford you to wander off."

I looked at him and furrowed my brows. "I'm fine," I whispered.

Oskar looked at me rather unconvinced. We looked up to see Michael nodding and slowly returning to us as he lit a cigarette on the way.

"Do not allow your family's death to be in vain

Sullivan," Oskar warned quietly. "If you're gone...this town is gone with it."

"I'm fine, Oskar...really," I tried to reassure him.

Oskar looked at me rather worriedly before patting my shoulder in acceptance.

I felt myself tense at the gesture as Michael returned to the group, inhaling and blowing out smoke.

"Everything all right?" I asked, breaking the silence.

Michael shook his head. "We're gonna have to burn these," he replied. "Quickly."

"Why?" Oskar asked.

"God forbid someone dares to come out this way," Michael explained. "They have plenty of evidence for the station to go through. At most they'll keep one."

"What?" I asked, confused.

Michael grabbed my arm pulling me aside, away from the patrolmen who were gathering the pigs away from the tree, grabbing anything they could use as firewood.

"Oskar," Michael called and Oskar straightened. "You think you're up for a challenge?"

"Anything," Oskar replied.

Michael motioned to the pile. "Pick one to bring back to the morgue," he said.

Oskar swallowed, looking back to the remaining carcasses. He pointed at one. "That'll do," he answered quickly.

Michael whistled to the ones with the matches. "Hey! Put that one in the car. Wrap it up in something so it doesn't stink!" Michael ordered.

The patrolmen nodded and grabbed the hog on either end with some difficulty despite not much left of it...it was still heavy.

"Connor and I got it from here," Michael added.

Oskar looked between us. "But-"

"I need to chat with Sullivan alone," Michael stated firmly.

My skin crawled from the sudden shift of energy.

Oskar nodded. "Gentleman," Oskar announced as he left the scene.

Michael was still gripping my shoulder as I watched the rest of the team prepare the burn.

"You don't think this is overdoing it?" I asked.

Michael leaned in out of earshot and I could hear his voice rough and firm. "We can't let the town panic," he whispered.

"We can't *hide* something like this either," I growled back. "Someone will find out."

"I know that!" he whispered harshly. "*However*, if it happens to be something feral, then I rather not let the animal come back to the smell of its kill."

The kill.

Michael reached into his pocket, grabbing another cigarette and struggling with the lighter.

He was right.

Whatever this thing was, it was vicious. Coming back to a kill would cause even *more* danger to the town. God forbid it attacked someone who was just wandering nearby. Besides, this scene alone would cause an uproar.

"What if we really are experiencing a curse..." I suggested as I watched his team gather up the bodies and find dry dead branches in the snow.

Michael rolled his eyes, cursing as the lighter wouldn't ignite.

I grabbed it from him, switched it around, and

struck it with one flick.

Michael sighed as he took the lighter from me, nodding in thanks, and shaking his head as he took a long inhale from his cigarette.

"Blackwood Hollow was *always* cursed," Michael stated, looking at his feet. "According to our parents anyway. Miss Shaw would know more than any one of us. She's one of the few people who lived through this hell. We're just dumb enough to face it head on."

"Should we evacuate?"

"And make people panic out in the streets for a person or *thing* to come and get them?" Michael demanded looking directly at me.

The world around us seemed silent as the patrolmen started burning around the pile. The smell was worse from the fire.

Michael stared at the carcasses of the animals. "I know you well enough that you'll agree with me," Michael scoffed. "I'm tired of people dying. I'm tired of families living in fear and hiding in church. My own children-"

Michael froze, taking an inhale of his cigarette. Maggie.

"She's pregnant isn't she?" I asked.

Michael stiffened. "Yeah..." he confirmed, nodding slowly.

"That's why...you've been so off lately," I scoffed.

Michael shook his head. "After Trevor..." he began, glancing at me. "I wasn't sure I deserved to have another."

I swallowed.

Michael was the best father I've known. The fact that he damned himself for an accident that wasn't even his fault.

"Michael," I whispered, feeling my chest tighten.

"All of them...Trevor, Catherine, Molly...Maggie," Michael raddled off their names as if they were vows and prayers to God. "I will *not* let this happen again. Or, so help me, I'll rip it's throat out myself."

I nodded in agreement. It had to be stopped.

Michael looked at me and I felt *my* body stiffen this time. I glanced at him. "What?"

"Is the boy with you?" he asked.

I nodded.

Michael raised his brows. "Evelyn too?" he guessed.

I nodded again.

Michael put his hand on my shoulder, and startled me when he gripped onto it.

I looked over at him and recognized that protective look on his face. "Do. Not. Separate," he said sternly. "I'm going to regroup with my jailer, make sure someone didn't move from their post."

"You think Avery could've gotten out?" I asked.

"He's a lot sicker than I thought if this is *his* doing," Michael replied. "In the meantime, I have some business with our poor Miss Shaw."

Michael turned and tossed his cigarette into the burning hog pile. "I'll meet you at your place," he continued. "I need to make sure I have bodies out on the streets at night. The curse of Blackwood Hollow ends with us. I pray my children will be the last to hear about the horrors of this place."

Michael turned, leaving me alone with the stench of burning, half-rotted pigs. My mind whirled at every possibly, but Michael was right...this ends with us.

Fourteen

I boarded up the windows as soon as I made it home.

I had found a few spare planks in the cellar, and covered the mess of broken glass and open air. The winter chill hit us hard as Bryan helped me hold each one in place while he and his mother questioned me up and down. They wanted answers, but my mind was racing with possibilities.

"You think the person was trying to hurt us?" Evelyn asked.

"I don't know," I replied as I started hammering another board in front of the bay window seating area of the study. "For all I know, it could've been just a warning."

"Warn us? With a bunch of pigs?" Bryan spat in disbelief. "Not much of a warning."

"You didn't see them," I continued. "They were shredded like they were attacked and possibly *eaten* by something. Michael wants to dig deeper. Lowe has one at the morgue for further examination."

Evelyn made a face. The same face she used to give when she'd find anything dead in the woods.

"I read that bears and even big cats can show up in the woods. Wolves even," Bryan mentioned, as he handed over the next board.

I rolled my eyes, frustration flaring. "The pines are different here. They aren't like the rest of the states. You know as well as I do that *nothing* dares to linger let alone *live* in those woods," I pointed out. Then I paused thinking of Trevor. "I'm surprised your friend was able to get the dog within a stone's throw of that place."

"It just feels like superstitious nonsense," Bryan growled.

"Bryan," Evelyn gasped.

Bryan rolled his eyes. "You and Sullivan *both* got too caught up in scary stories from when you were children," he accused. "Did you ever think your parents just planted them in your heads so you didn't run off?"

I paused. Our parents weren't moronic. They were scared just as much as we were. But then again...even I had doubts. Something about Bryan's insistence in his tone made it feel insulting though. I stopped and glared at him. He didn't seem to care.

"We should be *hunting* and getting this person this *thing* down," Bryan continued. "You expect the devil himself to just pop out of the woods."

"To us it very may well be," I warned the boy.

"This!" Bryan insisted as he grabbed the bottle on my desk, waving the whiskey in front of me. He tossed it into a nearby wastebin. "*This* is your devil, and it's making you paranoid."

"Bryan don't-" Evelyn tried to intervene.

The anger and frustration hit me like a ton of bricks. I pushed off the board and slammed the hammer to the floor. Bryan's frustration turned into fear as his mother gasped. I walked up to him slowly, my eyes boring into his. I watched the boy's face turn pale in front of me as I stood tall in front of him.

"Don't lecture me on *superstition*," I growled.

Bryan swallowed as I stared him down, daring him.

"By the time I was *your* age I had nothing left of a family due to this *superstitious* place," I continued. "And until *you* grow up I won't give you the reasoning. I have nightmares you couldn't comprehend. So don't tell me that it's all for show. Because the *victims* of it would say otherwise. And you *know* better, boy."

Bryan backed away, his eyes wide.

I took a deep breath to calm myself down and shook my head.

Before I could apologize, the boy stormed out of the room and up the stairs, slamming the door of his room.

Evelyn leaned against the doorframe staring at me.

"What? Here to scold me?" I asked.

Evelyn shook her head and walked up to me slowly. I suddenly felt her arms wrap around my waist, squeezing tightly. I hesitated for a moment before my arms wrapped around her shoulders and held her there. "He's never heard your story," she reminded me quietly. "It was never my place to tell him."

I leaned into her. I stared at the pictures that were facing the walls. They had always haunted my past. Now it seemed they were determined to take over my future here.

I shook my head as I made my way upstairs. The silence followed me with such suffocating energy. As I approached Bryan's bedroom door I hesitated. Finally, I worked up the nerve and knocked.

The knock on the door felt like a booming echo throughout the house.

I stood restlessly in the hallway.

Bryan had locked himself in the spare bedroom upstairs. Evelyn was right...it wasn't her responsibility to tell him my story. I'm not even sure after all these years she *would* remember the details. At least, not the way I did. The tragedy of everything still felt fresh in my mind some days.

And to her...perhaps a lingering reminder of how bad it used to be. How bad it *still* is.

"Bryan?" I called softly.

Nothing. I shifted awkwardly feeling the silence engulfing me. The mere moments felt as if I were waiting for an eternity. As much as my mind raced to find a potential way out, my feet remained rooted to the floor.

I had to be brave for the boy or maybe for myself at the very least.

"Look...can we talk?" I asked.

"You come to scold me more?" Bryan's annoyed but muffled voice demanded from behind the door.

I sighed as my body slowly moved to lean against the doorframe.

"I just," I sighed but then I just hesitated.

Words. Words would be good but I kept drawing blanks.

I shook my head in frustration at the vast emptiness. But there was some familiarity to it, perhaps a nagging understanding of feeling same at his age.

Just keep it simple.

"I'll," I began, swallowing the lump in my throat. "I'll be around I just...wanted to apologize."

I lifted myself from the doorframe and started down the hall when I heard the door click. I turned, seeing the door fully open slowly. A glimpse of Bryan's silhouette made its way back to the room.

I sighed. *All right then, into the trenches we go.*

I made my way back carefully until I hit the doorframe. I stopped, not wanting to accidentally cross any boundaries when I *finally* got him to open the door. He trusted me in the moment, but I had to treat this like every moment was a chance to screw it up or gain more from him.

I watched him as he walked back into the room, sitting on the bed. I cautiously placed myself again at the doorframe, giving the boy distance as he looked away from me.

"Do you *actually* mean it?" Bryan asked. "Or is it because mother told you to?"

I furrowed my brows in confusion. Evelyn? "What?" I asked.

Bryan rolled his eyes, standing up and pacing the room. The tension rose but I avoided fidgeting by crossing my arms. "I'm not an idiot. I've seen how you two have been acting lately," Bryan accused. "For all I know you could be apologizing just to *appease her*."

I rolled my eyes. Dammit. "It's not like that," I objected. I didn't sound very convincing even to myself.

Bryan stood his ground facing me, challenging me. "Really?"

"*Yes*," I responded.

Again...maybe I wasn't as convincing as I thought. I felt my voice stern, quick and almost regretted it. I was more offended or thrown off than anything. I sighed feeling the uncomfortable twinge of *how* to talk to him.

Bryan was more than capable of pushing back when he wanted to get a rise or a reaction. Or if he's trying to get an answer he's looking for, but this time it was different. He was no longer the small boy that busied himself in my study or in the library or outside in the yard. He was now approaching manhood and I had to treat him as such...even if the topic was grating on me.

Bryan's tension slowly dissolved. After a moment of silence, I shifted uncomfortably and his glaring gaze started to shift as he watched me. His eyes seemed to soften as I observed him, and he nodded in acceptance. I assumed he accepted the apology as he watched me.

I felt a sudden sense of relief. The judgement left his eyes, and curiosity filled them instead.

I cleared my throat. "Great...now that that's settled," I began quietly. "Perhaps we can clear the air."

I walked further into the room as Bryan straightened up. After a few moments of silence I made an offer.

"What do you want to know?" I asked carefully.

Bryan kept his eyes firmly on me, despite that look of processing every thought he might've had. "Everything," he whispered.

I felt my back stiffen, my mouth going dry. Of course he'd answer that way. His curiosity always got the best of him.

"Everything?" I repeated as if to reassure myself than him.

Why was it so damn difficult? It was just Bryan! The boy who watched every bit of my life in the last decade. God help me. The flashes of my past were starting to be overwhelming.

But...Bryan stood his ground and I swallowed feeling the pit of my stomach churning at the idea. I sighed, shaking my head. My eyes darted to the floor calming the scenes in my mind. Where to begin?

"You have a reason to believe in all this," Bryan pushed gently. "You're always looking for people."

"Of course I look for people," I answered him.

"Why?"

"No one else will," I stated simply. "And they become

part of these missing, forgotten souls that died in vain."

I glanced at a photograph on the wall that was turned around. They would want me to tell him. I needed to accept that.

"My parents...they believed in all these *superstitions*," I mentioned, walking towards a spare floral upholstered chair that sat across from the bed. I sat down. "My father was especially keen to getting to the bottom of it."

"What happened to your parents?" Bryan asked, slow and careful.

I shook my head. "Depends on who you ask," I replied.

Bryan sat on the bed across from me, leaning forward, arms on his knees. "What does that mean?" he asked.

"It means that...there is something here that has plagued this town for a *very* long time," I explained.

"Like?"

I sighed.

"I'm not a child anymore Connor," Bryan reminded, his voice quiet. "Please."

Connor...why the hell was he still calling me by my name? I tried to bat it away from my mind. I needed to focus on *how* to answer.

"I was...*younger* than you," I began slowly. "My father was found in those very woods."

I pointed out the window of his room where it revealed the ominous tree line.

Bryan's eyes then darted to the window as if he were looking for a ghost. "How?"

"My father was Sherriff long before Michael took the

job. He and his men were part of a rather large search party. They were looking for a missing girl, her mother had gotten worried when she didn't come home," I continued. "My mother even offered to help. But he wouldn't have it. He told her to stay here and protect me, and told me to protect her."

"Did they find her?"

"Yes," I nodded and smiled slightly.

"Is she still alive?" Bryan asked quickly. I nodded.

"It was *your* mother," I smiled softly in amusement.

Bryan froze.

My smile faded instantly remembering her reasoning for disappearing. "She was...trying to get away from your grandfather," I mentioned.

Bryan shifted uncomfortably. "I don't blame her," he groaned. "I barely saw the man and when I did he was...*pathetic*."

I nodded.

Bryan furrowed his brows, staring at the ground. "Wait, if you saved mother...then what happened to your father?" he asked. "What happened to Mr. Sullivan?"

I paused, gathering my thoughts as if I was still trying to figure it out. "One of the best officers in the world was...slashed and attacked by some...*thing*," I breathed. "Your mother said she heard something that night and my father saved her life."

Bryan sat there speechless.

"My mother well...it was that summer she was taken from me too," I added keeping my voice steady. "I lived with my aunt and uncle until they chose to leave when I was eighteen. And been living here alone ever since."

"What do you mean, taken?" Bryan asked.

I swallowed hard, my stomach heavy. "I saw

someone...drag her into those woods," I replied. "As if it was all a bad dream."

The silence of the room built until Bryan walked up putting a hand on my shoulder taking me out of my daze.

"She was found hanging on that ancient tree in the middle of the woods," I continued. "People claimed it was suicide. Though...I knew it was someone who made it look that way."

Bryan's hand moved as I leaned my arms against my knees, my hands folded in front of me and to my face.

"No one believed me," my voice a whisper. "I was fifteen."

I wasn't looking at him now, my mind racing with images and things I've kept suppressed for so long.

Bryan swallowed, nodding. I couldn't tell what he thought, but any former irritation was long gone.

"Why didn't mother ever tell me?" he asked.

I shook my head. "Unless you saw what we saw...what Trevor saw..." I began.

Bryan swallowed, sitting back down on the bed.

"There have been so many people," I continued. "Men, women, children who have *all* seen horrors here, including your mother. I was lucky enough to have friends that made me not feel like-"

"Lost?"

"A freak," I scoffed. "I became obsessed with finding out what was plaguing this place. And luckily, Sherriff Hughes and Mr. Lowe were...some of the best people."

"The drinking?"

I shook my head. "That...is *complicated*," I sighed, running a hand through my hair. "But...a sin I'm *trying* to remedy."

"Good...you were starting to smell," Bryan teased flatly.

I felt myself smile. We laughed for a moment before it became silent again.

Then Bryan just...stared at me and frowned.

"I'm...I'm sorry," Bryan commented.

I nodded. "I'd apologize to your mother more than me," I replied, smirking. "She's worried about you too."

Bryan then rolled his eyes. "I know," he grumbled. "I wish she wouldn't."

"She's your mother. It's impossible," I teased him, resting my face on the palm of my hand. "She's...always one to care and worry."

Bryan then looked at me. "Did you...and mom?" he asked.

I furrowed my brows.

Bryan raised his brows. He wasn't asking...he was.

I rolled my eyes getting up from my chair.

"That was a *long* time ago," I replied, reaching out my hand.

Bryan took it, standing up from the bed, gripping onto it for a minute. "How long?" he asked.

"Before your father and mother married," I commented. "But *that* is for another time."

"But-"

I tsked at him putting a hand up. "*Apologize* to your mother," I insisted lightly as I ushered him out and he rolled his eyes again.

"Fine," Bryan groaned. "But you owe me."

"Sure. Whatever you say."

***

"You can't seem to catch a break can you?" Bill asked sympathetically.

Bill sat there as I paced the living room of the clergy house that evening. The place was lit with a few candles as the sun started setting. The bitter cold couldn't fully stay out of this place.

Bill interrupted our security measures to catch up. It was hard to leave the others alone, but Evelyn had insisted as she assured me she'd have dinner ready when I returned. So, I sat in this frigid place as Bill started the fire.

"Michael's not exactly happy. It's bad enough we have to keep this from the public," I growled in frustration. I felt my arms wrap around my coat as if it would magically keep me warmer. But my mind was racing. "God knows what we will tell Shaw."

"First Elizabeth, then his boy...now this," Bill whispered moving his hand up to his face and rubbing it. "Pigs no less. I'd have to assume it *isn't* a new tactic with the butcher?"

"Michael's patrolmen are looking into it while Oscar does an autopsy maybe something can be found," I mentioned. "But you know as well as I do they're both meticulous with their work. This whole thing looks sloppy."

"What about Avery?"

"Do you have to ask?"

"Yes, as a matter of fact for the safety of," Bill began and paused when he looked at me for a moment. Evelyn. He must've been thinking the same thing I was. He cleared his throat and shook his head. "If he *is* somehow involved-"

"That man was already far gone and has been behind bars since causing a scene at the church," I commented as I immediately saw concern etch into Bill's face. "And forgive me if I no longer have sympathy for the man."

Bill raised an eyebrow.

I walked up, and leaned my palms the table to stare at him.

Bill leaned back a bit to give some distance, but his eyes remained on me.

"I should've asked," I whispered. "But did she come to you about him?"

Bill swallowed staying silent for a moment.

I could tell that the tension in the air was building.

"About?"

"*Anything*," I whispered. "His neglect, his cheating, his marriage being arranged on his own parents' dime? Maybe even *how* they got married in the first place? How he avoided Bryan from the start as soon as he was old enough to start walking?"

Bill swallowed and sighed. "You know as well as I do that I am a man of the church," Bill reminded me. "I can't just...*confess* someone else's grievances to you."

"Then why did you come to me now? Why did you wait for years to come to me?"

"What would you have done Connor?" Bill asked. "She had every right to leave him. As soon as she caught wind of the first woman he roamed with...she could've left, but she didn't."

"And you supported this?"

"Don't give me that," Bill objected.

I felt like my tone was getting harsher. Years of build up and were just eating away at me.

"I *begged* her to consider leaving," Bill continued. "But she had nowhere to go according to her. She was terrified of her father, and Avery's family was no better."

"You could've told me!"

Bills fist slammed the table and I felt a jolt through my body as if it was directed at my body. He glared at me angrily before taking a breath and then eyed me with sympathy. "What would you have done Connor? Whisked her away? Argued with her grumpy fool of a father and the Atwood family?" he pressed. "Whether you like it or not by then you were too far gone, and she didn't have the heart to tell you."

"Why wouldn't she?"

"That's something that you have to ask her," Bill sighed.

I paused, shaking my head as I sat down in the chair next to him. Bill reached over, and put a hand on my shoulder. "For us to make a future we cannot dwell on what was," he mentioned. "We have to cherish what is and how we now carve our future."

I sighed, allowing my anger to subside. It wasn't Bill's responsibility to answer for Evelyn's decisions regarding Avery. As much as *everyone* wanted him to be gone.

"She...looked happy when I saw her with you," Bill mentioned, giving a small smile. He nudged me. "It's like you two were yourselves again."

I swallowed. Was it really that obvious when we were together? I've been so distracted with what's been that I didn't think. "Is that why you came?" I asked. "To check in?"

Bill's face paled and he cleared his throat. "Mary...she was in a panic the other day," he shook his head.

I furrowed my brows in confusion. It's unlike Mrs. Donovan to be spooked. I leaned forward on the table, folding my hands. "What happened?"

Bill looked at me gravely. "You're going to think I'm crazy," he whispered.

"Trust me Bill, you are *far* from that," I assured him. "And after what I've seen the last few days...you can't surprise me."

Bill sighed. "The night you found the pigs," he continued. "Mary saw Ted Baker."

I felt the hair on my arms stand on end. The last time I saw him he was sweating and acting off. That felt like an eternity. "The man is grieving," I reminded Bill.

Bill shook his head and rubbed his hand along his face finding the words to describe it. "No...this was different," he whispered, keeping his voice steady but his eyes turned grave. He looked terrified. "He came to the house."

My eyes widened. Ted...Ted Baker who's been isolated since Elizabeth came to the house?

"It happened so fast," Bill continued. "She rushed home saying Ted was following her, but he wouldn't...*say* anything when she acknowledged him. He just stood there...stalking her."

My mind was racing. A six foot something man just looming over even at a distance could be terrifying. But this was Ted. The only thing he wanted to throttle was anyone who would hurt his wife.

"She rushed in," Bill continued, shaking his head. "He tried to break down the door and was making horrendous sounds. He was screaming nonsense. I finally grabbed the shotgun and threatened him." Bill looked at me dead in the eyes and I saw the fear as he continued. "He looked awful Connor...like he turned into something *inhuman*. Before I could do anything he ran off into the darkness, off towards those cursed woods. So...if I had to guess-"

The cloaked stranger flashed into my mind. The images of the person were blurred. I wouldn't be able to tell who it was in the dark. Was that Ted warning us? Or...is he the potential mastermind of the whole crime spree.

I got up.

"Then I need to pay Ted a visit," I said.

Bill grabbed my arm. I looked at him and he gave me a worried look. "Lock your doors Sullivan and don't go out alone," Bill warned. "Curse or no curse, this place...it's reeking of something dangerous, and I'm not sure even God could extinguish it so quickly."

I nodded and patted Bill's shoulder in thanks as I left the clergy house. I had to figure out a way to *not* lose another victim to this madness.

Fifteen

I felt my heart pounding as I ran, racing against the sun that began to set. I had to get to the Baker house before it got too dark.

The Baker's house rested on the other side of town. Not as far away as Avery's estate, but still a good walk from the church.

I was relieved when I finally spotted the place. It was so different than my parents' place. The two-story home was huge, displaying beautiful, colonial style architecture. The white siding was relatively clean while showing off many windows while pillars framed around the door. Everything looked to be in almost pristine condition despite the dreary season. A greenhouse peeked from behind the structure, clearly locked up until spring. The whole place was fit for a full family with its multiple patios and even a set of bay windows you could see from the outside.

Everything felt lived in and loved. My heart sank at the potential it had...and probably won't have again unless Ted were to remarry. That alone gave me a renewed sense of grief. Ted didn't deserve this. None of us did. I remember my father whispering to my mother about telling widows condolences after something tragic happened. It nearly broke him.

The sound of the wind filled the air as I walked up those stone steps, running my hands along the wrought iron rails. The iron chilled my hands and they were almost stinging as I steadied myself to keep from slipping on the ice. When I finally reached the door, I lifted the iron door knocker before standing silently.

Silence.

"Hello," I called, knocking again.

My voice felt louder than it should in the stillness.

Nothing.

I felt the hair on the back of my neck stand on end as I looked around the stone porch.

The glitter of broken glass caught my eye. One of the windows not far from the door was shattered. Broken glass hung in the frame, stained with...some sort of dark substance. I got a closer look, avoiding the shattered glass nearby. Blood.

I side stepped back to the door, breathing steadily to keep myself calm and alert. This time, the latch gave as if it were never locked and the door swung open lightly from the small bit of wind. I shivered as the door let out a sound like a pained moan. Still...nothing, no one rushing down to see who entered. No rustling of anything...no noise at all.

I peeked my head around not daring to enter yet.

"Hello?" I called out, feeling the deafening silence surround me.

I pushed the door further and finally saw the whole picture in the foyer. I felt my jaw drop.

The window was, indeed, broken, and the place looked like it had been ransacked. Pictures had fallen from the walls, dishes were shattered on the floor and even some bits of wallpaper were peeling as if ripped.

I dared to take a step and walked further in.

I reached under my wool coat to the holster on my belt. I grabbed my revolver and pulled it out slowly, keeping it at the ready.

I looked down at the floor, avoiding the destruction that littered the once warm wooden floors. I immediately saw the trail of blood from the window, leading up the stairs. I followed the trail up the stairs and heard a thump from one of the rooms.

Could it be Ted?

I quietly made my way up the stairs, revolver at the ready. As I approached, there was the movement of shadows I spotted in one of the rooms. I went to the door, turned, and pointed my revolver at a silhouette of someone's back.

I cocked the gun and the figure turned immediately. The person's hands went up. I tilted my head. "Michael?" I asked, my voice unable to hide the confusion.

Michael was also armed, his revolver in his hand. "Jesus Connor," he groaned, putting his revolver in the holster.

I looked around, before putting my revolver away.

"You could've knocked," Michael quipped, straightening his composure.

"I did," I said and rolled my eyes. "Where's Ted?"

"Gone, from the looks of it," Michael grumbled. "This place is a mess."

"What are you doing here?" I asked.

"I had a feeling and figured I'd check on things here."

"You could've warned me."

"The question is what are *you* doing here?" Michael asked.

I shook my head. "I got a lead that Ted wasn't acting himself last night," I replied.

"Really now?"

"He followed Mrs. Donovan home," I replied. "He was acting...strange and even threatened to attack them."

"And now he's gone, *again*," Michael growled as he grabbed a lighter and started to flick it in his fingers. I furrowed my brows at him. Something about the lighter looked different. I looked closer and noticed he wasn't wearing his wedding ring and there was an odd bracelet on his left wrist. He was holding something in his pocket that I couldn't see.

"You all right?" I asked.

Michael scoffed, giving me a smirk as he shook his head. "Yeah why?" he asked.

I motioned to his left hand. "What happened to your ring?" I asked.

Michael's eyes widened for a second as he patted his pockets. "Oh you know, I think I left it at the office," he sighed tiredly and rolled his eyes. "Didn't want to lose it."

I furrowed my brows but nodded.

Michael smirked. "Unfortunately for us, there's nothing here. Believe me I checked," he sighed. "Why don't you go home?"

"Aren't you worried about Ted?" I asked. "We haven't seen him in a few days."

Michael walked up to me, patting his hand on my shoulder as he led us back to the stairs. "We'll find him. Just give us some time," Michael encouraged. He put the lighter back in his pocket as we walked down the stairs, avoiding tripping on things. "In the meantime, I'll get my boys to search the house a little more thoroughly. Keep an eye out. Halfway wondering if maybe he *was* part of his wife's death."

I stopped as we reached the stone porch. "What are

you talking about?" I asked.

Michael turned as he hit the first step and rested his hand on the wrought iron railing. He sighed, giving me a weird look. "Come on Sul," he answered. "Clearly you heard the rumors with those two."

I looked at him and Michael raised an eyebrow. "No," I replied cautiously. "I don't believe I have."

"Well...I won't scar you with the details-"

"What are you talking about?"

Michael sighed. "Mr. Donovan, and Elizabeth were...having an *affair*," Michael stated, watching me. "And now the girl is dead."

I froze. Bill? No. Michael must've seen the look on my face because he became somber. "That's not-"

"I know you are fond of the man," Michael interrupted. "But we all have demons in our own little world."

I stood there in silence as he walked down the steps.

"We're getting closer Sul," Michael continued. "I can feel it. And we'll find Ted Baker soon enough."

Sixteen

"You can't be serious," Evelyn protested. "Elizabeth would *never*."

Evelyn, Bryan and I were sitting in the dining area having breakfast Evelyn attempted to make the next morning. She had stocked up on more food in the kitchen and surprised me when I came in late not having dinner.

"He did spend a lot of time with her," Bryan pitched in.

She did...Elizabeth was a volunteer at the church. But Ted was always there too, right? And Bill would never.

"*Stop it*," Evelyn growled, as Bryan shook his head. "She was *HALF* his age."

"Father found other people while we were with him," Bryan muttered. "Age doesn't seem to matter."

The forks dropped from Evelyn's grip as she moved her hands to her face distressed. I darted my eyes to Bryan.

"What?" Bryan asked, swallowing at my gaze.

"Why don't you...check on Trevor?" I suggested.

"But what about the pig thing?" Bryan objected lightly.

"What pig thing?" I asked.

"Trevor mentioned you brought a pig back to the morgue," Bryan pointed out. I rolled my eyes. They must've overheard Michael talking about it with his wife. "Weren't you going to go see?"

I raised my brows at him. "I *won't* bring you until you apologize to your mother," I objected lightly.

Bryan furrowed his brows in confusion. "For what?"

he asked.

"Mentioning your father's vices," I replied simply. "Now...I know you know better than to embarrass her."

There was silence. It seemed that Evelyn's cheeks turned red as she glanced at her son. Bryan's eyes widened as he realized what he'd said and he nodded, getting up from his chair. He grabbed his plate, tossed it in the sink and headed back to her. He glanced at me and pecked her on the cheek. "Sorry mom," he whispered.

Evelyn smiled sweetly as she waved Bryan off. He glanced at me as he went to the door.

"I'll pick you up at Mr. Hughes' place," I called out.

The door shut leaving Evelyn and I alone. Her eyes then went to mine. "You didn't have to do that," she stated quietly.

I shook my head.

Evelyn then looked at me in confusion. "I thought you all burned those pigs?" she remarked.

"We did," I replied. "But Oscar kept one for closer examination. Plus...I'm sure Michael needed evidence for Miss Shaw to confirm they were hers."

Evelyn kept her eyes on me shaking her head. "I need to talk to Bill," she insisted.

"No *I* will talk to him," I objected.

Evelyn glared. "Excuse me?" she demanded. "Elizabeth was my friend. I have every right to know if he was doing *something* behind our backs. And what if Mrs. Donovan-"

"Evee," I interrupted gently.

Evelyn stopped as tears started forming in her eyes. "It just...it can't be true can it?" she asked, her eyes searching mine.

I reached out, grabbing her hand and squeezing gently. "We don't know for sure," I answered. "But we can't risk you going in and talking to Bill. He's just as much of a suspect for Elizabeth's death as is Ted at this rate. If the affair *was* true, then Ted had a motive. They *both* do."

"But he," she hesitated, sniffling as tears fell from her face. "Ted was so *devastated*. He blamed-he even blamed Avery..."

"Then, maybe Bill is to blame, either way, we *will* get to the bottom of this."

Silence filled the room and I realized I was still holding her hand. I lifted it. "We know him better than anyone," Evelyn whispered. "Bill would *never* do such a thing. He loves Mary."

He did. The idea of him and Elizabeth having an affair hit me in the gut. She seemed happy, and an overall good woman. And Bill...well he's been a father figure to me for most of our lives. The connection didn't make sense. But...if Michael got an anonymous tip, it was still a lead nonetheless.

"That sort of thing unfortunately makes it easier for him to not be suspected," I warned. "As much as I would hate to think of him in such a light, I can't ignore a tip from Michael. He has no reason to lie about this."

I stood and grabbed my plate. Evelyn stood as well, reaching out and grabbing the plate from my hand. "I've got this," she announced as she and I held it between each other.

Evelyn stopped, staring at me as she kept her fingers on the plate.

I sighed. "I'll go talk to Bill."

Evelyn shook her head. "Please don't hurt the poor

man."

"What if he swings first?" I asked, raising a brow.

Evelyn took the plate from my hand and eyed me. "Then I'd leave it to Mary. God knows she'd set him straight," she replied, passing me as she went into the kitchen.

Knock. Knock. Knock.

The sun did very little to drive away the winter chill. Every day was getting colder, and my intentions for this visit were only making it more dreary.

Nothing.

I looked around the property, and saw someone coming out of the church. I furrowed my brows seeing Bill and some person walking out in front of him. He was almost chasing the man.

I descended the steps of the clergy house and focused on getting to Bill. He was yelling something and I'd never seen him so upset before. He was following a man dressed in a three-piece suit and a fur lined wool coat. His black hair was covered in a newsboy cap, and a bit of stubble showed on his face. His eyes…they were dark. He made it to the final step with the help of an elaborately carved cane. Something about it made my skin crawl. The carvings seemed like a relic, definitely nothing I'd ever seen.

"I'm sorry Reverend, but we've given you too many chances already," the man said.

"Mr. Adair, I assure you. We *need* to discuss this," Bill begged.

I slowed my pace as I approached them. Adair? Who's Adair?

"I'm sorry Reverend," Mr. Adair replied, with no sympathy in his lingering Scottish accent. "But we've been over this for a long time now. This *building* needs to be demolished. Condemned."

"I was getting *donations*! We were fixing it bit by bit. I promise you there has been *no* evidence of harm to-" Bill spat, his face turning red with rage.

"Bill?" I intervened. "What's going on?"

My voice must've spooked Bill since he jumped rather abruptly. "Connor," he greeted. "This *demon* of a man is taking the church."

"Now, Mr. Donovan," Mr. Adair objected smoothly. "Demon is...overkill don't you think? We had given you fair warning for a month now. And I'm not *taking* it. I'm *condemning* it."

"What?" I asked.

"The building is *old*," Mr. Adair answered with a bit of humor in his tone. "It's been around almost as long as the settlement...almost two hundred years!"

"My family has done *nothing* but bring this town peace through *this church*!" Bill exclaimed.

"And I'll ask again, *where* is the money for the repairs reverend?"

"Donations have been low and with good reason," Bill pushed back. "There are families in fear right now."

Mr. Adair reached into his pocket, pulling out a wad of cash. Hundred-dollar bills stacked on top of each other. I'd never known anyone to carry money like that before.

The hair on my neck stood on end at the sight. "Why don't we make a deal?" he suggested.

Bill's eyes widened. Something felt wrong and I immediately stepped beside him as the aura of the man reeked of something awful.

"Take the money as a way to get it out of your hands entirely," Mr. Adair offered. "Perhaps you can move to someplace less grim with a new church, a *better* church. I'm sure the missus will be more than thrilled."

Bill stepped forward and I grabbed his arm. This was insanity. This was his legacy. There's no way he could accept this.

"*Bill*," I whispered harshly.

Bill gave me a good hard look before nodding. It took only a moment more before I let go. Bill walked up to the man, narrowing his eyes.

"God forgive me for saying this, but *fuck off* with your money," Bill growled. He almost loomed over Adair his eyes filled with cold rage. "This is *my* church."

Mr. Adair smirked, and put the money away. "Consider your church *damned* then," Adair taunted in an amused tone. He pulled out a piece of paper, walked up the steps and nailed it to the door. "*Condemned* until I can reach the proper authorities."

We stared at him as he descended the stairs. "No one goes in or out of this building until then," he ordered. "Good day gentleman."

With that, he left us standing in the cold. Bill was livid, pacing and struggling to keep himself together. He finally stopped and turned to me. "I'm sorry you had to see that," he apologized.

Bill looked up at the looming sign on the door. He

then paused, noticing a few townsfolk gathering by the church and looked at me embarrassed. "Let's uh...," he stammered, pointing at the clergy house.

I looked around and saw a few people gathering to the sign around the church, whispering amongst themselves. I nodded and followed Bill to get some privacy.

Bill walked quickly to the clergy house steps, opening and shutting the door rather quickly. He locked the door behind us as well as the door that connected the church for good measure.

I stood as he motioned to sit. I refused politely as he sat down.

"What am I going to do?" Bill asked, his voice worn and desperate.

"*Who* exactly was that?" I asked, glancing out the window towards the church.

"A demon more like," Bill groaned.

I furrowed my brows at him in confusion. "I've never seen him here before," I noted.

"You wouldn't," Bill scoffed. "He only comes to represent the Atwood family."

Avery.

"For *what* exactly?" I asked.

"That pub down the way, used to belong to a nice English family since their grandparents. The grandson had lost everything from a fire, and the only way to repair everything was through a loan. That man...that man made a deal and it turned into the gambling den that it is. And...who knows what other sinful things. But it's in the Atwoods' name."

"I should've recognized him."

"From what I gather he only comes when he's called.

He's not from here. Boston? New York maybe? But he is sort of an enforcer for the Atwood family. And, now, he's after my church."

I swallowed, shaking my head as I sat down in the seat across from him. "He doesn't sit right with me," I grumbled. "Whoever he claims to be."

Bill leaned his elbows against the table. "Well," he scoffed in amusement. "At least I have a witness if things go awry."

Bill smiled at me and it immediately turned into a frown. "What will I tell Mary?" he whispered. "God knows what she will want to do."

Mary...then it hit me. I almost forgot why I came here in the first place. I sighed, looking down at the table. "How is Mary?" I asked. "Any other sightings of Ted?"

Bill shook his head. "No, but like it or not we're more than a little on edge. This whole spiel with Adair just made things worse," Bill said and sighed. "And it all started with Elizabeth. Poor girl."

I stayed silent for a moment as he folded his hands.

"You seem rather distraught over her death," I pointed out.

Bill furrowed his brows at me. "Of course I am. She was a huge part of the church," Bill replied. "One of the few positives in the last few years. Always smiling, very close to her faith-"

"Close to *you*," I interjected, staring at him intently.

Bill shook his head. "And yet I let her down," he whispered somberly. "Perhaps the only thing I did right by her was helping her best friend."

There was a bit of silence before I took up my nerve. I had to let him know.

"Bill...be honest with me," I insisted.

Bill looked up and sighed as he drummed his fingers on the table. "Anything."

"You and Elizabeth...there wasn't anything..." I asked, trying not to be crass.

Bill tilted his head looking utterly confused. "Anything what?" he asked.

I rolled my eyes. There was no way he was having any affairs. That wasn't the look of a lover at all.

"Michael warned me there was an anonymous tip about you and Elizabeth," I stated. "Stating you two might've had some love affair."

Bill's eyes widened before he gave a disgusted face. "Are they mad?" he groaned. "Heavens no. Lord help me I need some tea."

Bill stood up and walked over to the tea kettle.

"So...you didn't?" I asked.

The tea kettle clanked loudly as Bill set it to the fireplace. He shook his head and then faced me. There was some somberness in his expression. "Connor...I would *never* do that to Mary," he stated firmly. "I treated Elizabeth like my own daughter. Evelyn too. All of you."

"Yet someone is pointing to you or Ted Baker as prime suspects in her death."

Bill's face paled as he leaned his back against the counter.

"Do you think someone has it out for you?" I asked.

"Outside Adair this morning...no. I would *never* harm the girl, and I know Ted loved her to bits. I was there for their wedding," he replied as he walked over to sit back down in his chair. "I hate to admit it Connor..." he continued as he sighed and shook his head. "Whoever or *whatever* is doing this to Blackwood Hollow is trying to rip us apart from the inside out. Just like when your parents were young."

"It ends with us. One way or another," I stated plainly, and he nodded as I stood and headed to the door.

"Connor," Bill called out as I grabbed the door knob. There was a tear forming in his eyes. "I'm sorry...for all of them."

I knew he didn't mean just Elizabeth. I knew he meant every single person I witnessed leave this world for whatever curse had been put on Blackwood Hollow. All the missing people. All the souls that were growing in numbers to haunt this place. Bill and Mary were there. Every funeral where a child like me turned into an orphan.

I gave Bill a nod. "Lock your doors," I said. "Find protection. Do *not* leave your home unless it's necessary."

"I'll say extra prayers," Bill agreed.

"I meant *real* protection."

Bill smiled at me with such mild confidence. "That *is* protection my boy," he replied. "Hopefully, soon enough, you will see it."

Seventeen

"This is...*fascinating*," Oskar whispered as his gloved hands moved deftly, working with various tools to dissect on the hog.

I waltzed into Oskar's office after seeing Bill, surprised to not see a body...but a pig resting on the embalming table. It or rather "she" was still pale and looked cold from the scene as well as the chill of the morgue. The wounds, despite being dried out, managed to look even more grotesque than any victim we'd encountered the last several days.

I stepped back to hover over Oskar's shoulder as I tried to stomach the stench. He examined the face and the eyes were even blacker than on the scene. The throat had bled but...there were punctures. It was different than the stomach that was completely torn. He lifted the opening in the stomach. There was almost nothing left and it wasn't the work of a butcher.

"There's no blood," Oskar said, and shook his head. "Everything was taken and drained. It's unlike anything I've seen before."

I motioned to the neck. "Did you see that?" I asked.

Oskar then looked at the throat, then back at me, his eyes weary. "It's almost *identical* to that poor girl," he replied. "Could be teeth. From whoever or *whatever* this thing is trying to imitate."

"Have you seen Ted at all?" I asked.

"No...and it's a shame because I needed someone to work out the proper funeral arrangements. I guess I'll have to run it by Michael and Reverend Donovan."

I shook my head. Ted had been gone for way too long. "I don't think we'll see him anytime soon," I remarked.

Oskar took his gloves off and placed them in a nearby sink. He motioned for me to follow him into his office, where he grabbed a glass and bottle of the same liquor Michael complained about. He offered it to me but I put up a hand. "When did you last see him?" he asked as he poured himself a glass and leaned against the desk.

"Few days," I recalled. "Mary saw him roaming about so I decided to check in at the Baker house."

"And? He wasn't there?"

"Worse," I swallowed. "His place was...it looked ransacked, but *nothing* was missing."

Oskar cursed in German, shaking his head. "Grief can do horrible things to people, especially with a death like this," he added taking a large swig of the alcohol hissing at the contents as he put his glass down. "I should know better than anyone."

Oskar looked over my shoulder.

"I'm worried about him, Lowe. It's not like Ted to disappear," I remarked.

Oskar's face immediately turned pale and his eyes widened.

I furrowed my brows in confusion, but then heard rustling behind us and a crash.

I turned my head to see the pig thrashing from the embalming table and onto the floor. It was *screaming*. Oskar in a fit of fear, grabbed a nearby shotgun in his office. He hesitated as it thrashed on the stone floor.

"What in God's name..." I started.

BOOM!

A slug of Oskar's shotgun went straight into its head, and it finally stopped moving with a hole in its skull.

"You mean *hell*," Oskar corrected.

We looked up to see Michael at the door frame, just as dumbfounded as we were. "Michael," I greeted Michael, keeping my eyes on the pig to make sure it was actually dead this time.

"Is it dead?" Michael asked, barely able to get the words out.

Oskar walked up to it and kicked it lightly. I flinched, waiting for it to get back up, but it didn't.

"I'll make sure it stays that way," Oskar promised as he put the shotgun down in arms reach. "I suggest we burn the thing."

"Well I was going to keep it until Miss Shaw came to claim it," Michael pointed out.

"We burn it," I objected.

"Connor," Michael groaned.

"No, he's right Michael," Oskar agreed. "We can't have this thing start roaming. It would cause the town to panic."

Michael swallowed and nodded in agreement. He pointed at me. "You, me, going out, now," he ordered lightly. "Bring protection."

I raised a brow at him.

Michael noticed my confusion and shook his head. "One of my boys went up to the farm to tell her about the incident," he explained. "They haven't seen any sign of her. Not there, not anywhere in town."

Jane Shaw missing? Why would she be out of her home when there's danger all over?

"We're going to the farm."

***

Knock. Knock. Knock.

The sun was setting faster than I would've liked. Michael kept his revolver hidden in a holster under his wool jacket. Ever since the first incident, the cold had gotten far worse, especially with the darkness coming as fast as it had. I wasn't expecting to make so many house calls that day.

Michael and I stood there, waiting for a response. Nothing.

Michael grabbed his case of cigarettes and lighter from his pocket as he looked around the perimeter of the house.

I felt my hand go to the coin in my pocket, flipping it in my fingers. Something didn't feel right. My instincts were blaring and my hair was trying not to stand up.

"Is it always this quiet out here?" Michael mumbled as he lit his cigarette.

I looked towards the barn as I took my turn at knocking on the door. "No it isn't..." I replied. "She has a donkey that screams every time someone comes by."

"Maybe it's asleep," Michael commented as he blew out some smoke. "Hell I'd be hibernating too if I was out in this damn cold."

Nothing.

We were out in the cold with nothing but utter silence. Maybe she wasn't home.

"Do you have your flashlight on you?" I asked.

Michael nodded, as he reached into his coat pocket.

I reached into my own pocket and grabbed the small, portable metallic thing from my pocket. "Keep it on you," I suggested. "We might need it."

I walked around the wrap around porch. There was no sign of a lantern, fire in the fireplace, or anything. I turned on the flashlight and checked inside through one of the windows.

There was no sign of anyone.

I rolled my eyes as I approached the door again.

"Anything?" Michael asked.

"I'm not sure," I replied.

I reached down and the knob clicked. It was unlocked. I traded a puzzled look with Michael.

"What?" Michael asked.

I turned and pulled the knob, allowing the door to creak open slowly. He raised his brows. "Miss Shaw!" Michael called out from the porch. "It's Sheriff Hughes and Detective Sullivan."

Silence.

Something wasn't right. She wasn't the type to leave home.

I crossed the threshold first, taking quiet, easy steps. The kitchen was the same as I had remembered it, with odd trinkets, herbs, and other things on display.

Michael followed quietly behind me. He made a low whistle. "Jesus..." he whispered. "What is all this?"

I walked into the kitchen. Something smelled awful in a pot on the stove, and it was still mildly warm. It didn't look like anything I'd ever seen. The color was off, and the contents looked like some concoction versus something that was edible. I couldn't help but make a face.

Michael walked over making a similar face over the

pot. "Hope that's not dinner..." he whispered.

"It's still warm," I observed.

Michael glanced around the room. "Couldn't have been gone long then," he said as he walked towards the odd taxidermy statues and trinkets.

Michael furrowed his brows as he looked towards the hall.

I walked up to him, and noticed a door that wasn't like any of the open rooms.

I walked over, realizing the door was out of place and not only because it was closed and locked.

I looked around. The rest of the rooms were simple bedrooms and a washroom. This...this was different. A tapestry laid on the door, something that maybe would've been a Scottish ancestral picture but...it had that same crow on the coin and in the living room.

"Move," I ordered lightly as I tried to open the door. It was locked.

I cursed.

"I got it," Michael groaned as he rolled his eyes. He turned to me and motioned to the door. "Grab hold."

Michael grabbed a pocket knife out of his coat and flicked it open. He wiggled the knife around between the doorframe and the latch before we heard the click.

I smirked at him. "Should I ask *how* you know how to do that *Sheriff?*" I quipped.

"Trevor taught me after his sister locked herself in the bathroom when she was younger," Michael chuckled. "Been real easy to get into places I'm needed since."

Michael nodded as he unholstered his revolver, I pulled the door open with a creak that echoed angrily through the whole house.

A set of stairs behind the door led down to a cellar.

Michael motioned for me to pull out my revolver as he reached for his flashlight. "Miss Shaw," he called. "It's Sheriff Hughes. Are you all right?"

Nothing.

Michael went down first, each wooden step whining as if about to give at any moment. I pulled out my revolver as we walked down into the dark. It seemed as though it was even colder than outside, and the few windows in the basement offered very little light from the setting sun.

Michael made it to the hardened dirt floor and stepped further into the basement. I followed shortly behind him and shined the light into another corner. There wasn't much other than some shelves of jarred and canned goods, a tarp that covered some stacks of wood, and a shallow, old well that was frozen over from the cold.

I made my way to the storage shelves. All the jars were molded and they reeked. Everything was disgusting and far from edible as if they were forgotten about for months, maybe even *years*. Cobwebs covered the goods and nothing from the supply made any sense to keep. I covered my nose as I finally caught a horrid stench.

"My word! Does this woman have *any* luck with this place," I commented.

"Connor," Michael's voice was barely a whisper but in the dead quiet it felt like yelling in comparison.

I turned.

Michael was staring at something in front of him. I approached Michael as he aimed his flashlight to the ground. "What's that?" I asked as I bent down to look.

There was a pile of poorly kept blankets and ripped tarps and something sticking out from under it. I holstered my revolver as I pulled on my gloves. Michael stayed behind me his revolver still in his grip. I moved away the blankets and the odd looking tarp: fingers, but...far from alive. I winced the smell filling the air.

I quickly lifted the rest of the tarp as a few rats sprang away from the lump and ran squeaking.

Michael cursed under his breath as he steadied a shaking hand to keep the flashlight on the body.

The fingers led to a hand, which led to a decomposing body. We put our scarves over our noses.

The smell.

The skin was gray and rotting.

"*God* that smell!" Michael coughed.

I dared to approach the body. The clothes were far from new as the simple farm dress splayed out. Long black hair was now gray and white, the face was torn from being eaten as were other parts of the exposed body. I then looked at the face and froze.

I swallowed hard as I slowly stood.

"Jesus how could Miss Shaw hide a body without anyone knowing?" Michael asked.

My throat went dry as I motioned to the face. He shined the light to it and winced.

"Michael," I said. "That *is* Jane Shaw."

✳✳✳

"Two...maybe three months tops," Oskar concluded as Jane Shaw's body remained sprawled onto the table. "**If it wasn't so cold I'd think she'd be worse.**"

The graying in her skin looked worse under the morgue light. Pieces of her flesh had been eaten away, but the frigid basement kept her body somewhat preserved, except for the rodents feasting on her.

"How is this possible?" Michael swallowed, turning away as if he was going to be sick. "She was just in my office days ago complaining about her damn pigs."

"Clearly it was an imposter," Oskar pointed out.

Michael rolled his eyes. "How?" he demanded, pointing at the body in frustration as he kept his distance.

"Michael...we never really saw her until a few days ago," I pointed out. "Not since we were children. The only ones who really knew what she looked like were our parents."

Michael rolled his eyes. "Well clearly unless she is like her possessed pigs!" he objected angrily. "*THAT* right there wasn't walking around last week. I *think* I would've *noticed* that!"

Michael leaned against the counter far from the body and started breathing quickly.

Oskar walked around the table and made his way to Michael. "Michael..." he whispered urgently. "You need to breathe."

"I *am* breathing," Michael spat.

Oskar rolled his eyes, and closed the morgue door to the rest of the hall before heading to the office. He grabbed a crystal glass and poured some of the strong liquor into it. "This is insanity," he muttered.

Oskar came back and gave Michael the glass. Michael glared at the glass as he grabbed it and immediately downed it. He cursed under his breath and coughed violently. "She was standing *in* my office. Not *that thing*," he insisted.

The thought hit me like a train. Jane Shaw had come into the office and before that...Avery had been stalking her like a predator when she arrived.

I stood from the counter and left the morgue.

"Where are you going?!" Michael called out as they followed me down the hall.

I found myself charging towards the jail cells and burst through the door. The guard jumped from his seat as I walked towards Avery's cell.

I noticed something was wrong almost immediately.

Avery...was *fine*. He was smiling, leaning against the bars, and his undershirt was neatly tucked in even though it was still stained from sweat. He looked *completely* normal as he smirked. "Mr. Sullivan...to what do I owe the pleasure?" he greeted me casually.

I furrowed my brows at him. "Just a few days ago you were raving like a lunatic," I remarked.

"Grief does that to people," Avery replied smoothly, eying me up and down. "I'm sure I can convince the psych ward to reconsider my application."

I swallowed as Michael and Oskar approached from the hall.

"Aww the trio is all here," Avery teased. "Such a treat."

"What do you know about Jane Shaw?" I asked.

Avery raised an eyebrow at me and laughed. "The old crone up on the hill?" he asked for clarity. He backed up, laying on the cot on his bed and putting his hands behind his head. "Other than she's probably the *worst* farmer in the entire state of New Jersey. What about her?"

Avery reached into his pocket, pulled out a coin, and

made it to dance across his knuckles.

"She's dead," I told Avery bluntly.

Avery stopped, flicking the coin into the air and catching it as he sat up and approached the bars in a quick flash of speed now standing in front of me. "Really?" he asked, his voice filled with intrigue. "You sure the old hag didn't have it coming?"

"And what of the woman who came a few days ago?" I asked.

"What woman?"

"You know the woman."

Avery grinned. "I'm sorry Connor...the last few days...are just a blur to me," he replied.

I couldn't help it. I reached through the bars and dragged him closer. Oskar jumped as the guard yelled in protest but Michael motioned him to stand down.

"Don't you lie to me," I growled.

Avery's laugh lowered and he showed his teeth.

"Jane Shaw is dead. We found her in the basement," I said.

Avery smirked. "How do you know she didn't kill someone?" he asked and then started to sing, "The pig lady with the ax-"

"Shut up," I commanded, my voice firm.

Avery's grin widened.

"Who *was* she?"

"Connor," Michael intervened.

I looked over and saw the guard on edge. I swallowed, looking sternly at Avery. "You know something," I whispered harshly. "And one day I'll figure out how and *what* you know."

I let go and Avery let out a low laugh.

"I don't know what you're talking about Sul," Avery replied pointing a coin at me from his fingers.

I furrowed my brows then grabbed his hand and twisted his wrist. Avery yelled in pain until I plucked the coin out of his hand and let go of his wrist.

A coin of similar markings as the one Shaw had given me, but this one had the outline of a bat.

I tilted my head at him. "What's this?" I asked.

"It's nothing," Avery replied, brushing off the question.

I smirked, closing it in my hand. "Fine...then you don't mind me keeping it," I informed.

Avery flinched but quickly covered it with a scoff. "I'm sure you'll find many places to keep it safe Sul," he said with a nonchalant smile as he walked his way back to the cot. "Now if you don't mind."

He waved me off. He *dismissed me*.

I rolled my eyes and put the coin in my pocket with the other one. Michael nodded to the guard who gave me a glare.

We were well into the hallway until I finally spoke. "You keeping good eyes on him?" I asked Michael.

"You know me, all eyes are on him. He's priority."

Eighteen

I was staring at the woods. I could hear her.

"*Connor*," her voice sang through the air, melodic as it ever was.

My mind had no control of my body as it moved into the clearing of the woods. I heard another voice behind me, but it was so faint, that I couldn't make out what it said. That other voice felt insignificant.

I moved further and further until finally saw her.

The woman in the photographs. The woman I chased down as a small boy.

Mother.

She turned, smiling at me. I felt my body stiffen as her hand reached out to me. I should be happy to see her. She'd been gone for so long, but here she was smiling at me. Still something in my gut told me to be very, very afraid.

She beckoned me sweetly.

"Connor!" another voice yelled from behind.

I jumped, turning to see Evelyn standing behind me. I smiled at her motioning to my mother.

"She's here," I whispered in disbelief. "But...why are *you* here?"

"Connor...we *need* to go home," Evelyn begged. She watched my mother with fear in her eyes. "I've been looking for you."

Evelyn reached out her hand, grabbing mine instantly. It tightened to give me a fair warning as I looked behind her. My heart stopped seeing the dark piercing eyes of Avery coming out of the shadows, glaring at us. Then a hideous hiss resonated from behind. I turned to see my mother's eyes becoming just as dark and menacing as Avery's.

We were trapped. And not by the people we knew...but by demons.

Outside of her eyes, my mother's skin had turned to a sickly gray with an almost leathery appearance, and her teeth had become elongated and sharp. She stared at us as if we were her next meal as her fingers transformed into hideous talons in seconds.

I felt my body itch to run far away from this place. I grabbed onto Evelyn and put her behind me as I kept her separated from Avery as best I could.

"She's *mine*," Avery growled his voice a low, and unfamiliar hiss. I turned, and his features matched the same monstrous structure as my mother. "*Give her to me*."

"No!" I yelled.

There was a piercing shriek, and Evelyn was out of my grip. Avery tore her from me and Evelyn's screams were torture.

I was about to run towards her, but my mother grabbed me, trapping me in her grip, my back to her. She hissed and screeched as her hands forced me to watch as Avery was on top of Evelyn.

Avery's mouth opened hungrily as his teeth sank into her neck. That scream. That horrid scream wrenched from her mouth. I yelled as his claws dug into her.

"*Evelyn!*" I screamed in horror.

Then there was silence.

Avery stood, glaring at me. His scowl turned to an evil grin with blood dripping from his mouth. He picked Evelyn up, she was limp at first, but then she stood up straight with little effort. Her eyes opened and they looked blank. I watched Evelyn as she stared at me with cold, dead eyes, blood still draining from her neck.

"Evelyn?" I whispered.

Evelyn moved towards me and Avery grinned. "Now you two can be together…" he laughed lowly.

I glanced at him confused.

Evelyn's skin had turned paler, and her eyes black just like them. Her teeth grew into fangs, and she eyed me like a piece of meat.

The monster. She was becoming a monster.

My mother's talons let go, and I felt the weight lift off.

Evelyn lunged at me clawing and ripping into my skin as I started screaming.

✱✱✱

***SLAM!* The sound of a door forced me to bolt upright in my bed in a cold sweat, and adrenaline still rushing through me.**

My heart was pounding as a sudden rush of cold air hit me from under the door.

What?

I got up, still shaking from the nightmare, as I was suddenly presented with one in real time.

I opened the door, hearing the gentle creaking as I peeked out into the hall. Where was that coming from?

I looked down the stairs.

The front door was wide open.

My heart continued to race as I looked down the hall to see Evelyn peeking through her own door. Her eyes were wide with worry. She must've heard the sound too.

Not long after Bryan was doing the same, his head peeking out of his own door. They both changed into warmer clothes, slacks and sweaters to investigate the noise.

We all stood there, staring at each other in confusion for a moment.

I motioned towards the door downstairs. They looked at me, their eyes wide. I motioned them back into the room as I crept toward the landing.

There was nothing, I felt as if each step would alert an intruder to my presence.

Finally, I found myself facing the open door of the study. It was messy, as if someone rushed through the house. Sudden flashes of the Baker residence started showing in my own home in an odd sense of déjà vu.

The cold chill ripped through me as I moved closer and closer to the front door.

Creak. I nearly jumped as I looked up to see both Bryan *and* Evelyn approach me from the top of the stairs. They fearfully watched the front door. Bryan was a bit braver than his mother as he walked his way down steadily.

I pressed a finger to my lips and he nodded quickly. I finally proceeded further down the full set of stairs. I motioned for Bryan to check the kitchen and he nodded, walking quietly away from me as I approached the study.

Evelyn crept up behind me as I moved closer to the source of the chaos. She approached from behind, grabbing my arm and gripping it tightly. My heart was racing at full speed as I leaned my head through the door frame. I looked around cautiously expecting to see some source of the racket.

Nothing. Nothing but silence and the mess from the previous night.

I had to tell myself it wasn't just a bad dream. The door was *wide open*.

I shivered at the cold chill I felt from the front door. There was nothing between us and the outside world. Maybe I had forgotten to lock it.

I stood for a moment, but then the hair on my neck stood up and I heard a quiet gasp.

I turned my head as Evelyn stood covering her mouth and closing her eyes. I furrowed my brow at her as she pointed a finger, motioning upwards in the study.

I swallowed as tears started forming in her eyes. I looked along the shadows of my ceiling.

A large looming figure was covered in the darkness, hovering above us like a spider on the wall. The silhouette was facing us and, despite the dark, its eyes were blacker in the moonlight peering into the room.

My eyes adjusted and I stood in terror. It wasn't just a looming figure.

"*Ted...*" I whispered.

A sudden growl came from Ted as his body shifted in the light. His clothes were torn and bloodied. His teeth were shining in the little light that entered the room. They were more like those of a wild animal than a man, sharp and pointed.

God what happened to him? He was just...

The flashes of him sweating, his anger growing. What...what was this?

"*What*?!" Evelyn gasped.

My eyes never left Ted as he sniffed the air like a wild dog. His eyes finally found us, and he sneered viciously.

"We need to go," I whispered urgently and everything happened so fast.

Ted peeled off the ceiling and landed on the floor with a massive *thud*.

Evelyn screamed, and he slowly approached us grinning with a low rumbling growl that shouldn't have come from a man's throat. Then, he lunged.

I pushed Evelyn out of the way, then turned to Ted shoving him with all my might as he made his way towards her.

"*RUN!*" I yelled as I grappled with him. Considering his build I wasn't going to last very long. He was like fighting with an ox. His eyes were dark and focused as he pushed forward. I felt myself push against his weight as he relentlessly pushed back. "I NEED YOU TO RUN!"

Evelyn hesitated before sprinting out to the kitchen.

I held Ted there as long as I could, keeping him from getting to anyone else. Finally, I shoved him back into the room to create distance, still maneuvering over glass and the normal mess it was.

He tried to get past me, but I challenged him, blocking him from leaving the room. If he was strong before, which he was, he was *much* stronger now.

Within seconds, I was on the floor with his hands gripping onto my legs as I tried to get up. I saw a bottle and took the chance. I grabbed it quickly and threw it at his head and managed to hit him hard.

Ted growled, shrieking almost an inhuman shriek. "DAMN IT CONNOR!" he hissed, some of his voice seeping through a new inhuman tone.

I scrambled out of his grip and raced to the door.

As I finally made my exit, Bryan came storming in with a fire poker from the kitchen. The poker was glowing red and hot in front of me. I nearly grazed it as Bryan appeared and shoved me out of the way. He thrust the end into Ted's shoulder. Ted yelled in agony as the three of us pulled out of the room and slammed the door in his face.

We all leaned against the door as Ted's howling continued.

"What *IS* that thing?!" Bryan's voice cracked as Ted began pounding on the door against our weight.

"*That*," I flinched under the power of the door being punched, "is Mr. Baker."

Bryan's eyes widened in terror.

"Help me!" I ordered and motioned to the chair across the hall.

Bryan nodded, as he quickly got up and shoved the back of the chair into the doorknob.

We wedged it as best we could with the raging lunatic behind the door. They grabbed their boots from the door, frantically pulling them on and grabbing their wool coats.

"Why does he look like that?" Bryan demanded.

I grabbed my own coat as we bridged the gap to the entrance. I grabbed Bryan by the collar and grabbed Evelyn by the arm as I dragged them out of the house with enough force that they nearly stumbled. I'd apologize for that later.

"I don't *know* boy," I growled feeling my mind racing with everything happening. "But we're going to need reinforcements."

The cold chill was biting at us, I knew where to go.

Nineteen

The race to the sheriff's department had already felt like an eternity.

Not even the bitter cold could wake me from this nightmare. And, now, the only place we should've sought for refuse only continued that hell.

The door of the sheriff's office gaped like an open wound. It hung listlessly from its hinges, shattered glass littering the floor. The whole from door entrance looked like it had been rammed by a car. The hell happened here?

Bryan stayed close behind, and I felt Evelyn's hand reach out, her fingers interlacing with mine. I glanced down, noticing her knuckles turn white as her grip tightened. I forced myself to move forward, giving Evelyn's hand a reassuring squeeze as we ventured to the lights near the center of the station.

The empty sheriff's office greeted us with nothing but darkness and silence. "MICHAEL!" I yelled.

Our eyes slowly adjusted to the dim moonlight that barely seeped into the station. It provided the only light except for the occasional bulb that was left on around the halls. We ventured deeper before we saw the first sign of life.

A small, steady light illuminated a sliver of the hallway outside Michael's office.

I let go of Evelyn's hand as I rushed to the door, and pulled it open without thinking.

Michael turned quickly and aimed his revolver at my chest. Oskar was sitting in Michael's chair looking pale. His clothes were ripped and spattered with dark spots.

Evelyn gasped, pushing Bryan behind her protectively as I stood between them and Michael.

"Thank God you're all right," I greeted Michael and Oskar.

"Tell me where he is?" Michael demanded, his eyes wild.

I stared at him in confusion. "What?" I replied.

"He *saw* you," Michael growled pointing at Oskar. "You came to the cell."

"Michael," I started, keeping my tone calm. "I have *no idea* what you're talking about."

I looked at Oskar, and he let out a sigh of relief.

"Connor..." Oskar greeted me.

"Don't *Connor* him," Michael growled. He holstered his revolver before slamming my face into the desk. He wrenched my hand around my back and produced a pair of handcuffs from his belt. "Don't *move* a *muscle*."

Oskar stood from the chair, putting his hands up.

Evelyn shrieked. "MICHAEL!" she exclaimed, grabbing him by the arm.

"Back up," Michael ordered.

Bryan stepped forward to stand between Michael and Evelyn, his hands up in surrender.

"Michael...we need to focus now," Oskar breathed.

"Sheriff...It's okay it's just us," Bryan added quickly.

Michael kept me pinned to the desk as I struggled against his grip handcuffs still in arms reach.

"Michael..." I groaned. "We have a *problem*."

"Damn right we do," Michael snapped. "You released the man who was *insane* with fucking Ted next to you! Oskar saw the whole thing!"

"Michael I-" I tried to begin again.

"Where are they?!"

"I wasn't HERE! I was at home."

Oskar looked at me and swallowed before looking at Michael. "Michael...he's right," he said. "There's no way that was him. Even if the person *looked* like him, something was terribly off."

Michael looked at me, back to his friend and then to the others.

"Michael...we just came from the estate," Evelyn insisted, her eyes wide in horror. "What on earth did you see?"

Michael took a moment that felt like an eternity. Finally, he let go of me, twirling the handcuffs in his grip and walked around the desk, shaking his head. I picked myself up as he grabbed a cigarette case from the drawer. I furrowed my brows at him. His ring was very much on, and that bracelet was nowhere to be seen.

"I see you found your ring," I mentioned and he looked at me funny.

"You lost your marbles. I never take this off," Michael scoffed. "You know that. Maggie would kill me."

"Where's the bracelet?" I asked.

Oskar looked for a lighter as Michael scrambled silently. He tilted his head in confusion. "What bracelet?" Michael asked.

I shook my head. "Back at the Baker house, you had a bracelet on," I explained. "You were missing your ring and said you left it in your desk."

Michael looked at me as if I had two heads while he took a drag of his cigarette. "I thought you said you'd quit drinking," he snapped as he rolled his eyes at me.

"I did!" I shouted. "Michael, you were at the Baker's house. I *saw* you. We had a conversation-"

"Watch it," Michael warned, his tone getting firm as he pointed at me. "I'm telling you I *didn't* even set *foot* in that place."

Then it hit me. We all looked amongst each other. That couldn't be possible...but after what we found of Jane. Maybe...no.

"Don't lie to me Michael," I whispered. "Please."

Michael looked at me with the same uncertainty in his eyes.

I shifted uncomfortably.

"Just like you're telling me you weren't just here?" Michael asked.

"This is madness," I whispered, shaking my head as I ran a hand through my hair.

This whole night was a nightmare.

There was a long pause as Michael took another drag from his cigarette. He looked at me dead in the eye for a long moment.

Oskar looked between us with fear in his eyes. "Something very, very wrong is happening," Oskar commented. "There's some wicked evil at play here. I can feel it in my bones."

The hair on my neck stood and Michael shook his head. "You're acting like we're seeing double of each other," he stated skeptically.

"Maybe we *are* Michael. This is far beyond ghost stories from the funeral home," Oskar whispered. "What if there's an imposter? Just like Miss Shaw..."

God someone that looked like Michael *and* me? That seemed absurd. But...

"I'm...afraid I'm starting to think you're right," I whispered.

Michael rolled his eyes. Apparently, it was just as ludicrous to him as it was to all of us.

"Fine let's say that *wasn't* you. How did you get in?" Michael asked as he pinched the bridge of his nose and put his hand up at me.

"The door was wide open," I replied.

Michael stared me down, reading my face as he took another drag of his cigarette. The man was breaking, and I didn't blame him. How in the hell did he see another well...me?

"What are you doing here?" Oskar whispered. "Did something happen?"

"We have a problem," I replied.

"Damn right we have a problem. The *original* problem," Michael growled, moving to sit on his desk facing us. "Avery's *gone*."

I stiffened and Evelyn gasped. Bryan stood wide eyed behind me.

"What do you mean *gone*?" the boy managed to ask. "I thought he was locked up here with you?"

"He *was*, but something happened to one of the guards. After *he* supposedly walked into the jail cell," Michael growled in frustration as he pointed at me and waved it off.

"What do you mean?" I asked.

"The guard...he's dead," Oskar replied.

Silence descended on the room.

"How?" I demanded.

"Ted Baker," Oskar answered as he swallowed. "Or whatever was *left* of him was here with 'you' maybe about an hour ago."

"So...Avery's missing?" Evelyn asked.

I could tell she was trying to clarify the situation. We all needed it. The man wasn't exactly sane. One minute he's sweating a storm talking nonsense. The next he's acting like nothing happened.

"Oskar called me when it all happened," Michael explained.

I cursed under my breath. I couldn't imagine facing both Ted and Avery alone in their states. And whoever this other me potentially was.

"I was working late," Oskar recalled, looking between us still shaking. "I heard someone come in."

We all turned to look at Oskar as he paused, his hands tightening into fists.

"I called out quietly, but only heard the jail door open. As I went to check, the guard was already dead and Ted and well 'you' were letting Avery out. Something was very *wrong* with all of you," he continued, swallowing hard. "Then...she," he stopped.

"*She?*" I asked.

Was it Jane?

"I saw her get up," Oskar whispered, shakily.

"Who? Not Jane."

"No...it was Elizabeth."

I stared at Oskar wide eyed. Elizabeth Baker was walking around? What the hell was happening?

"It was like they were calling to her. I barely made it out alive," Oskar finished quietly.

I started taking in Oskar's appearance. His clothes were torn, there was blood splattered on him. But it didn't look like *his*. A sudden flash of Ted's clothes came into my mind. He was covered in blood. Maybe this was why.

"You can't be serious," I whispered.

"Dead serious," Michael objected. "Elizabeth is a walking dead."

Evelyn gasped, her eyes filling with tears.

"Why not Jane?" Evelyn demanded. "I don't understand."

"That is strange," I agreed.

Oskar then went pale. "She...she didn't have the puncture marks," he informed us. "All of them had some sort of puncture mark. She must've been murdered some other way. And it was a long time ago. If she was affected, we would've seen her...like *that* a long time ago."

"Then...what do we do?" Bryan asked.

Michael shook his head. "Find them before they hurt someone else," he replied. "Though, we have no idea where they *went*."

Silence.

I sat in the spare chair and rubbed my face. It gave me a moment to think.

"We have to think quickly. Who knows if they'll come back here," Evelyn pointed out, turning to check the door.

"I could name *one* place," I grumbled as I rolled my eyes.

"Where?" Oskar asked.

"Ted Baker," I breathed, looking up at Oskar and Michael. "Was on my *ceiling*."

They both paled. Bryan and Evelyn nodded in agreement.

"That's why we're here," I finished.

"Whoever or whatever *that* is," Oskar whispered. "That's not Ted anymore."

"Then what do we do?" Evelyn asked.

I turned and looked at her as Bryan stood protectively over his mother's shoulder.

"I'm going by my gut," Michael interrupted with the cigarette in his mouth.

Michael lunged into his desk calmly, calculated. He motioned us to follow him out of the office.

We walked down the hall, and stopped at the door that read *"Armory"*.

Michael grabbed a set of keys, unlocked the door, and strode in. He walked around a table set in the center, approaching the gun cabinets. One by one, he pulled out weapon after weapon, gun belts, their appropriate holsters and ammunition. He was ready for a war. He pulled on a shoulder holster, grabbing both revolvers placing them all on the table in front of us.

"Go on take them, we need all the help we can get," Michael ordered as he placed down a revolver.

Oskar nodded, leaving the armory to go into the morgue to grab the shotgun down the hall he'd used on the hog. He also seemed to move around his own desk while I peeked down the hall at him.

Evelyn looked at me wide eyed as Michael continued towards another weapons cabinet. He pulled out a shotgun, checking and loading it. Ammunition was locked and loaded into every weapon.

"Michael...you can't be serious," Evelyn breathed, fear in her eyes.

"Eve, I've seen what these things do to anything that comes in their path the last several days, we need to take *all* precautions. And I don't think they'll wanna talk."

Evelyn glanced at me, and I nodded in agreement.

There were tears in her eyes and I felt my gut twist at the side of it. She's been through so much for so long and now she has to face a friend in such a state. She had to see Elizabeth not as a friend...but as a monster.

"We do what we do with a rabid dog. Only this time it's worse," Michael remarked. He looked at me. "Are you armed?"

I nodded, showing him the revolver at my belt.

"I'll give you something better," Michael assured, motioning the gun to Evelyn. "Eve can have yours."

I swallowed, taking the holster off my belt. Michael then walked over to Bryan, handing him a spare revolver. I hadn't trained him as much as I would've liked. The boy would have to go by instinct.

Michael approached as if he were talking to his own son. "One, always treat it as if it's loaded. Two keep your hand *off* the trigger until you're ready to shoot," Michael instructed. "And three...don't point that at something you don't want to destroy," he warned.

Bryan nodded, as Michael gave him a spare holster and Bryan looked at me as he proceeded to buckle it around his waist.

I motioned to Evelyn and gave her mine butt-end towards her. She swallowed. "Are you sure?" she asked, worriedly.

I nodded. "Do you know how to shoot?" I asked.

"Outside of your father teaching me?"

"We need all the protection we can get."

Evelyn looked at me for a long moment, nodded and then grabbed a spare shoulder holster. Then she holstered the revolver quickly. I never thought I'd see *her* armed and ready like that. Evelyn Fields...ready to fight a monster.

Michael shoved a shotgun towards me, along with a bandolier with spare shells. He passed a thick baton over to Evelyn and did the same for Bryan. I watched as the boy twirled the rod in his hands.

"Remember what we practiced," I told him.

Bryan nodded, putting on a brave face.

I wasn't sure what would happen after tonight, but I had to be sure no one left this room unarmed.

Oskar returned to the room, having armed himself with his own personal shotgun and a small pistol he had hidden in his office desk. I nodded in approval.

"My father was a very cautious man," Oskar quipped, trying to lighten the mood. "He wouldn't run from superstitions again. And I won't either."

"You said Ted was at your place?" Michael asked.

I nodded. "Locked up in my study," I confirmed.

Michael looked at us as he extinguished his cigarette. "Let's go pay a visit, shall we?" he said.

❊❊❊

From the outside, it felt as if I was walking into a warzone: quiet, and dangerous.

We stood in front of the estate in the cold as I stared at the door, armed to the teeth. Michael nodded to me ready to proceed. I felt my adrenaline hit me as the others readied themselves. I grabbed my handheld flashlight to carry through the darkness.

The little orb of light was all I had as we approached the door.

I walked slowly and felt myself hesitate before pushing the door open. It gave a long whine as it presented the empty house.

Nothing. The winter chill felt worse as I stepped into the house. The study door was just as beaten and still as it had when we left. The others followed, keeping their distance. Michael was still outside looking behind us. We didn't want an ambush.

As I walked closer to the study door, I saw that it was still locked tight. The chair that kept it sealed while we were away. Thank God for that.

I stepped up to the door and leaned my ear against the wood. I listened carefully, a chill ran down my spine when I heard absolutely nothing. I wondered if Ted found a way out.

I furrowed my brows, motioning Michael to the door. He nodded, and readied himself.

I pulled out the fire poker from alongside the chair and I slowly unlocked the door, while Michael pulled out the chair away to give us room.

I pushed the door open quietly, Michael went in first. I followed suit, shotgun at the ready. Oskar, stayed in the hallway with Evelyn and Bryan keeping an eye on the staircase and the front door. We were all keeping on our toes and I couldn't help but wonder if this is how my father felt when he had gotten a call like this.

As I stepped into the study, I felt myself gaping.

It was destroyed now more than ever. I glanced at Michael who cursed under his breath, his gun still at the ready.

The map was torn, and pictures were scattered everywhere. My entire life's work was in shambles. My father's work.

I looked down and saw my mother's cross on the floor, still intact. I bent down, picked it up, and immediately pocketed it. Bill would kill me if I left this behind.

There was no sign of Ted. I even glanced at the ceiling out of caution half expecting him to spider crawl down towards us. We were met with nothing but the eerie silence.

Then I heard Evelyn come into the room behind me. She approached, looking at the torn map and swallowed as she took in the state of the study. "Good lord..." she whispered, her eyes wide at the debris. "Where could he have gone?"

That's when I felt it. The gust of wind that brushed into the room. My head turned, seeing the fresh planks on the windows torn and splintered allowing the cold air to seep into the crime scene.

"Oh that's *fantastic*..." I growled.

I almost stomped towards the window, feeling the fury of this whole ordeal rush over me. There was some blood in the glass no doubt from Ted escaping.

"Jesus, Connor. What happened?" Michael asked.

I rolled my eyes. "The same thing that happened at the Baker house," I whispered. "Total destruction."

I noticed Evelyn examining the map, and picking up a few pictures. She picked up one with Elizabeth and Ted at the church.

Michael shook his head, and leaned against my desk.

"This is a whole other level Connor," Michael remarked.

We walked around as we were interrupted by a sudden ringing sound.

I furrowed my brows.

"What's that sound?" Evelyn asked.

I realized it was on me. I reached into my pocket, and I found the source. The coin I took from Avery was glowing and hot.

It was ringing like an alarm and it was *loud*.

"What in God's name is that?!" Michael demanded, covering his ears as Evelyn did the same.

The coin suddenly flared and grew hot to the touch. I yelped.

"Get rid of it!" Evelyn yelled.

I instinctively threw it out the shattered window.

The ringing followed all the way outside until there was silence again. I felt my breath quicken at the sudden adrenaline.

We looked at each other in utter confusion.

"Was that," Michael started.

"It was a coin that Avery had on him," I replied, then reached into my pocket. I found the coin that Miss Shaw gave me. "Like this one."

Michael swallowed. "I don't like this," he commented, straightening up with his hands gripping onto his gun.

"What do we do?" Evelyn asked.

"We go on a man hunt is what we-" Michael started but was briefly interrupted. There was a thud, then a yell from Oskar followed by another bang against the wall behind us.

We turned to find Oskar pinned to the wall by Ted. My eyes widened in horror as Bryan stood in fear behind him. Everything happened at once.

"Bryan," I felt my voice whisper as Ted pinned

Oskar.

Bryan yelled, grabbing the baton in his hand and swinging profusely. Ted only got angrier as he growled, dropping Oskar. Oskar coughed and growled in frustration.

Then in a flash Ted had Bryan in his grip and rushed out the door with inhuman speed.

Everything slowed down as we watched in horror.

"BRYAN!" Evelyn screamed as she rushed outside with Michael.

I ran behind him until I stopped to check in on Oskar who was rubbing his throat.

"Get the boy," Oskar growled harshly shoving me away from him.

"I don't want to leave you!" I growled back.

"Get...the...boy," Oskar demanded and shoved me further.

I made sure he was standing before rushing out the door.

Evelyn and Michael were running as Bryan was being carted away. I forced my way forward as I watched the dark silhouettes running at full speed.

"*MOTHER!*" Bryan yelled as he was being dragged further out.

This can't happen again. It won't happen again.

Evelyn raised her revolver, she shot near them but kept missing. "Connor *help me!*" she screamed desperately as she raced to follow Ted's form rushing further and further away.

Michael stopped, aimed and took careful shots with his revolver. The .38 special didn't faze whatever Ted had become. It was an utter nightmare.

Oskar finally caught up with us, shouldering his

shotgun. He aimed with a rifle he got from the house. He stood silently, aimed carefully, and hit Ted's neck.

Ted howled fiercely, that same inhuman shriek. He stumbled...but he didn't stop. He only pushed further and further ahead.

I felt my heart pounding as we sprinted down the hill.

Not again. I will not have another one die again.

Ted threw Bryan over his shoulder effortlessly as the boy kicked and punched in his arms. He outpaced us easily and, within moments, they disappeared into the pines.

Twenty

"BRYAN!" Evelyn's desperate cry pierced the night as we charged forward.

Nobody stirred in town, a fact which triggered a queasy feeling in my gut. Someone should have heard the racket. Someone should've at *least* come out to check, but there was nothing. We ran through a tense silence as if it were a bad dream.

My mind raced through a repeated nightmare, but for the boy this time. I caught up with Evelyn as we pushed into the trees, armed and ready.

"How the *hell* can he run that fast?!" Michael growled in frustration as he stepped over a few branches.

It was dark and Ted was moving too fast for us to keep up. We had to rely on tracks that we prayed weren't from us walking around the pig incident.

Oskar stayed towards the back. He occasionally checked behind us as we fanned out with Evelyn in the middle.

"I'm not sure, but whatever it is...something is *different* out here," Oskar warned, his shotgun at the ready.

I felt it too, a sense of being outnumbered in the silent forest.

"I'm not going anywhere without the boy," I replied.

Bryan was *not* going to be pulled into this hell any more than he already was. First his father, then people dying or getting hurt around us...now this. I wouldn't let him be a victim of this chaos.

A branch snapped.

We all stopped and looked in the direction of the noise. The clearing was a few yards out...and that horrible twisting tree.

"*Bryan?*" Evelyn called out quietly as she made her way towards the noise.

I picked up my pace to stay beside her as Michael and Oskar followed close behind. I finally saw movement ahead and it set me on edge.

Ted's shadowed silhouette dragged Bryan and dropped him off at the bottom of the twisting tree.

I sprinted out in front only to find myself face to face with a cloaked figure standing over the boy.

Bryan tried to avoid the figure until another appeared from behind the twisting tree, and stood next to them. "Well, well...Looks like we got a little lucky," a feminine voice greeted us. She approached Bryan, her voice playful. "Seems we have a party, don't we, Avery?"

The hood fell and Avery stood smiling. But his teeth were...unusual. "*Yes*, I say we do. Don't we boy?" Avery greeted Bryan with a grin. Fangs...he had *fangs*.

Bryan swallowed, backing up as he tried to crab walk towards us. He was intercepted by Ted, who appeared from the darkness and dragged him back.

"No!" Evelyn screamed as she leapt towards Ted before I could stop her.

Ted hissed as he pulled Bryan further away.

A sick grin crossed Avery's face as he reached out and grabbed Evelyn.

"Hello *Evee*," he whispered as he turned her around to face me.

Evelyn struggled, but she couldn't break his grip. She watched me with fear in her eyes. I felt...trapped.

I risked a step forward, but Avery tsked at me as he kept Evelyn still in front of him. I hesitated, trying to feel out what he might do.

The cloaked woman laughed as she made her way towards me, moving with an unnatural grace. "Connor Sullivan," she greeted, and I noticed a hint of a smooth Scottish accent in her voice.

I furrowed my brows.

The woman pushed back the hood of her cloak as it fell to her shoulders. As the moonlight hit her, it revealed a young woman with dark hair, pale skin and dark eyes. She smiled. She was a strange beauty to behold, but my body, my very *soul* was screaming that I was in danger. She felt...*familiar*.

"You don't recognize me?" she asked.

I shook my head slowly.

The woman grinned as she reached out a hand, touching my forehead and a flash immediately sent me. The screaming in my mind of my nightmares. *MOTHER!* The cloaked figure...would that be *her*. My eyes widened in horror.

She smiled. "You were such a little boy," she said playfully. "Now look at you all grown up."

I stepped back as dark black shadows swept around her as if becoming night itself. My jaw dropped when the shadows disappeared. She looked at me from her wrinkled face, her hair was in disarray and she even seemed to have put on extra weight.

"Jane Shaw," I whispered as she smirked at me.

"Not quite," she laughed.

"You?!" Michael snapped. "You're the imposter?!"

The woman grinned and laughed as the darkness

swept about her again and revealed the dangerous beauty from before.

Oskar remained still behind me, his gun at the ready, and pointing at Ted. "Witch!" he gasped.

Michael leveled his gun at the woman. The woman walked up to me. Though, Ted, and Avery seemed incredibly still. "Very clever, Oskar," she grinned. "And to correct *you*."

"You know who I am?" Oskar asked, his face turning pale.

"Of course I do," she chuckled and the shadows swarmed about her again. "For I am many things."

The man who was harassing Bill Donovan stood before us, Mr. Adair.

I swallowed hard. "You took the church," I said.

The witch looked at me, her grin getting bigger. "I need it for preparations," she stated in Mr. Adair's voice.

I walked up to her, and she poked the cane which Adair walked around with at my chest. "Easy boy..." the witch warned.

I narrowed my eyes. The bracelet. I reached into my pocket, and pulled out the coin. "You were with me at the Baker house," I concluded.

A swarm of shadows engulfed her and then there was a duplicate "Michael" in front of me. I glanced at Michael. He was pale as he readied his revolver.

"My, my, you are a smart one aren't you...just like your father," the witch mocked at me in Michael's voice.

Michael stiffened, cursing under his breath.

"Easy Hughes," the witch continued in his voice. "You wouldn't want your wife to end up with the wrong Michael now, would you?"

BANG!

The witch's head snapped back, and she toppled back into the snow. There was a swarm of shadows as her normal form laid there, bleeding in the snow.

"No one uses my face," Michael growled.

The witch sat up, and with a slow smirk as she stood carefully, bleeding as she faced me.

The blood drained from her neck, darker than any human blood I had ever seen.

"I applaud your enthusiasm," she chimed as her wound healed rapidly. "But that won't work here."

I revealed the coin in my hand and her eyes darted to it.

"You had this at the house. You gave me one at the station," I reminded her calmly.

"And what do you think it is boy?" the witch asked, getting close to my face.

"Whatever it was it sent a huge racket," I replied. "So much for protection."

She tilted her head, laughing at me. "Don't you see young one?" she asked. "It has eyes."

I swallowed and looked down at the coin. Th crow and sigils glowed on the almost black coin. It had been tracking my every move. "You were spying on us," I snapped and threw it at her.

The coin dropped in the snow in front of her and she bent down to pick it up into her fingers.

"Who are you?" I dared to ask.

The witch smiled at me. "I have gone by many names over the centuries. But your simple mind can settle for *Clara*," she replied.

Centuries. That couldn't be right.

"What's that supposed to mean?" I asked, feeling a fury building inside of me.

What was with this woman and how the hell did she get here?

"It means I've been around *well* before any of you walked this earth," Clara whispered.

I swallowed. Impossible.

"And I did it," Clara continued, shadows swarming around her. When they dissipated she had turned into...*me*. "By hiding in plain sight thanks to you and your friends," she added in my voice.

"You really are a witch..." I whispered.

Clara grinned at me and I felt a growing urge to *run*. "Very good Connor," she said in my voice. The shadows danced around her once more and she turned into her *original* self. "You are a clever man," she continued as she began circling me. "You know not everyone believes me. Those who do...don't unfortunately live to see my plans. Including that poor old woman. She was probably the *hardest* to convince."

Jane. That was an unexpected punch in my gut. The poor woman was left all alone with this wretch of a human being. And no one would've believed her because of her legendary reputation.

"So...you killed Elizabeth from the start?" I concluded.

Clara smirked. "She...got in the way..." she admitted motioning to Avery.

I swallowed. All these people were just victims of some sick plot.

"Wait, " Evelyn whispered.

Clara turned and faced her.

Evelyn's eyes widened. "I recognize you…" she whispered.

"Shut up," Avery hissed, keeping his grip on Evelyn.

Clara grinned. "Do you now?" she asked. "And when was this?"

"Avery," she insisted. "She was the one that went with you at the courthouse. You signed everything under my name."

Clara raised her brows at Avery. "I told you she was smarter than you gave her credit for Avery…" she sang.

"You took my face?" Evelyn asked.

"It's very easy…" Clara replied with a grin, she transformed for a moment and mimicked Evelyn's face. Evelyn stared at her in fear. Then Clara looked at me. "She's such a pretty thing. I can see why you fancy her. And I used it to my advantage more than once."

My blood ran cold as she faced Evelyn like some evil twin. Was I always seeing Evelyn…or was it this woman?

"So, you were the one he went out with…" Evelyn continued.

Clara winked at Avery and he grinned. The damn monster grinned at this woman. "He was doing me a favor," she chimed. "Like we have for a long time. We go *way* back."

Evelyn swallowed as the witch turned back into her "normal" self.

Bryan looked at his mother in curiosity and fear as he stayed in Ted's grasp.

Before Evelyn could say another word, Clara looked back at me. "I must admit, I was not expecting you to just prance onto my doorstep," she remarked smoothly. She reached out her hand as if to touch me. "But then again…it's hard to stay away from the one you love isn't it Connor?"

I felt frozen.

"You've grown so much from that little boy. And now you bring me another."

"Mr. Sullivan!" Bryan grunted and shifted under Ted Baker's grip.

Ted hissed and growled for Bryan to be still.

I snapped out of some sort of trance, pulling myself back from her fingers near inches from touching me. I pulled my revolver on her, pointing at her.

Clara simply smirked. "Tsk, tsk. That won't do," she sighed.

Clara waved her hand, and I suddenly felt as if my hand was on fire. I yelled and dropped my revolver.

Evelyn shrieked in fear.

I grabbed my hand and saw the shape of the revolver's handle burned into my palm.

Michael immediately raised his rifle. He fired and couldn't have missed. She flinched for a moment, but then stared at Michael. She only grinned at him.

Nothing.

There was *nothing*.

I saw Evelyn and Bryan's eyes both widen in horror at the display.

I drew my revolver, and pointed at her. "I don't care *who* you are," I growled. "Let them go."

Clara narrowed her eyes at me. "You already saw that this doesn't hurt me," she stated.

"I know," I admitted, then I aimed towards Ted and Bryan. "*MOVE!*"

Bryan ducked as far as he could away from Ted.

I managed to graze Ted's ear, but he screeched nonetheless and lost his grip on Bryan.

Bryan grabbed a large nearby branch and started running towards Avery.

Oh my God...he was taking the offensive.

Avery seemed caught off guard by Bryan and put his arm out to block him while using Evelyn as a shield in front of him. Bryan halted immediately to avoid his mother.

Avery grinned widely as he growled at Bryan. "What now boy?" he mocked.

I aimed and fired at Avery's free arm. He yelled and struggled to keep his grip on Evelyn. She stepped on his foot with her heel and used the baton in her hand to swing across his head. Avery growled, hissed and cursed under his breath as Bryan pulled her away to some form of safety. The relief lasted only for a moment.

"You *wretched thing*," Avery growled as the two of them dodged around Ted and Avery who were both bleeding and snarling.

Clara just smiled at us. "As much as I would *love* to continue this charade," she began, then snapped her fingers. Avery and Ted seemed unharmed from the recent scuffle, staring at all of us. "I have things to do."

The bloody form of Elizabeth appeared from the darkness of the trees. She was breathing heavily, panting with her skin gray and ghoulish. Her teeth were monstrous fangs and talons had replaced her nails. It was as if the things in my nightmares were really happening.

Evelyn gasped, pulling Bryan behind her. Michael and Oskar readied themselves as now we faced *four* monsters, seemingly unfazed by bullets.

"I suggest you'd put down your weapons if you know what's good for you," Clara suggested.

"Like hell," Michael spat back.

We weren't outnumbered, but if no weapons could kill them...what could we do?

I pulled Evelyn and Bryan over to me, keeping them far from the feral looks of Ted and Elizabeth. "Michael," I whispered.

"Yes Michael, keep fighting...then you'll end up like your boy," Clara sang tauntingly.

Michael was fuming but Oskar put down his weapon and put up his hands.

"Live today..." Oskar whispered to Michael.

Michael kept his guard up. "What will you do with us?" he demanded.

"Keep you out of the way until we have everything prepared," Avery replied. "And I know just the place."

"Unless you want to die here," Clara laughed. "Or become one of them."

I looked between the monsters in front of me and glanced at the others. I swallowed and nodded to them.

Clara followed with her hands behind her back, amused as Avery took charge. Avery grabbed me and I struggled in his grip. He threw Michael and Oskar over to Ted.

"Careful he might bite," Avery teased with a smirk.

Avery gripped onto me while pushing Evelyn over towards Elizabeth. Evelyn grabbed Bryan as Elizabeth hissed and snarled at them.

They marched us out of the woods and we made our way back to town in the dark.

Twenty-One

SLAM! We were thrown into the jail cells of the emptied and raided holding area.

Not too long ago it was Avery here, pacing, rambling; and, now he was there, grinning at me as if nothing happened in the last few days.

I was thrown into the cell, the locks secured as Avery stood there, laughing.

Michael and Oskar were thrown in the cell across from me. We had to comply with the monsters that stood before us and Clara being…whatever *she* was.

"Get comfy," Avery mocked us as he leaned against the cell bars.

Evelyn was still in his grip, and Bryan remained held in Ted's grasp. Elizabeth stood by the door like a guard dog.

Something didn't feel right as Avery started walking away.

"What are you doing?!" Bryan demanded.

"Oh you'll find out soon enough pest," Avery spat.

Ted pulled Bryan towards the exit as he fought to stay with us.

"Connor!" Bryan yelled. "I'M NOT LEAVING WITHOUT MY FRIENDS!"

Avery kept his grip on Evelyn as he watched. He pushed Evelyn towards Clara as he approached Bryan who struggled in Ted's grip. Bryan let out a pained groan when Avery grabbed him by the jaw, forcing the boy to look at him.

"You do as I tell you," Avery hissed. "Like the good

sniveling brat you are."

Bryan narrowed his eyes and spat in Avery's face.

Avery gave a disgusted look, then glared at the boy. I felt a swelling of pride for a moment.

"I fucking hate you," Bryan cursed.

Avery scoffed as he wiped his face. He walked up, and punched Bryan in the face.

Bryan grunted at the impact and Evelyn screamed at Avery.

"AVERY!" Michael growled from behind the bars.

Oskar stood as well, glaring at the man.

Elizabeth ran in, hissing and snapping her monstrous teeth at Michael and Oskar, forcing them back. Ted gave a growl unlike anything I'd heard to force them back. They put up their arms. Avery and Clara had taken our weapons, and we had no chance of fighting back whatever they turned into.

"If it's anything...I wasn't very fond of you either *boy*," Avery spat as he leaned down to Bryan's ear level. "You are and always will be what I need at my disposal. Your mother can't change that both you *and* her belong to *me*."

"HEY!" I shouted at Avery.

Avery turned his glare to me with a grin flashing across his face. "You got something to say Sul?" he asked, waltzing back over to hover over the cell.

I leaned close to the bars.

"What are you going to do?" he taunted smoothly.

"I'll kill you," I growled. "Mark my words, jail is not good enough for the likes of you."

Avery reached through the bars of the cell, his fingers turning into talons as they gripped onto my throat. "That's funny...because it looks like I've already won from where I'm standing," Avery replied with a grin, showing off his fangs as he squeezed at my throat. "I will do what I *please*."

"No!" Evelyn yelled in protest while Bryan wiggled in Ted's grip.

"Stop it!" Bryan shouted, as his face started to bruise from Avery's punch.

Avery kept tightening his grip, and I felt my breathing cut off. He was much stronger than I remembered. He smiled, and I saw the fang that formed from his canines, his eyes dark as night. *He* was no longer human.

"Let him GO Avery!" Michael shouted from the other cell.

"Avery," Clara's voice sang in warning and smiled at him.

Avery glanced at Clara, eying her up and down. "Darling Mistress," he sang back with almost a hiss. "Are you sure we can't make an exception?"

"We need him for the preparations," Clara sang as if to remind him.

"Once we prepare...I'll make sure you have the most painful death for stealing her from me," Avery threatened. "But I'll make you watch her turn and your boy die."

Avery let go, a laugh in the back of his throat as I gasped for air.

Clara waved and Ted followed her out with Bryan as Elizabeth hissed at Michael and Oskar before following her so-called mistress.

Avery grabbed Evelyn from Clara and she resisted. "Please!" she begged looking at him in the eyes. "One request."

Clara smirked at Evelyn and nodded. "Sure," she agreed.

Avery rolled his eyes.

"Let her," Clara sighed. "Clock is ticking."

Avery snarled, shoving Evelyn away.

"You have five minutes," Avery growled, but Evelyn motioned to the door.

Avery reluctantly obeyed as he shut the door and locked it to make sure that no one could to leave while he stood outside with the others, including Bryan.

Evelyn walked up to me as I got up to stand in front of the bars. She grabbed my hand and squeezed, putting a hand on my face and examining my neck.

"I'm fine," I whispered, trying to reassure her even though my voice was hoarse.

"Shut up," Evelyn objected, she kept glancing at the door. "I need you to listen to me."

I swallowed.

Evelyn's eyes desperately searched mine. "Bryan," she whispered. "I need to protect him as long as I can. I need to go with them."

"Don't you dare," I objected. "I will find a way. *We* will find a way."

Michael and Oskar sat in the cell, watching from their places, and shaking their heads doubtfully.

"We'll find a way out," I repeated in a whisper.

I looked over, the prison keys were missing from their place. Well...there was no way of getting to that plan.

I felt her hand grabbing mine, gripping it lightly.

"Please...promise me you won't die," Evelyn whispered.

I swallowed. "Evee..." I sighed.

"I can't lose you again," Evelyn whispered as she lifted my hand and kissed the back of it. "I need you...Bryan needs you."

I couldn't promise anything. I was stuck in a cell while her and the boy were some sort of sacrifice.

"I know," I growled. "God...what do we do?"

Evelyn smiled sadly. "What you've always done. What you've always promised me," she said.

The door opened. I grabbed Evelyn, pulling her close to the cell.

Avery stood in front of her snarling. "Times up," he announced, grabbing her as I kept my grip on her.

"That wasn't five minutes," I growled protesting. But Avery just grinned.

"*Please*," Evelyn begged as I gripped onto her tighter.

Avery pried Evelyn away from me and I felt her leave.

I felt myself yelling at him.

"You *bastard*!" I cursed.

Avery came back and punched me square in the face through the bars.

I was pushed back, but the adrenaline kicked in and I lunged to the bars of the cell. I tried to grab him, but he stepped back grinning.

Avery smirked. "See you on the other side Sul," he sang as he grabbed Evelyn and dragged her out of the cells.

"*Connor*!" Evelyn screamed as she fought.

I banged on the cell bars and screamed in rage.

He took her and Bryan and I felt the walls closing in. Not again...

***

I found myself sitting on the cold floor.

I sat in the darkness of the cell, but it was far from quiet.

Michael had been trying to pry open the cell he and Oskar resided in. He was trying to find *any* weak point in the doors.

"You'd think after *all* this time being here, I'd *know* the tricks of this damn thing," Michael grumbled to himself as the clanging continued.

The keys were nowhere to be found. They must've hidden them after the first raid when Avery cleaned out the patrol. Maybe they planned this all along.

"Sullivan come on!" Michael called out angrily. "I need a little help here."

"If *you* of all people can't unlock your jail cells, how do you expect me to do it?" I asked, pinching the bridge of my nose.

I felt as if my world was collapsing. My mind couldn't hold it together. It was spinning with the image of Bryan getting beaten and Evelyn getting dragged. How in the hell was I supposed to be the hero now?

Michael cursed, pacing up and down in the cell he shared with Oskar.

Oskar sat on the cot, his elbows leaning against his knees. He took off his glasses and rubbed his eyes. "God, we're going to die, aren't we?" he asked. "The curse of this place is going to finally swallow us whole like everyone before us."

"Like hell we are," Michael growled back. "I'm not ending up like those *things*. And GOD FORBID that woman becomes *me* again!"

How do we stop someone who could literally turn into any of us? Someone will notice the change in behavior, right? They'll know we're really missing.

I wanted to object, to find *some* form of hope. But I couldn't help but feel as if Oskar's fears were right. What if we couldn't get out of this? And Evelyn...Bryan...what was going to happen to them?

I leaned my head against the wall as I sat on the floor. The winter's chill was the only thing keeping me alive.

Then I heard Oskar muttering under his breath. I looked up, seeing his hands clasped and whispering. I overheard bits here and there, clearly showing he was praying, his head bowed in his hands.

"You really think God is going to help us right now?" Michael asked in irritation as he looked around then proceeded to go back to the cell door. "Ask him for a crowbar in the wall or something?"

After another shove, Michael stopped, sighed, and leaned against the bars.

Oskar kept praying and I watched him for a moment before leaning my head back, my eyes were closed and I drifted off before I knew it.

Twenty-Two

February 1905

I felt a hand rest on my chest and a steady breathing as a body rolled over to meet mine.

My eyes slowly opened only just barely noticing the outline of a beautiful woman sleeping next to me. Evelyn. My *wife*. I glanced at the floor seeing our clothes lying about carelessly. A sweeping memory of the vows, the rush of coming home and being in each other's arms. Flashes of the feverish joy that we shared. The whole night we were caught in each others passion we have waited for so long to embrace. It felt like a spell that kept happening over and over again. Now I lay here...looking at her. The woman I will forever lay in this bed with.

I stared at her sleeping form, finding a smile on my face.

Evelyn shifted in her sleep, then her eyes fluttered open looking at me in the morning glow.

"Good morning," I whispered and she groaned, burying her face into my chest. "How are you feeling Mrs. Sullivan?"

Evelyn looked up at me and raised her brows. "Forgive me but I used to call your mother that," she commented. "Now I bear a heavy title."

"Heavy?"

"Have you *seen* your mother?" Evelyn chimed, smirking. "I have *massive* shoes to fill."

I grinned back. "She would be *proud* of you," I

disagreed. "She *adored* you."

"I miss her..." Evelyn whispered. "I miss your father too. He was a good man."

Despite the pang of guilt in my chest, Evelyn leaning against me gave me a sense of peace. I knew in my heart my parents would've been thrilled.

Evelyn sighed, as she looked at me. "If only I could say the same about my family," she groaned as she shook her head. "I still have to get my things."

"I'll be with you. So will Mr. Donovan," I assured her.

Bill and Mary Donovan made sure to be available for Evelyn at my request, especially given her father's horrendous gambling problem. Her mother's death hadn't helped. It only made him worse and her more isolated.

Evelyn nodded, leaned up to kiss my lips and smirked. "Shall I make you breakfast Mr. Sullivan?" she teased.

"You may do whatever you want Mrs. Sullivan this is *your* house now after all."

"Well...not until we sign the papers today. Make everything official."

"Breakfast first then."

✳✳✳

"Ah you finally made it home!" Mr. Fields greeted us as we walked into the living room of his home.

I froze in the rather chaotic room. Everything was filthy, dusted, bottles were littered everywhere, and dirty ash trays filled the coffee table. Even the pictures of family were left askew. The once tidy, beautiful brick house at the end of town had become a wreck after Evelyn's mother died.

Evelyn's father, George Fields, looked somewhat out of place in his three-piece suit, holding a pocket watch that looked worn and scratched. His hair was thinning, and his beard was flecked with white.

Evelyn looked up.

"Yes well I've come to get my things!" Evelyn announced.

George grinned. "Yes of course! I heard the news!" he exclaimed. "Avery told me all about it!"

I furrowed my brows in confusion. "Avery?" I asked.

"Yes," Avery's voice came from further back into the room as he stepped in. "Very, very exciting news indeed."

I swallowed hard as I glanced at Evelyn. "Avery," she greeted. "I hate to tell you but this isn't a good time to be asking my father for a debt collection."

Avery grinned, walking over to us. "You must be mistaken Evee," he said. I was actually telling your father the very good news."

George finally seemed to notice me. "What is he doing here?" he demanded.

"He's here to help me pack my things," Evelyn replied. "I'm leaving."

"Well that's very gentlemanly of him," Avery remarked. "Now that we're married. Mrs. Atwood."

I froze. He's not married. *I'm* married.

Evelyn's eyes widened in horror. "What-?"

"I told your father that we signed the papers this morning," Avery replied.

"I didn't-"

The door swung open and Bill Donovan walked in heated. "There you are!" Bill growled, glaring at Avery who straightened grinning at him. "I don't know *who* you think you are or what *imposter* you had in that courthouse but this is not going to fly."

"What is all this Reverend?" George asked in confusion. "I would think you'd be *happy* for my daughter!"

"*We* got married Mr. Fields," I growled as I corrected him.

"The paper says otherwise Sul," Avery said.

"When could you have gotten married?" George demanded in disbelief.

"Last night," Evelyn insisted. "We had Mr. and Mrs. Donovan there."

George rolled his eyes. "I saw you this morning," he protested. "You told me yourself you were heading to the courthouse."

"That's impossible!" I objected. "She was with *me*!"

"I can agree to that," Bill grumbled, keeping his composure.

George scoffed in disbelief. "I'd rather *die* than have her marry you."

I glared at George and was about to approach him, but Bill grabbed my arm and shook his head.

Evelyn froze. "Are you drunk again?" she spat.

George's face reddened in anger. "Don't insult me brat!" he scolded.

"I *was not* here!" Evelyn pushed. "Clearly you are *mistaken*."

"Mr. Fields," Bill interrupted firmly getting George's attention. Bill cleared his throat. "Perhaps we have a misunderstanding. I was personally on my way to the courthouse this morning to finalize the legalities. And whether you like it or not sir, Evelyn is of age to marry who she wishes under the grace of God and I as her witness."

"Yes, and she *chose* me. And we're leaving *today*," I growled at Mr. Fields who was fuming.

That's when Avery reached into his pocket. "Really? Then how do you explain this?" he asked as he took out a piece of paper.

My eyes stared at the paper. A marriage certificate with both signatures.

Evelyn's eyes widened as she saw her signature. "I did *not* sign that," she whispered.

"Sweetheart we don't need to hide it from your father now, do we?" Avery drawled. "It's signed, it's done and now you're coming home with me."

"Like hell she will," I growled.

I walked up and tried to grab the certificate from Avery, but he backed away.

"Oh I'm sorry to hurt your feelings Sul, but it's official. She's *mine*," Avery stated, grinning.

I punched Avery in the face, and he grunted hissing as he grabbed his nose.

I turned to Evelyn. "We're leaving," I said flatly.

Avery grabbed me, turned me around with such force, and punched me back across the face. Pain rushed through my head and I could already taste blood.

Evelyn screamed as Bill grabbed her to pull her away from the sudden brawl in the living room. I wouldn't let up. I hit Avery back hard enough it hurt my knuckles.

"HEY!" George called out.

I turned at the red-faced man as he charged towards us. He grabbed my shoulder and pulled me off

Avery in one forceful shove. I hit the wall behind me as Evelyn rushed over to me.

George grabbed Evelyn and forced her away. Bill was trailing behind him to grab her but George reached into his coat pocket, and pulled out a revolver.

Bill put up his hands in surrender.

"This is my house," George growled as he kept the revolver on me. He looked at Evelyn. "You don't have your mother to save you anymore."

"I hate you," Evelyn whispered but George kept his grip on her.

I was about to charge him, but Bill held me back.

"She's going with Mr. Atwood," George announced, his breathing heavy, his face reddened by the ordeal. "I gave him my blessing."

"More like your money," Evelyn spat.

George growled, pushing her to the floor in front of Avery. Avery then picked her up as she fought.

"Tell your family to send for her things," George ordered and Avery nodded in approval.

Avery looked out the window. "Speaking of that's my ride," he announced.

I looked out to see a shining black car pulling up in front of the house.

"Let's go darling," Avery commented. "Say goodbye to dear old dad."

"Connor!" Evelyn screamed as she was dragged out with Avery.

I was about to follow but heard the click of George's revolver.

"Now you," George threatened and I glared at him. "I don't care if you married her under God. Legally, she belongs to them. And rightfully so."

"Mr. Fields-"

"You come near my property again while I'm still breathing, I promise you, you won't be," George threatened lowly. "I don't want you anywhere near my daughter."

"George...please, let's not do this," Bill protested calmly.

"Get out before I call the Sheriff," George barked. "Now!"

Bill grabbed me, pulled me out of the house, and closed the door behind us.

I watched, as a few feet away, Avery had slammed the car door while Evelyn was yelling at him from the inside. He was talking to the driver when I charged him.

"Hey!" I called out as he backed away from the car and took a step towards me.

Avery gave a smug look of victory despite his bloodied face.

"You're not getting away with this," I growled.

Avery grinned. "And what will you do Sul?" he asked mockingly, pulling out the paper. "I have it all in writing."

I grabbed it from him. The signature was perfect. It was *actually* in Evelyn's handwriting.

"I'll call the Sheriff's office for fraud," I spat. "You forged her signature."

"The judge will say otherwise," Avery sang. "She was even with me."

"What poor girl did you trick to come with you?" I growled.

"Forget it Sul, I have a very good lawyer and my own family was there to witness the signing with her," Avery chimed. He grabbed the piece of paper from me and folded it neatly. "Now...if you excuse me. I have a honeymoon to start."

Avery turned, but I grabbed his arm.

"We're *not* done here," I spat.

Avery's head slowly turned, his face still bloody from the first hit. He then grabbed my wrist, gripping it hard as I grunted, letting go. He leaned down eye to eye. "Let me be very clear," Avery said smoothly. "You touch me again, I can't promise I won't kill you and I'll make it look like an accident. Or...if you'd rather I go after her."

I spat at him and Avery snarled as he gripped onto my arm and punched me in the ribs. I yelled as I fell to the ground.

Bill bent down to me. "Avery!" he scolded.

"I know you love that girl," Avery said, a grin forming on his face. "But she's mine now Sul. It's time you accept that."

Avery turned on his heel and headed to the car.

"Connor!" Evelyn's voice muffled into the car.

I sat on the ground as I watched Evelyn try to push herself out, but Avery rested his hand on her chest. She froze when he whispered something in her ear. Tears formed in her eyes and I swallowed as she slowly settled herself back into the seat. He shut the door behind them.

"That bastard will get what's coming to him," Bill growled as he twisted his jaw. "We'll find a way to stop this."

I watched as Evelyn was taken away from me. I had no idea if I'd see her again.

Twenty-Three

I bolted upright, realizing I was back in reality as I heard the creaking of the door.

Both Michael and Oskar were already in a fighting stance.

The door opened a little further, and a woman's head popped out.

It was Mary Donovan. I wondered how she got there as a smile spread across my face. She investigated the jail and made an exasperated sound. "Mrs. Donovan?" I greeted her.

"Our prayers are answered…" Oskar whispered, looking up at the ceiling.

Michael glanced at him and raised his brows. "Remind me to come to church more," he scoffed.

"Bill, quickly! They're in here!" Mary whispered as if she was worried about strangers coming out of nowhere.

"What are you doing here?" Oskar asked.

Bill quickly entered the room and grinned. "Connor, Michael, Oskar," he greeted us. "My aren't you boys hard to find."

"How did you get here?" I asked.

Mary nodded over to Michael "Mrs. Hughes was looking for you," she replied. "She was worried, so Bill and I went searching everywhere."

"Maggie…" Michael chuckled. "Bless that woman."

"We saw what happened at Connor's…it was like the place was ransacked," Mary added.

"What happened?" Bill asked, staring at me with

concern.

I swallowed. "They took her. They took her and the boy," I found myself stuttering.

Bill's eyes widened. "Who?" he asked.

"Avery...and that witch of a pig lady," Michael growled.

"Miss Shaw?" Mary asked in shock. "But...I thought she was dead? How on earth would she-?"

"It's not Miss Shaw," I interrupted and looked at Bill who looked at me in confusion. "It's an imposter. She's...using some kind of evil magic."

"You can't be serious," Bill sighed.

"She was Mr. Adair, she was Miss Shaw, she has been walking through this town without ever being noticed," I continued. "*She's* the reason why people are missing. She's not from this world."

"Oh my Lord..." Mary whispered. "Connor...please this is serious."

"He's *dead* serious I'm afraid," Michael objected. "We all saw it with our own eyes."

Bill and Mary looked at us, terrified and confused.

"This is something so much bigger than us," Oskar replied. "Lucky for us...we're the only ones who know now and she'll try everything to get rid of us."

I walked up to the door of my cell and rapped my knuckles on the bars. "We need to find a way to break these cells open," I interrupted.

"I'll look for the keys," Mary suggested, rushing around the room.

Michael sighed in relief leaning on the cell doors as Oskar stood up, straightening his clothes and his nerves.

Bill then looked towards me and shook his head. "I

knew Avery had something to do with it. But this?" he said.

"She's been his mistress...or *something* I can't explain," I growled. "He's been with her since Evelyn at the very least."

Bill shook his head in disbelief. "It was happening right under our noses," he muttered.

"If we don't get to him, Bryan will die first..." I warned.

Bill froze and swallowed hard. "Are you sure?" he asked.

"They're *evil* creatures. They're the reason people go missing," Oskar interrupted. "That witch is their sole keeper, the thing that's controlling them."

I paced toward the window looking out into the darkness. "Bullets don't do anything against them," I growled. "God...what are we going to do?"

"I don't care *how* many bullets we need," Michael growled. "This stops tonight."

I nodded.

Bill shook his head and swallowed. "Looks like the man is finally getting his revenge," he said.

I furrowed my brow, puzzled. "Revenge?" I asked. "No, you know as well as I do he hated me from the start Bill. I didn't think it would take him this long to properly threaten to kill me. I just wish he didn't go after Evelyn...or the boy."

Bill scoffed in disbelief. "I'm not surprised about the boy," he commented.

I rolled my eyes. "Why because it's her son?" I said. "It's still a cowardly thing to do."

Bill looked at me oddly. "Didn't she tell you?" he asked.

"Who?" I asked.

Bill furrowed his brows and tilted his head. "Evelyn," he answered simply.

I looked at Bill, my mind racing. What could he mean?

Bill was reading my face and shook his head. "I wish there was a better time," he sighed. "I figured you would've known by now."

"Bill...what are you going on about?" I demanded in frustration. "What in God's name are you keeping from me?"

Bill smiled slightly. "Connor, Avery is going after *him* for a reason," Bill stated carefully. "Bryan...is *your* son."

I felt like my heart stopped and my body felt lighter. Michael and Oskar stood watching me with surprise on their faces.

"What?" I whispered.

It couldn't have been, could it?

Flashes of Bryan's features, his behaviors...that night with Evelyn. The night we were married...just us and no one tearing that away from us.

"I knew it," Michael grumbled. "Had *Sullivan* written all over him."

"Gee, thank you, Michael," I groaned as I paced over and sat on the cot with my head in my hands. Bryan...he was *my* son. "How...how could she not tell me...?"

"He threatened to hurt you the day she was taken away. She was trying to protect you...Evelyn told me when she first had signs," Bill explained. "It's why I was so...*reluctant* with Avery's treatment."

"How do you know for sure?"

"They were never...*intimate*. He tried but she

refused," Bill scoffed. "Besides...he had mumps on his sixteenth birthday. When he found out she was pregnant, his family admitted he couldn't have children. The marriage was a cover up. Evelyn told me everything. Or at least that's what we thought. Could be whatever the hell *he* is too."

That's true...did a monster like that breed? There's no way.

"The keys!" Michael called out as he snapped his fingers. "Mary! There are spare keys in the jailer's desk!"

"Found them!" Mary's voice called back, muffled from the hall.

My mind was swirling. Bryan...was *my* son.

Mary came back in grinning victoriously. "Here," she whispered, giving them to Michael.

Michael fumbled through the keys until he found the one that unlocked their cell. "Yes!" he celebrated as came over to me, grinning victoriously.

"What do we do now that we're out?" Oskar wondered following Michael out of the cell.

"Kill the bastards," Michael replied. "Save the girl, save the boy."

"But how?" Oskar asked. "We'll be outnumbered for sure."

I looked out of the barred window and I saw the church standing alone in the darkness.

I saw Avery, Clara, and the others dragging Evelyn and Bryan to the church in the moment. They seemed unphased by the grounds. Wasn't the area condemned? I furrowed my brows. How were they able to walk into the church if they had some sort of black magic behind them? Something wasn't right, and we had to stop it before it got even *more* out of hand.

"If these things are in fact evil," Bill mentioned. "Then perhaps the answer is simple."

"Defeat it with something holy?" Mary guessed.

Bill nodded.

Michael fiddled with the cell door before it finally swung open.

I turned and scoffed. "Well looks like they set themselves up in their own trap," I remarked as they all looked at me in curiosity. "They just *walked* into the church."

"How?" Oskar asked. "That's holy ground, isn't it?"

"If Clara was playing at Mr. Adair...they did *something* to the place," I suggested.

"Desecrating my church?!" Bill growled.

"Most likely," I replied.

Bill was fuming as he looked at his wife.

"Did you see our weapons?" I asked.

Mary nodded and pointed down the hall.

"Good," Michael replied as he rushed out and headed in the direction of our stash.

"What are we planning?" Oskar asked.

I walked out of the cell. "With the Reverend's permission," I said, patting Bill on the shoulder. "I'd say trap the evil within the holiest place in town."

"The church?" Oskar asked.

"The church," I agreed.

Michael stomped back in, distributing our weapons back to each of us. "Well reverend, you up to putting that to good use?" he asked as he handed a shotgun off to Bill.

Bill smirked. "You know sheriff," he said, cocking the shotgun. "I think I'm ready to do God's work. This evil ends tonight."

Twenty-Four

I rushed back to the house for my father's arsenal. The years this plague tormented us, this curse surrounding us...it was finally our chance to end it.

I grabbed my father's shotgun, a spare hunting rifle, and a revolver. I even managed to find a hunting knife stashed in an old chest. I was armed and ready as I dressed for the cold while I looked around the house.

I saw the pictures on the wall facing away. No...not anymore.

As I went down the stairs, I found myself flipping the pictures around, facing the ghosts of my mother and father, even the younger version of me. I stood there for a minute, remembering every line on their faces, and their eyes, their vigor of life.

My eyes drifted to the photograph of a boy. It was me, but I realized how much Bryan really did look like I had at his age.

I was going to end it that night. No excuses.

I loaded the weapons, and grabbed my old cross in my desk. I even grabbed my father's cross necklace and pulled it around my neck as I walked out the door.

I had to meet the others at the church.

As I stepped out of the house, I felt my feet finally hitting the hardened ground free of the icy snow from the past several days.

The last few days had turned our town upside down, but that was nearing the end. I felt a fire building in me as I drew closer and closer to the church.

It would not take Bryan. It would not take Evelyn. I wouldn't let it.

I saw a few silhouettes hiding along the front entrance of the church, away from prying eyes. As I drew closer, Bill, Mary, Michael, and Oskar were waiting each with their own weapons. I heard Bill whistle lightly and beckon me over.

Mary's eyes widened at all the weapons. "Are we fighting a bear?" she whispered harshly.

"Much worse I'm afraid," I replied.

Michael smirked as he checked his weapons. "Agreed," he said. "Bears would be *much* easier."

Mary's eyes widened in horror. "I can't believe we're doing this in *God's* house," she whispered.

Bill smiled and patted his wife's shoulder. "It's God's work, remember that Mary," he reassured her. "And it's *our* house of the Lord."

"We're casting out the demons," I agreed.

Mary hesitated but then nodded in acceptance. Bill handed her a rifle, and she checked it before slinging it over her shoulder. It was odd seeing the older couple armed to the teeth, doing *God's* work.

"Can you handle that thing?" Oskar asked.

"You all forget, Mr. Lowe, I wasn't always a pastor's wife," Mary reminded. "Even *I* have a past."

Oskar chuckled in amusement.

I nodded to the others. I never felt more love, energy, and willpower to put this thing down than with the people I was standing with. I tried to hold in my pride.

"Keep your eyes peeled," I instructed. "Evelyn and Bryan should be here somewhere."

Bill pointed towards the back of the church. "We can

go this way," he suggested.

I looked over at Michael and Oskar. "What do you want to do?" I asked.

Michael sighed. "Oskar and I will scout the front," he ordered. "You lot find the others."

I could see the tension build in Michael's posture, but he was ready for a fight. He had that determined look on his face he always got when he was going to square up with a bully or any idiot who was about to be arrested. Calm, collected, earnest.

"You got this?" I asked, looking at Oskar.

Oskar smirked. "God sends his most trusted people," he said. "I'm ready to end this plague on my family."

I patted Oskar on the shoulder, and nodded at Michael.

"God be with you," Michael said. "If you still believe anyway."

I swallowed nodding slowly. I had to...after of everything I'd seen.

"Demons be damned," Bill whispered, readying his weapon as he led the way toward the back. "Not in *God's* house."

I nodded to the others as I followed Bill and Mary down the lot toward the back of the church. We came to the side door, and Bill fumbled with some keys.

"I won't be with you long," he told. "You need to find her while Mary and I look for our real arsenal."

"That being?" I asked curiously.

"Holy water," Bill supplied with a grin. He put the key in the lock and finally started unlocking the door. "Everything's safely in the clergy house."

"You think that'll work?"

"You said it was evil. Then all evil will be afraid of a blessing," Bill stated. "However, I wouldn't be surprised if what you claim is true that witch took advantage of the years this place has been standing. Needs a proper cleansing. That's got to be the only way they're here."

"If you say so," I said as the door quietly swung open.

Bill motioned into the darkened church. The door led to a part of the lower level, with darkness overwhelming the entirety of it.

Bill patted me on the shoulder. "Walk with God," he whispered. He stopped, placing something in my hand and walking off. I looked at it and saw it was a lighter. "Let Him be your guide."

I nodded as Bill winked at me. Mary nodded and kissed me on the cheek like a mother would. "Be brave," she whispered. "Your father would be proud."

I felt a sinking feeling as she smiled then followed Bill back to the clergy house.

I took a breath before I walked through the door. *Here we go.*

I stepped in and the darkness was overwhelming and almost colder than the horrendous outside chill.

The stones seemed to suck in all the winter air and trap it in the walls.

I was alone, struggling to find any sign of *anyone*. I stepped into the darkness, my eyes adjusting to the little light I had. I grabbed the lighter Bill gave me, I had to flick it a few times before it finally came alive.

I walked through the basement and heard movement.

I stopped. Then I heard a muffled sound, a voice?

I furrowed my brows as I inched my way deeper into the basement. The meager light from my hand outlined a silhouette in the darkness. I approached the figure cautiously.

Evelyn. She was gagged, blindfolded and strapped into one of the church chairs.

I reached out to touch her but she flinched, screaming in the gag. I held her down for a moment. "Evee," I whispered. "It's me."

Evelyn tilted her head at my voice and immediately stopped.

I pulled off the blindfold gently and her eyes blinked in the darkness. She sighed in relief as she saw my face, and I leaned my forehead against hers.

"Let's get you out," I whispered.

Evelyn nodded quickly as I frantically helped undo the bindings. I tried the knots first but opted for the hunting knife. Even then, they came off after a few moments of sawing.

Evelyn lifted her hand, and pulled the gag off her mouth. "Thank God," she whispered and as soon as her arms were free, she wrapped her arms around my neck.

I wrapped my arms around her as she stood holding me tightly with tears streaming down her face.

"How did you get out?" Evelyn whispered.

I smirked. "The priest and his wife are *very* observant," I chuckled.

Evelyn laughed quietly in relief, but her laughter faded instantly. "They have Bryan," she whispered. "He's in the church with them."

"Great," I growled in frustration. "You go with the

Donovan's to the clergy house. I'll get Bryan. Cause a distraction."

"Are you insane?!"

"Michael and Oskar are out guarding the door. If things go wrong...we have backup," I reassured her, but she was tearing up. "Go, Evee."

"Are you always this stubborn?" Evelyn demanded.

"I'm sure you can forgive me," I replied.

I turned to leave but she grabbed my arm.

Before I knew it, she pulled me in and kissed me. Her face was serious when she pulled away. "Make it out alive, and I'll consider it," she quipped.

I felt my heart flutter, along with the need to protect this woman. I led her out the door I came from and grabbed a spare small cross from the storage shelves.

"I'll bring him back," I reassured Evelyn, putting the cross in her hand.

I pushed her out the door.

It was time to face my demons head on.

Twenty-Five

I went up the basement stairs and peeked out at my enemy through the door leading into the church.

It was wide open as I leaned against wall along the door frame out of sight.

I could vaguely see Michael and Oskar keeping their distance in the darkness along the back wall of the church. I looked to the front of the church as the small team of monsters gathered around the altar. A strange book, and a few odds and ends sat on top of the altar. The cross had been taken down, and it made the place feel empty.

Bryan sat in front of the altar, tied up the same way I found his mother, although he wasn't blindfolded.

I readied my shotgun. I was more than ready.

Ted and Elizabeth Baker stood on either side of him, looking more feral than ever. Avery paced back and forth in front of him...there was no sign of Clara. I couldn't imagine what she was planning to do that wasn't already heinous.

I leaned out just enough to keep watch over Avery.

"I should've known what you were from the start," Bryan growled.

Avery smirked. "Well, now you know you little brat," he taunted smoothly.

"He'll find you," Bryan threatened.

Avery stopped, standing in front of him.

"He'll make you regret siding with that witch," Bryan added.

Avery charged Bryan, grabbing his hair as he grunted in pain.

I struggled to keep my temper under control.

"*You* my dear *boy*, have *no idea* what I'm capable of," Avery growled.

Bryan yelled, squirming away and grabbing the man's wrists. He dug his nails into Avery's skin where he hissed.

"And with you out of the way," Avery growled. "I can deal with your mother *personally*. And as for that *scoundrel* of a man," he continued, pulling Bryan to his face, glaring as Bryan scowled back at him. "I will *break him*."

I reached into my pocket, throwing the cross out in front of the door frame. It thudded against the pew in front of me as I hid back into the darkness.

Elizabeth's feral eyes darted in my direction. She made a monstrous hiss as she approached the doorframe.

As soon as she came into view, the shotgun's blast roared in my ears.

The ringing, the stupid ringing I had to get over. She shrieked, spilling back into the aisles as I marched forward. I was now in the church with these monsters.

Elizabeth was writhing and shrieking in pain as I stepped over her.

"Connor!" Bryan yelled.

I nodded to him in acknowledgement, I still *hated* that he called me that, but I let it slide. He was my son after all. He'll get the truth soon enough.

I glared at Avery's seething eyes. "I guess we'll start this party early," he growled as he snapped his fingers at Ted. "Go!"

Ted's eyes then shot at me, and a massive growl escaped his throat.

"You wanna to join her?" I taunted motioning

towards the screaming Elizabeth.

Ted made a shriek before jumping onto the high ceiling and started crawling across the church's ceiling like some twisted inhuman spider.

"Come on not again..." I muttered, as I kept my eyes on the man...well *creature* at this point.

Avery was about to pounce, but Michael and Oskar came out of their cover from the back of the church.

Michael shot Avery first, hitting him in the shoulder and forcing him back.

I looked back at Michael and nodded in thanks. That man was literally my guardian angel.

Avery growled and lunged in Michael and Oskar's direction. Elizabeth, despite her flailing, struggled to get up, and headed towards Oskar.

I kept a bead on Ted and slam-fired the shotgun. I saw the shot and wad tear apart his shirt, but *nothing* seemed to affect him.

I growled at Ted as he grinned.

"Why don't you come down here instead of being a coward?!" I yelled out.

Ted's expression changed, and he unhooked his fingers from the wooden beams.

Thud. He was massive. His skin started changing into a sickly gray, his fangs showed, and his eyes turned piercing black. His over six-foot frame was now looming over me. What the hell was this?

"Connor!" I heard a voice yell from the back-room doorframe. "Move!"

I felt myself backing away as quickly as I could. The sound of another rifle boomed through the church, and Ted screamed. He *actually* screamed.

"Mother?!" Bryan called out.

I looked over and saw Evelyn with a hunting rifle in her grip. Ted was crying out. She rushed over to Bryan to help untie him.

"What did you do?!" I asked in shock.

"Dosed the bullets in holy water in the basin downstairs," Evelyn answered. "Seems to have worked right?"

Holy...they were affected by *holy* things.

I felt my hands grip onto father's cross and went over to Ted. I pulled the cross over my neck and wrapped it along my wrist and grabbed him.

For a split second, Ted contorted and hissed. Then his eyes flashed. "Connor," he breathed harshly, his normal voice filtering through his monstrous look.

I hesitated as I dropped him, and he growled monstrously.

Ted's eyes flashed as he looked at me desperately. "You need to finish me," he breathed harshly.

I looked at Ted and he shifted over, grabbing me by the shirt as I pulled away. He snapped his teeth at me, but I grabbed him and he flashed to normal again for a moment.

"B-bless the church," Ted choked out. "Save us. Save Elizabeth."

Was Bill's theory true? Get something holy.

I looked at Elizabeth who had been shot by Oskar and was flailing on the floor again.

I looked at Avery who was attacking Michael with terrifying talons and ripping at his shirt. That's when I felt a grip that drove my attention back on Ted. He gripped me and he bit hard into my wrist.

I yelled in agony.

"*Connor!*" Evelyn screamed.

I grabbed my revolver, and shot Ted straight in the head.

Pain radiated down my wrist like fire, my breathing becoming heavy.

Michael was on the floor.

Oskar was guarding Elizabeth preventing her from lunging again.

Avery suddenly froze, his body turning rigid. Then his head snapped around and his eyes bored into me, utterly devoid of anything that had been human. I looked down. Blood...was he smelling the blood?

I started moving back towards Evelyn, and Bryan, who was now free, stood between me and Avery as the monster started charging at us.

It was no use. Bryan, despite his best effort, was tossed aside like a rag doll.

Avery reached out and grabbed onto my neck, holding me still in front of the altar.

Avery grinned. "I was going to wait for the party to start with the boy," he said. "But I think I like this order better."

I felt the rush, like my body and even my *soul* were struggling to survive against the pain of the bite, and Avery's grip around my neck wasn't helping. I struggled to get a grip on his wrist. Then his eyes glanced at my father's cross dangling on my wrist.

For a brief moment, whether it was imagined or not, I could've sworn I saw Avery hesitate. Then, he grinned. "A man of little faith, has no power in this place," he gloated.

"Avery please," Evelyn begged next to me. "Let him go!"

Avery's eyes darted to Evelyn. "You'd like that wouldn't you," he growled. "Why not have all of you on display? One big happy family."

Then he paused, a big grin on his face. "Or maybe," he continued. "I'll have him come after you. It's only a matter of time."

The bite...was I going into one of them?

"Now, now Avery," Clara's voice rang through the church. "Why don't we drop him and get started."

Avery kept his grip for a few moments before he complied and dropped me to the floor.

My lungs were on fire as I coughed and gasped for air.

Evelyn and Bryan ran up to me to help, but Evelyn was immediately picked up by Avery while Clara grappled with Bryan.

"Ah, ah, ah," Clara chided Bryan with a grin. "We don't want you to get in the way of the process now, do we?"

Bryan struggled, but Clara waved her hand. Instantly, Bryan was pinned to the floor along with the others wherever they were.

They all screamed and shouted.

Clara only grinned. "Now...shall we proceed?" she asked as she came up to me and tossed me into the chair.

Avery stood guard, licking his lips as Clara showed off my bitten wrist.

"What do you want with me?" I demanded.

"It's not just *you* Mr. Sullivan," Clara sang. "This town is mine for the taking. Beyond that...who knows. But you will make a *fine* addition to my collection."

"You can control them?"

Clara revealed her wrist, the punctures. "Comes

with its benefits..." she said with a smirk.

She grabbed my bloodied wrist as she beckoned Avery over. I watched his eyes turn dark, and Evelyn screamed behind me.

The others were struggling to get up from whatever spell Clara put on them.

The world around me was crashing. The chaos of everything was swirling around me. Avery's grin widened.

My heart was racing in fear and adrenaline.

Clara was whispering something that made a blackish tendril spawn out of her hand. It swirled and I felt trapped. It wrapped around me.

I was going to die.

Avery's fangs latched onto my wrist while Clara chanted in whispers I couldn't understand. Power...there was *power* in this room.

I yelled in agony. Fire spread up my arm, forcing my veins to feel like I was being swarmed with electricity.

My life started flashing in front of me.

My mother, my father. They were all smiling at me. Every waking hour with them felt like a lifetime passing me. Then...Evelyn. We were children and finally adults. The smiles she gave when we were standing alone. The heartbreak of her leaving to go with Avery. Every waking heartbeat felt like an eternity.

I looked down as I saw the cross around my other wrist, as tears of pain washed down my face.

I closed my eyes. Evee. I had to live for her and Bryan.

A man of no faith has no power.

I opened my eyes.

God. I'm praying...You hear me? Let me live for them!

I grabbed my father's cross with my free hand and slammed it into Avery's face. It steamed and burned around my hand, but it did the same to his face. Avery screamed, and Clara was so thrown off that she stepped back in shock.

"*You lowlife BASTARD!*" Avery screamed.

I felt the rush of adrenaline hit me, again. The pain was driving me to move forward. I stood, and punched Avery in the face hard to keep him down.

Clara stood and lunged at me, but was brought short by the sound of a pistol.

BANG!

I looked over and Bryan was up along with the others, now free from the spell. He had shot the revolver directly into Clara's neck.

"You *brat!*" Clara screamed.

"Go! NOW!" I yelled at everyone as I grabbed Bryan and Evelyn.

We rushed out of the church, with Michael and Oskar already outside.

We all made it out. We slammed the doors shut and barred them from the outside.

I turned, Mary and Bill were already gathering all the holy water outside the clergy house.

My arm was stinging and driving me mad.

"Help them!" I ordered as Michael and Oskar grabbed a few bottles of holy water.

"What do we need to do?" Evelyn asked as she did the same.

"Make a perimeter," Bill instructed. "Keep pouring the water around the church. Quickly!"

We all did our part, bleeding and battered. My mind was racing.

This has to end. This has to end with us.

Bill grabbed his bible and searched through it frantically.

We ran around the church spilling every drop of holy water as dawn was approaching. Bill's prayers could be heard as we made our way around the church.

Bill had one more phrase when we all met up back at the start. "Amen," he concluded.

"Amen," we all confirmed in unison.

Inhuman screaming erupted from inside the church. Evil finally had something to fear.

I looked into the windows.

They weren't dead.

I grabbed the others.

"They're not done," I growled.

"Maybe we still have to kill them?" Evelyn suggested.

"Fine by me," Michael growled, making his way up the steps.

We all charged up the steps of the church.

As we went back in, armed and ready for another fight, we saw that Ted, Elizabeth, and even Avery all looked...*different*.

They were almost human again.

Avery was worse than the rest.

Clara looked at us with pure hatred in her eyes. "*WHAT* did you *DO*?!" she screamed. "You ruined *EVERYTHING!*"

I motioned the others to take care of Ted, Elizabeth, and Avery. Elizabeth, I noticed, was long dead. Her body wasn't moving at all. Ted...he was still alive, but barely.

Avery was furious.

Ted turned to Oskar with a pleading look. His eyes were on Elizabeth. It was like a grieving husband all over again. "Please...just save me," he whispered.

Oskar swallowed as he shook his head.

"I want to be with her," Ted begged.

And with that, Oskar aimed, fired a shot, and Ted was gone.

Avery growled at Michael. "*Hungry*..." he groaned, his eyes got dark again, feral and predatory.

Michael unholstered his revolver as Avery started to get up and shot him. The man slumped over, his breathing grew rapid for a moment and then his chest finally stopped moving.

Clara glowered. Then her eyes changed as I pulled out my cross. She flinched and then smiled. "Now, now, now. Let's not be *hasty*," she sang. Everyone kept their guard up as she walked to me. "Why don't we make a deal?"

"What makes you think I'll listen?" I asked.

Clara pointed at my wrist.

I flinched.

"You want to be cured, don't you?"

I hesitated.

Evelyn gasped at the mark and the others kept their eyes on me.

I felt as if the whole world was watching. This had to be a trick.

Clara only grinned. "I cure your little curse and you let me go. I'll be miles and miles away from Blackwood Hollow like a bad little dream," she offered. "You're always trying to be the hero, right? The good man?"

I looked at the others, then I found myself stepping away from them.

I glanced at Evelyn as her hand reached out to my arm, but I brushed it away gently.

I stepped closer to Clara who gave me a young, pretty smile.

"Yes...I am," I answered.

Clara grinned.

I shook my head. "How does the curse work?" I asked.

"It's all started by those who created it," Clara assured me with a disarming smile. "I can start it as much as take it away. Isn't that what you want?"

"Yes," I answered and scoffed. "And I think you just gave me my cure."

Clara furrowed her brows, tilting her head in confusion.

I noticed the coins on the altar and motioned to Bryan.

The boy nodded, then walked over to the altar where the tracking coins were on the table. He grabbed a spare bottle of holy water and splashed them.

The coins burned...and disintegrated.

Clara flinched and shrieked. "Little brat," she spat.

I drew my revolver before Clara could react and shot her in the chest.

Clara's eyes widened. "I know you...you don't believe in all this," she motioned to the church. "Allow me to heal and be free, Connor Sullivan."

I hovered over Clara and she stared at me.

"After the last few days...I am a man of God," I growled at the witch. "And you answer to me."

I backed up just enough and shot her again and she gasped.

"You are *not* welcome here."

Clara collapsed onto the floor and something happened that I was...shocked to see.

The witch looked up at me, her mouth still trying to move with her last desperate gasps. I was about to shoot her again when she stopped clinging for life. Her skin turned sickly gray, then started fading away like powder. It spread from her wounds as she turned before my eyes.

I shook my head and looked around only to see the same thing happening to her three former thralls.

I felt a stinging in my arm, and looked down. The vicious bite on my arm was closing, not leaving even a scar in its place.

The curse...whatever it was...it had to be gone.

Everyone exhaled at the same time the feeling of relief flooded the room.

"Well, this is going to be a mess..." Mary objected.

"What do we tell the others?" Oskar asked.

"Nothing...and if they do ask, just tell them the truth," I suggested. "That whatever luck this place has...there's nothing to be afraid of anymore."

Everyone took a breath as dawn broke around us, flooding the church with early morning sunlight.

I found myself mindlessly walking out of the church, the cold air hitting my face.

I walked out to the woods and fell to my knees.

Before I knew it, tears of relief were falling from my face. I looked up at the cross above the church. "I hear You," I breathed. "I *finally* hear You."

Epilogue

3 Months Later...

It had taken us over a week to clean out *just* the study...not to mention repair the broken window.

I even called a team of people to repair it because Ted's destruction was so...difficult *not* to just rebuild it, but things *had* changed.

Pictures of the family were turned the right way around. Any bottles and bad habits were tossed away thanks to Bryan. Michael and Bill helped replace the window.

I made a deal with Bill that I'd help with the next church function if he was willing to help rebuild. Of course, he agreed to it now that he'd managed to clear up the fraudulent condemnation of the building by the so-called Mr. Adair. *Anything to get me back into church.*

Evelyn had a habit of making food for everyone who needed it. Since she was still a part of his will, she sold Avery's estate after his death. His family on the other hand...*left*. They were rumored to have gone to New York, tired of this wretched place. As a result, she was...Evelyn Fields again. Officially. And she was staying with me.

I had decided to talk to Bill about making her Sullivan title official again...without *anyone* getting in the way this time.

I had no lasting effects of that bite.

Oskar believed that the curse was lifted since the witch was dead.

I sure hoped that was the case.

I have to admit I had a few vivid nightmares but that was it...a reminder of how lucky I am.

It was oddly calming to see my parents faces in the portraits again. I made sure to have Elizabeth and Ted's portrait next to their house on the map as a reminder. I still feel guilty about how that played out. They might've been at peace, but that didn't mean Blackwood Hollow would ever feel the same without them.

Bryan...we told him the news of who he was to me. He seemed to have taken it rather well. I felt myself almost tear up when he actually hugged me, out of sight of his mother of course. It would be embarrassing at his age.

A part of me felt *whole* again knowing he was my own flesh and blood. But I had to be careful. He was a part of me after all.

I found myself sitting by the wood line staring into the dense trees. There was still a sense of foreboding that I couldn't quite shake.

Footsteps approached as I felt my eyes wander. What if there were more of these things still lurking in the woods? Was it possible?

"Dad," Bryan called.

I jumped a bit at the greeting. I was still thrown off from that.

"Everything all right?" Bryan asked as he sat down next to me.

I nodded slowly then looked back at the woods. "I've been...thinking," I mused. "About all those missing people."

I looked over at Bryan and he nodded slowly before he looked back out toward the tree line. "You think they're still alive?" he asked.

"I'm not sure," I answered honestly.

"Do you think there are more of those things?" Bryan asked.

I swallowed. "If there are...we'll be ready," I replied.

There was silence for a moment. Bryan then looked at me. "Dad?" he said.

I hummed in acknowledgement.

"If the missing people are alive, shouldn't we be the ones looking for them?"

I looked at him. "Why's that?" I asked.

"Because that's what good men do, right?" Bryan replied like the answer was obvious.

I laughed at the answer as if it was the truest thing I could've thought of. I got up, holding out a hand. He grabbed it, lifting himself up and brushing himself off from the cold dirt.

"I taught you well," I quipped, and wrapped around an arm around his shoulder.

Bryan smiled.

"Let's get you home, before your mother starts to worry."

ACKNOWLEDGEMENTS

The story itself I knew from the very beginning it was a *"living and breathing"* project after writing it in my grad school class (with a different title). That class changed my whole perspective of how I really had a knack for storytelling. But after the script was completed, the pitchbooks, etc. it's been clawing its way out and I *needed* to have it out. At first it was a feature script, but I felt like it was missing so much. So...I rewrote it to what it is today. And honestly...I'm so proud we took the time to really develop this town, the characters and the story.

When it comes to the rest of the "acknowledgements", I'll keep this short and sweet since I'm not even sure who would read this far! I also have *so* many people to thank that I could *specifically* acknowledge but I don't want to forget anyone by accident. So here it goes:

The first is obviously a thank you to my husband who has read, edited, and encouraged me with all my endeavors of art, film, and writing. With this story especially he was my biggest cheerleader even at the very early stages of it as a feature film script. We did a lot of work to make it what it is today. Thank you to my parents and family who let me be the weird artistic creative kid growing up, and now can hold something everyone can see and read. And believe me this won't be my only story. It's just the beginning.

Thank you to the friends and former peers in the academic world that have been with me through different stages in my life and stuck by me through all of it. I also want to acknowledge my amazing professors in the film and tv world, both undergrad and graduate because without you this story wouldn't even exist. You made me see that my calling is being a storyteller.

Thank you to my *new* friends of 2025 (you all know who you are) who have been nothing but amazing on my new beginnings that are terrifying. You are the reason I'm still going.

I only hope that from this story on, I will continue to reach my calling. It's terrifying knowing people will read what you put your heart and soul into, but in the end I hope I can inspire other people to do what they are called to do. Remember, you have *one life* and you should strive to live it to be happy for *you*. The path will never be easy, but I promise you it's worth it.

Thank you, *all* of you...for letting me be me. This is only the beginning.

About the Author

Courtney Adkisson was born and raised in the small town of Mays Landing, NJ before venturing off up and down the east coast. She pursued her BFA and MFA in film combining her creative talents into the storytelling world. She's always had a passion for writing stories since she was young, being surrounded by her favorite comics and movies she would read and watch on repeat. She loves writing and playing music, video games, and painting. Follow her all her future stories on Instagram: @courtney_adkisson.

www.ingramcontent.com/pod-product-compliance
Lightning Source LLC
LaVergne TN
LVHW091628070526
838199LV00044B/979